Women and Other Animals

WOMEN

&

Other Animals

STORIES

FOR BETTY

Bonnie Jo Campbell

Bonnie Jo Campbell

University of Massachusetts Press Amherst

This book is the winner of the Associated Writing Programs 1998 Award in Short Fiction. AWP is a national, nonprofit organization dedicated to serving American letters, writers, and programs of writing. AWP's headquarters are at George Mason University, Fairfax Virginia.

Printed in the United States of America

LC
ISBN 1-55849-219-4

Designed by Kristina Kachele
Printed and bound by Sheridan Books
Set in Monotype Walbaum, Serlio, and AT Sackers Italian Script by
Keystone Typesetting, Inc.

Library of Congress Cataloging-in-Publication Data
Campbell, Bonnie Jo, 1962–
Women and other animals : stories / Bonnie Jo Campbell.
p. cm.
ISBN 1-55849-219-4 (alk. paper)
1. Michigan—Social life and customs Fiction. 2. Human-animal relationships—Michigan Fiction. 3. Mothers and daughters—Michigan Fiction. 4. Working class women—Michigan Fiction. 5. Poor women—Michigan Fiction. I. Title.
PS3553.A43956W65 1999
813'.54—dc21 99-15159
CIP

British Library Cataloguing in Publication data are available.

ACKNOWLEDGMENTS

Thanks to my writer pals Carla Vissers and Heidi Bell—I toast you with every glass. Thanks to Jaimy Gordon for her wisdom and her unwavering confidence. Thanks to Stuart Dybek for his practical approach, which has made writing both less and more mysterious. As my deadline neared, Lisa Lenzo's help was a godsend. Susanna, harsh critic and devoted fan (and also my mother), has inspired much in these stories, and my darling Christopher has kept me honest.

These stories first appeared in somewhat different forms in the following magazines:
Alaska Quarterly Review, Spring & Summer 1998: "Old Dogs"
Controlled Burn, 1999: "Shifting Gears"
Kiosk 8, 1995: "Sleeping Sickness"
Michigan Quarterly Review, Winter 1999: "The Bridesmaid" (herein "Shotgun Wedding")
Moonlighting, 1998: "Rhyme Game"
New Delta Review 16, no. 2 (Spring/Summer 1999): "The Sudden Physical Development of Debra Dupuis"
North Dakota Quarterly 66, no. 1 (Winter 1999): "The Fishing Dog"
Oxford Magazine 13 (1999): "Taking Care of the O'Learys"
Passages North, Summer 1999: "Bringing Home the Bones"
So To Speak, Spring 1999: "Celery Fields"
South Dakota Review, Winter 1998: "Running"
Southern Review, Winter 1999: "The Smallest Man in the World"
Story, Summer 1998: "Circus Matinee"
Third Coast, Spring 1999: "Gorilla Girl"
And three cheers for the Detroit Auto Dealers Association for making "Shifting Gears" the official story of the 1999 Detroit Auto Show.

CONTENTS

Circus Matinee, 1

Rhyme Game, 10

Gorilla Girl, 15

Old Dogs, 30

Eating Aunt Victoria, 34

Shotgun Wedding, 56

The Fishing Dog, 62

The Perfect Lawn, 86

The Sudden Physical
Development of Debra Dupuis, 100

Sleeping Sickness, 109

Celery Fields, 125

Running, 135

Taking Care of the O'Learys, 143

Shifting Gears, 162

The Smallest Man in the World, 171

Bringing Home the Bones, 181

Women and Other Animals

Circus Matinee

THOUGH Big Joanie senses something is wrong, she does not turn to look at the tiger. Instead, she places snow cones into the outstretched hands of three black-haired girls, making certain that each girl firmly grips the plastic cup before she lets go. Big Joanie accepts clean dollar bills from the girls' father, who wears a denim shirt, probably washed by a wife who buries her face in her husband's shirts to remind herself of him when he's gone. In less than two minutes, Big Joanie must move out of this cramped front row because the lights will go out, and when they come back on, Helmut, the world's best animal trainer, will appear in the center ring with his Asian tigers. Big Joanie can't quite straighten her body against the hip-high barricade between the front row and the arena floor, but she raises her arm and holds her snow cones high in the air like an offering.

Behind the oldest black-haired girl, who is about eleven and wears a silver cross with Jesus crucified on it, a man in reflector aviator sunglasses holds up his finger to signify a snow cone. More than once, Big Joanie has carried a man as big as this man from his truck to his bedroom, then pulled off his boots and unbuttoned his shirt. She has gotten undressed and folded her pants, blouse, and bra into a neat pile on a chair and crawled in bed beside him.

Big Joanie need not look behind her to know that Conroy has wheeled the first tiger cage into position, to know that Conroy, who invited Big Joanie to his room fourteen times last summer, has gone behind the velvet curtain to retrieve the second tiger. Everything is the same as every other show, she tells herself, but she senses a disequilibrium, the kind of apprehension a flightless bird must feel before an earthquake.

The band and clowns clamor on, and the audience bites into snow cones. Big Joanie lowers the tray to her shoulder. Her nostrils itch, and she smells the sweat of the crowd beneath the mask of aftershave and perfume and the orangy scent of her own deodorant. Ignoring the hair standing up on the back of her neck, shoving aside the thoughts of men she's known for just one night, she leans across the oldest girl carefully, so as not to drip cherry juice onto her blouse or jeans. Big Joanie offers the sunglasses man the snow cone, and his hand closes around it, but as she lets go the cup slips and crashes to the floor. The man's face changes, stretches as though made out of clown rubber. Big Joanie has never seen a man struck dumb like this. Some men have regarded her with disgust in the morning, seeming to have forgotten the way they whispered to her the night before, but she didn't sleep with this man. She only handed him a snow cone, the way she's handed snow cones to thousands of men.

In the same moment, the expressions of people sitting near the sunglasses man freeze the same way. Have they all just noticed Big Joanie's over-large head and her hips as wide as the length of an axe-handle? Are they stunned by her acne-pocked face? By her lightning-struck hair? Then she sees the answer reflected in the man's glasses, a double rearview vision of a compacted and curved circus world in which a miniature tiger stands in front of, not inside, its cage.

Scraping feet and muffled screams are not quite drowned out by the circus band. People at the top of the section and in the aisle seats escape toward the exits, falling upon one another. But at the bottom center, those sitting in a half-circle around Big Joanie are trapped in their seats.

"Stay still!" shouts a voice from the floor, Conroy's voice. Big

Joanie has heard it in ninety-seven arenas, in the pie car, and whispering in his lower bunk in train car eighty-five, but never has she heard such urgency. Conroy is the assistant to Helmut's assistant Bela; Conroy is the person who makes sure the six-inch steel pin is dropped through the slot to secure the doors on each tiger cage as it is pulled into the arena. Conroy shouts, "Y'all stay still. We'll get her back in." Whenever Big Joanie went to Conroy's room on train car eighty-five last summer, Conroy's roommate eventually stumbled in drunk and turned on the light. Conroy would pull the blanket over Big Joanie's head, uncovering her feet which hung off the end of his bunk.

"Just stay still. Nobody'll get hurt if you all just stay still." Conroy's voice cajoles in an attempt to soothe the tiger. "Queenie, take it easy," he says three times, as if trying to convince a small, pretty woman to come to his room. "If y'all move," he says to Big Joanie and the audience, "this girl might get excited."

Big Joanie can imagine Conroy—he has small hands and a bald spot the size of a copper pot scrubber—but that doesn't help her now. She tries to feel Conroy in her nerves and bones, the way she felt him last summer, but she senses instead the tiger pacing. Each stride is longer than the last, looser, as though in the pads of its feet it has stored a genetic memory of life in the Asian forests where its ancestors took down game.

Big Joanie doesn't move. Her size twelve canvas shoes stick to the snow cone juice and flattened cotton candy as the tiger's feet meet clean floor mats, swept and scrubbed after each show. For six years, in sometimes three shows a day, Big Joanie has seen this tiger pour into the caged center ring, but she never considered the possibility of the tiger walking free. Now she imagines tiger feet prowling her spine, stepping on vertebrae which float up her back like bone islands.

The three black-haired girls are crying, but their sobs are so quiet Big Joanie must strain to hear them. She has never looked squarely into the faces of frightened girls, has never watched their pretty cheeks being sliced by tears. The girls have just seen a woman no bigger than the eleven-year-old and clad only in a glittering bikini let go of the rope and spin by her braid; they have seen the Polish acrobats pile atop one another, stretching upward in a human tower of Babel, risking everything to get their body language to the upper tiers of the arena. A daredevil rode a motorcycle upside down, but nothing prepared the girls for this.

IN two of the cheapest seats, way up in section P, a manager of a regional sales office sits with his girlfriend, who compares to his wife as filet mignon compares to a cubed steak. During the first half of this matinee, people filled many of the seats, but by twos and threes they have migrated to lower sections into better seats than they'd paid for. The loudspeaker behind the couple bangs out a sped-up version of "The Entertainer," but their distance from the arena mutes the action. The manager watches clown stooges hit each other with handbags and plastic hammers far below. A female clown whose figure is camouflaged in polka dots hangs shirts on a clothesline. When she turns her back, a little dog jumps up and tears them down.

The chain-link enclosure appeared miraculously in the dark of the center ring while that tiny woman spun by her hair in the spotlight above, and now a tiger has been wheeled out in a cage. The tiger is the brightest toy in this toy circus, a butane tiger-torch, a brilliant carved bit of amber the manager might hang on a chain. In China, he has heard, men increase their virility by eating the powdered penises of tigers.

Christ, he loved that sparkling little woman who spun by her hair. She had seemed small enough to fit in his hand, as perfect as a wish, a bikini-clad genie he could conceal in the pencil holder on his desk. His girlfriend loved the animal acts—the camels, the bareback stunts, even the ridiculous bow-tied and skirted poodles.

His girlfriend hasn't noticed the tiger. Her fingers have been sliding upward from his knee and now she unfastens his fly. He shifts in his seat to help her. There is nobody else around, and even the pushy vendors won't bother coming here for only two people. This is precisely what he hoped for, precisely why he didn't buy better seats. His girlfriend is a district sales manager; she has thick dark hair and an apartment not far from the office. She reaches through the fold of his shorts. They have eaten restaurant meals at corner tables, and she has never done more in public than touch his leg. She lowers her head into his lap, and he strokes her shoulders. Two men emerge from behind the purple curtain with a second tiger cage, but they stop halfway across the arena. The manager sees what they see. The first tiger is stepping out through the open door of its cage, the powerful head first, then front paws, back paws, and long, muscled tail. Or is he imagining this? His girlfriend doesn't even notice when the music slows.

BIG JOANIE wonders why they don't stop the music altogether. The faces before her are pale with fear. Behind her, the cat stretches farther with each stride. The memory of prowling Asian forests travels from its feet into the muscles of its legs. The tiger spikes the air with growls, tests its space, tastes its freedom.

When Joanie was twelve, a year older than the oldest black-haired girl, she was working alone in her mother's garden, on the far side of the barnyard, along the road. She was weeding a row of bush beans, straddling the plants on her knees, when she heard noises behind her. Instead of investigating the noises, she kept weeding. She sensed danger up and down her spine, noticed her spine, maybe for the first time, as if it were a closely planted row of beans or seed corn sprouting in her back. The men came from behind, through the garden gate with a gunny sack which they pulled over her head without even shaking out the last of the chicken feed.

She had never breathed the fine dust of chicken feed so deeply, or felt it cake her eyes, or filter into her hair and catch on her scalp. The men pressed her into the sand and garden dung, so that the grit worked itself into her armpits.

Joanie was as big as a grown-up, and probably those men had mistaken her for a grown woman, her mother said later, scrubbing chicken manure off brown eggs with enough force that she would soon break one. A few mornings later when Joanie was standing in the driveway with her arms across her chest, her father, who was a big man but not an ugly man, said those men were probably from out of town. He looked as though he wanted to say more, but he grew unsteady watching his only daughter—who was already as tall as he was—hug herself and rock back and forth, and he slammed the truck door and left for work.

The first man pinched her breasts and called her ugly. "You'll like this, you ugly bitch." Coming from a grown man that word "ugly" stung her. The second man spoke sweetly. "Oh baby, this feels good." When he said, "I want to kiss you," the first man kicked dirt on them and said, "She'll see us, you asshole." With the first man, Joanie just prayed for it to be over, for the day to be over so she could go to bed, for this life to be over so she could start again and run when she first heard the noises. As the second man whispered kind words to her, Joanie felt dulled by a sympathy toward him, a sickening camaraderie which slowed time.

"Don't take that bag off," the first man said, "or we're coming back." Joanie lay across the bush beans, sticky, pasted with sand and dung, her T-shirt pushed up under the chicken feed sack, her throat clogged by the mash. The men tore through the garden, trampling her mother's tomato and squash plants as Joanie lay listening to the mockery of crows above. She felt herself separating, the way a garden divides into rows of snap beans and corn and tomatoes. Her spine had only just come alive minutes before, but now she thought of the way vertebrae boiled apart in oxtail stew. Her mind halved, and halved again, endless halving. She lay swathed in an awful calm, feeling the rhythm of the men's bodies long after they were gone.

"Doughnut move," says Conroy's boss, Bela, the assistant to Helmut. "Stay calm, everybody. Doughnut move."

Big Joanie wishes she could sink behind the barricade, but there is no room, and she wants to stand up straight, but the ledge on the barricade cuts into her, so she continues to bend slightly forward, touching the eleven-year-old's knees with her own big knees. When a drop of cherry juice is poised to drip from her snow cone tray, Big Joanie shifts so the drop doesn't fall on the girl's white denim but instead runs ice-cold down her own chest inside her uniform shirt. The smallest girl buries her face in her father's sleeve, but the older girls shrink against their own seats. Big Joanie feels herself stretch wide across the tiger's field of vision. She wonders if she will be ripped open and devoured like a milk cow, like an Asian water buffalo.

"Freeze," comes the voice of Helmut, the world's best animal trainer. "Nobody will move." In less than a minute, Helmut should be performing, so he is wearing silk pants and a vest with no shirt. His blond hair lies perfectly in place, even as sprigs of her own hair snap loose from her pony tail. The tiger Helmut has trained continues to pace, orange, black, orange stripes rippling across big cat muscle. "Nobody will move," commands Helmut.

Though she always has remembered that afternoon in the garden, has used it as a marker, a zero point on her own time line, she has never had a good hold of it. She knew those men with voices but no faces about as well as she knew God. Big Joanie obeys the world's best animal trainer, but she hates it that every person in this arena except her can see the tiger. Only about a minute has passed since the sunglasses man dropped the snow cone; the cherry color hasn't even begun to fade from her remaining snow. But the air has changed, become as empty as before a tornado. If she dares look up, the roof of the arena will be sucked away, and open sky will mock her. In arenas across the country, she has held her snow cones high as an offering, but today God has made it clear, he will not bargain with Big Joanie.

THE manager's girlfriend begins to lick him. He blinks to clear his vision and loosens his tie. The girlfriend samples him, tastes him. Small, insignificant circus people scatter in the tiger's wake. A dozen men in blue coveralls draw near the tiger, then back away, like the tide coming in and going out. Still, the music blasts. The manager presses the bleached cuff of his shirt sleeve against his forehead. The tiger pads back and forth between the cage and the front center seats. His girlfriend's mouth closes around him.

Below, that big-headed, big-assed snow cone girl is wedged against a low barrier between the arena and the seats, her back to the tiger. That girl lugged herself up and down the stairs of this section early in the show. She was double-bag-ugly but oddly voluptuous, her breasts and hips pornographic in their proportion. Lying with that giantess, eyes closed, a man might feel he'd come home after a long journey. Still, even a man who liked them big couldn't get past the face. A man who would take that to bed was a man who entertained no illusions of himself. That's what the manager had been thinking when she looked right at him, through eyes as close-set as double barrels of a shotgun. She seemed to know what he'd been thinking and that he'd lied to four creditors on the phone this morning. Then, just as abruptly, she looked away.

His girlfriend purrs, her breath raspy. He grabs a handful of that glorious hair and pushes her head down harder, establishes a better rhythm. Sweet God in heaven, he thinks, but his pleasure is lashed to his fear that she will stop. He knows she would like nothing more than to look up and see this tiger loose on the arena floor, but he can't bring himself to tell her.

TIGER muscles flex behind Big Joanie, close enough that the sharp smell of tiger urine is overpowering. Helmut, Bela, and Conroy draw near, pushing the tiger closer to the barricade and closer to Big Joanie. Helmut speaks to the tiger in German, words that sound as if they emanate from some private train car where the three men sit, smoking cigars and drinking liquor in comfortable chairs. The tiger stops. Big Joanie hasn't realized the world could be motionless, but the tiger stops pacing, and the world is like a still-life: ugly woman and tiger.

"Nobody will move," whispers Helmut in English. "Everything will be fine." He speaks so softly that Big Joanie wonders if she is reading his mind rather than hearing him. The voice mesmerizes her, connects her to him. He will lift her from danger before the audience of thousands.

But the tiger growls and severs their connection. Of the two creatures, Helmut is the weaker. The tiger's eyes cut into Big Joanie, sending twisty patterns of electricity through her. The tiger is aware of her rushing blood and of the muscle beneath her fat.

"You will not move." Helmut's voice travels easily into her, and if Helmut or any man had ever declared loyalty to her, Joanie might stop.

"Doughnut move, girl," says Bela. But Bela has never cared for her either. Remembering the men she's known is futile, though she can't stop herself. Pictures of them rattle through her like strung-together boxcars.

"Big Joanie, stay still!" commands Conroy. If he had invited her to his room last night, she might obey. If Conroy had covered her head to protect her and not to hide her, if he had ever sat beside her in the pie car or held her hand, she would become meat for him now.

Instead, Big Joanie wills herself to turn, and as she does, lost vertebrae line up and reconnect. Big Joanie feels puzzle pieces snap into place. She turns broad shoulders to face the tiger, straight on, full frame. The creature is as strange as Asia, as familiar as her own reflection.

She rests her snow cone tray on the barricade. She sees the tiger more clearly than the hair-spinning woman sees the husband who controls the rope that holds her aloft, more clearly than Big Joanie's mother ever saw her father, more clearly than any pretty woman will ever see an ordinary man. The tiger is more golden than orange, its black stripes as delicate as smoke trails from a cigarette, as painful to Joanie as whip marks. One pale front leg barren of stripes reveals an asymmetry. Shaggy feet with claws like dark quarter-moons grip the rubber mat uneasily, as if testing foreign soil. Big Joanie has seen this tiger jump through a ring of fire, yet she has never really seen its yellow god's eyes or read the calligraphy of its war-paint face. The tiger stares back at her. She weighs what it weighs. If the tiger pounces, she will be overcome, but the tiger must look at her and acknowledge her, and Big Joanie will know the face of the animal that devours her.

Tiger muscles tense and contract as they do before springing at Helmut's bidding. But the tiger hesitates. It shifts its weight and looks away from Big Joanie, retracts its claws. The tiger glances toward the empty cage, and shifts its weight again. Seconds flash in Joanie's mind like glimpses of sun between boxcars. The tiger twists its body, tilts its head, and roars into the bank of lights.

Rhyme Game

TINNY MARIE and her mother rattled along Halfmoon Road in the pickup truck, heading east toward the risen sun. Bits of trash flew out of the cans and barrels in the back—a plastic bag from Spartan egg noodles, a popsicle wrapper, grocery store receipts. Tinny Marie's mother had canceled weekly garbage service because she could save money by storing the trash until she had a truckload and then dumping it herself. The longer she saved it, the more she was getting out of her eight-dollar compactor fee. Between compactor visits, cans of garbage lined up outside the back door, waiting.

Tinny Marie's mother was driving with one hand and holding a cup of coffee with the other. Coffee sloshed with each bump, spilling and soaking into the foam rubber where the bench seat was ripped. The smell of burned coffee made Tinny want to gag. She knelt on the seat sideways and leaned out the window to watch the swamp glide past. The tips of marsh grasses were white with frost. When the pickup crossed the stream which flowed under the road and later crossed their property, Tinny spit out the window toward the water. She turned her side-view mirror in all directions to see the road shimmy up from behind.

"That coffee smells real bad," she said.

"Best coffee I ever had," said her mother.

"Does the coffee make you glad? Or mad?"

Tinny's mother honked and waved at a man coming toward them in the opposite lane in a Martin's Excavating dump truck. In order to wave, she let loose the wheel, causing the truck to swerve right. Tinny closed her eyes and clutched the cracked seat and door handle. Her brothers had promised to take her with them to the auto parts junk yard, but the way her mother drove, there was no guarantee she'd be alive to go. Loose gravel spit up as Tinny's mother jerked the truck back onto the pavement.

"Looks like we're here," said her mother as she braked to turn into the compactor driveway.

"Let's have a beer," said Tinny Marie.

"Did you peer in the mirror?"

"I'm a queer reindeer."

They backed into the unloading zone, and Tinny helped her mother empty the blue plastic oil drums and galvanized metal cans. The more an object was unlike garbage, the better Tinny liked throwing it into the pit. Her favorites included pieces of busted furniture, appliances, and books. A handwritten sign on the side of the operator's shack said "No TVs!" Tinny Marie would've liked nothing better than to see a TV explode.

After they had emptied the cans and barrels and swept out the rusting truck bed, Tinny climbed on top of the cab. The roof bowed and made a sound like thunder beneath her weight. From inside his shack below her, the compactor man turned on the hydraulics and a chunk of the world began to compress. Lengths of wood splintered and snapped like bones. Cans flattened and bottles popped. Tinny imagined a stray cat jumping into the hole. She closed her eyes and hunched her shoulders against a shiver.

"Tinny Marie, what do you see?" asked her mother from the ground.

Tinny opened her eyes. "I see a tree and it sees me."

"What if I were you?" asked her mother. "And you were me?"

"What if bumbles was a bee? What if there was a flea on that bee? On his knee?"

Tinny's mother carried her empty cup into the shack with the compactor man and closed the door. Hands on her hips, Tinny surveyed the field beyond the mowed grounds. She could see all the way through to Indian Road from her perch, nearly all the way home across the yellow scratch of fall. The reds of the sumac trees are like scabs, she thought, on hills that are like knees. "These trees are bees' fleas' knees," she said aloud.

From the top of the truck, she could see Jimmy Poke's red and white cows lounging in the sun beside the farm pond edged with frost. The cows didn't seem to care that winter was coming. They lay chewing as if seasons didn't change. Jimmy Poke was a friend of her mother's. He dragged one leg behind him as he walked and called all the women "Dahlin'." He always kissed her mother on the mouth. Tinny Marie said "Dah-lin" twice out loud but couldn't find a rhyme.

Late last winter, Jimmy Poke had called their house to say that one of his cows had walked out on the ice and fallen through. If there was a thaw, he said, the carcass would poison the water. Her mother could have the meat if they could get the cow out. Tinny had gone along but stayed on shore while her mom and two brothers went out with a rowboat. They took lengths of rope and a chain saw as well as a splitting maul to bust up the ice.

The cow in the water was frozen solid, and that was why they had to cut her legs off. As the chain saw buzzed, Tinny had buried her face in the shoulder of a Guernsey heifer. Her brothers tossed the legs one at a time toward the shore. The legs clattered as they skipped across the ice. If those cold white legs were there now, she would kick them into the compactor and bravely watch them snap. Last winter they had carried the frozen cow home in the back of the truck, and her brothers had skinned her and hung her body in the garage. The weather broke, and over the next few days the boys cut the meat from the bones. Her mother finished the job on the kitchen table, wrapping ugly five-pound chunks in freezer paper and gray tape.

The truckload of garbage was smashed into a tight package, and through the window of the little hut, Tinny Marie could see her mother laughing with the compactor man. Their mouths moved in speech she couldn't hear. When finally another truck pulled in and honked, the two strolled out, her mother with a full cup of coffee.

From the truck cab roof, Tinny watched her mother place the cup on the dashboard below her. A ghost of steam formed above it on the windshield. Her mother turned the key and the truck made spiraling sounds until the engine caught. She yelled up, "Tinny Marie, what do you see?"

"The hill is my knee," she said. "My scab is a tree."

"Come on down and get in with me."

"I see a cow right now."

"Get in. We've got to go," said her mother.

"How about a one-legged crow." Tinny laughed at the vision she'd conjured up: a one-legged crow standing on that one leg, then flying off with no problem. She slid into the passenger's seat through the window. It'd been years since the door opened. They turned back onto Halfmoon Road and her mother waved goodbye to the compactor man. As they bumped over the pavement, Tinny watched Jimmy Poke's cows chew their cuds in the rearview mirror until they were lazy dots of fur. The pond shone like an icy mirror, then disappeared behind a hill.

"There's a *two*-leg-ged crow," said her mother.

"So?" Tinny hung partway out the window.

Her mother began to sing, "There lived an old Lord by the Northern Sea, bow down . . ." Tinny watched the marsh. The sun was warming the air, and the iced tips of the grasses were melting. When they crossed the shallow stream again, Tinny threw one of her yellow plastic barrettes into the current and watched it float and turn and fall behind them. When she got home, she'd run to the creek to wait for it and see how long it took to travel. Slowly, as if in a daydream, a giant black bird lifted itself into flight with a bony stretch of wings.

"Look! The biggest crow in the world," said Tinny. As her mother turned to see, the truck hit a pothole, and hot coffee splashed down the front of her mother's shirt. She swore and pulled the shirt cloth away from her. Tinny saw another truck was coming toward them, and her mother was not paying attention. She squeezed her eyes shut and gritted her teeth until she heard her mother resume singing, "I gave my lo-ove a gay gold ring, the boughs they bend to me . . ."

Tinny Marie opened her eyes slowly. The truck had not hit them. Their own truck had not been reduced to shattered glass and bent steel, nor she and Mother to bloody muscle and splintered bone. Their limbs would not be severed, and they would not be tossed piece by piece into the compactor to be crushed. Her mother apparently hadn't noticed how close they'd come to dying, for she just smiled at Tinny and took another drink of what coffee remained in her cup. The truck bounced and rattled on. Tinny spotted the big crow soaring above the marsh. It swooped clumsily to rest at the top of a swamp oak, on a tiny branch that bent beneath its weight. Tinny Marie turned backward in her seat to watch the crow flap its wings to keep its balance. She longed to view the world from such a height.

"I'll fly to the top of that big crow's tree," said Tinny Marie.

"Long as I can see you, and you can see me," said her mother.

Gorilla Girl

WHEN beer is mixed and left to ferment and bread is set out to rise, they sometimes collect wild yeasts; these foreigners drop out of the jet stream or rise up from the bowels of the planet, unwelcome particles which give the finished product a sharp flavor. I suspect this is what happened to my mother when she was pregnant with me. Sometime during the first trimester she must have let her guard down, perhaps in the public toilet at the flea market in Paw Paw; in a moment of inattention, something airborne and bony slipped inside her to poison the brew, something like a curse.

If I cared to describe the details of my birth and the ecstasy of release from that suffocating maternal clench, you might question whether I actually recall such an early event. In fact, I recall in miserable detail this and every sensation that has followed in the tangled and knotted lifeline connecting that howling newborn to me, seventeen years later. I recall that despite the humid heat of the southern Michigan summer, my parents kept me at optimum temperature with air conditioning, and in the bitter winter I was warmed by a clean-burning gas furnace whose filter they changed regularly. Despite these ideal conditions, I was an unhappy baby, screaming during the day and most of the night as well, whether flat on my back or rolled onto my stomach, whether a gentle breeze blew or the night was still. When I found toys or even blankets in my crib, I tossed them out, unwilling to submit to their paltry comforts. On my parents' shelves are the guidebooks they purchased during this time: *Doctor Spock's Baby and Child Care*, *Bringing Up Baby*, *Saving Yourself from Baby*.

It seems foolish to suggest that my having resulted from an accidental conception should have made any difference. And certainly my mother was wrong about my problem ever having been colic, for had it been colic, I'd have been feeling better by the time I was using complete sentences to demand rare-cooked meat and glass after glass of cool water. For years my parents tried to sustain the illusion that I was a normal girl, but my siblings learned by trial and error to keep away from me. My brother broke his wrist the time I pushed him off the roof—before ordering me down, he first should have considered how precariously near the edge he stood. As a kindergartner, I bit my sister's leg so badly that she needed six stitches. Throughout those early years, I yelled for food at the first pang of hunger, bathed irregularly, and threw things, so my bedroom floor was a pool of broken dishes, torn books, and drywall dust. My father, a dedicated actuary, replaced my broken windows with plexiglass. In photographs from this time, I have a red and swollen look.

At school I tried to wait my turn for the playground swing or a particular crayon, but after a minute or so, I would yield to my monster and seize the object of desire. Even the most mundane acts—such as my fourth grade teacher, Mrs. Mitschlager, straightening and restraightening the stack of papers on her desk—could drive me to a frenzy. The school psychologist was averse to prescribing Ritalin or other drugs to "bright" children such as me, and my sense of self-preservation told me that in this man's presence I ought to be on my best behavior. He scolded my parents and teachers. Weren't my verbal skills superb? he said. When I did apply myself to math, wasn't I doing it at a level above my classmates? I needed to be loved and challenged, he said, and my fits of rage would diminish. And if Mrs. Mitschlager complained that I snarled in response to her questions, then perhaps she shouldn't call on me.

During the day, my outbursts reduced my tension and body heat, but nights alone in my room were nearly unbearable. In order to go to sleep, I practiced cursing, and sometimes could enunciate verbal strings such as, "Fucking-motherfucking-sonofabitch-cunt-sucking-cock" without degenerating into animal sounds. If this didn't help me sleep, I banged my head against the headboard or squeezed my hands together until the bones ached. Apart from this occasional self-infliction of pain, however, I did not touch myself. If my hand fell across my stomach in sleep, I soon awoke to a sensation of burning skin. Sometimes even the brush of my blankets and pajamas was too much, and I tossed them off as I had done in my crib and slept naked with my legs apart and arms out to my sides.

Tommy Pederson was the biggest and meanest boy in our fourth grade class, and every day at lunch, he and his cronies hung kids upside down from the monkey bars to empty their pockets. The time they grabbed me, they flipped me so my underpants were displayed for all. As if that were not enough, Tommy pushed his grubby finger under the elastic of those underpants and touched the folded skin between my legs. As gravity sent blood to my face, I willed myself to become a superstrong monster—Frankenstein and Rubberman in one—and I twisted my new form around to bite Tommy Pederson's forearm through his jean jacket. He screamed and fell, and we wrestled in the sand. At one point he straddled me, pinning my arms, but when I knocked his head with mine he let go. Once atop him, I grabbed a plastic lunch box and clobbered him with it until his head fell back into the sand, until drool and snotty blood rolled down his face. I recall both the pleasure of winning and the disappointment of realizing that Tommy was not going to fight anymore.

In earlier matches, I had kicked kids or smacked them or wrested swing set chains from them but had never engaged in a full body match, unfurling all my strength. In the afterglow of this contest, my head was clear, and my body felt as calm as the center of my own storm, released momentarily from both the volcanic pressure within and the oceanic weight pressing from outside. My limbs swung loose, and I free-floated as though gravity had been lifted. When I got home that afternoon, my mother was sitting near the phone, sobbing into folded arms.

After school I spent time out-of-doors in our quiet neighborhood of ranch homes attached to two-car garages, and I took pleasure in capturing insects. A tight vibration of wings sounded against my teeth as I held a grasshopper steady between my tongue and hard palate, anticipating the thrill of biting into that alien skin and extinguishing life. Crickets snapped against the top of my mouth until I ground them between my molars. Sky green praying mantises raked their arms against my gums, begging for reprieve even after I'd severed their thoraxes from their abdomens.

"What on earth are you doing?" screamed my mother the time she saw me put a june bug into my mouth.

"Nothing." I closed my teeth, crunched the shell, and swallowed.

"What's in your mouth?" She moved closer, right into my face.

"Nothing." I thrust my tongue toward her. The corners of her mouth recoiled from me, and she released a little shriek. I felt with my finger and found a june bug leg with ridges the length of it, ending in a small black foot. I smeared it onto my jeans. Rather than admonish me, she walked away, plump arms dangling in defeat.

The Sandersons, four houses down from us, kept a pit bull. He paced in his cage like a zoo beast, jaws slavering, mottled stripes stretching and contracting over his torso. Often I approached to watch him throw his body against the chain link. With his armor of muscle pushing out against his skin, he seemed to embody the turbulence of my own corporeality. I could fall asleep to the crazed barking as peacefully as another child to a lullaby. If I knelt on hands and knees before his cage and concentrated hard enough, my own body began to change. My teeth sharpened and grew longer—I could feel them with my tongue. My limbs thinned, my chest pulped with muscle, and I flinched at the sharp pain of sprouting a tail from my backside. As I became an animal, the pressure inside my skin lessened, the feeling of too much heat and too much blood racing through tiny venous caverns subsided. One day, however, I forgot to hide behind the Sandersons' inkberry bushes and attempted my transformation in view of their living room. Father and mother, brother and sister, the cartoon family clutched each other in horror. I should have stopped when I saw them but was loathe to leave my sublime state. When I threw my head up and growled at them, they phoned my mother, who revived me with a yank to my front paw, propelling me too quickly back into my own pink and inadequate flesh, ruining me.

I snarled and tugged at her slacks with my teeth. The thready affections I felt toward my mother further shriveled beside the sturdiness of my rage, and yet something always prevented me from physically harming her. It didn't take a near-genius IQ to recognize that I was to blame for her misery, and something like guilt even pricked me on occasion, but such feelings were pebbles at the bottom of my stomach while madder passions rushed through me like white water. After she dragged me home, I stomped upstairs, kicked a new hole in the drywall under my window, and began chewing my hand, working it the way the pit bull worked his rawhide, biting to feel the force of teeth on both sides, stopping just short of puncturing the skin.

Perhaps if my parents had beaten me, or even spanked me, there would have been some relief. Perhaps by transference, the release of their anger would have diminished some of my own. But the anger of the family—if not of the whole lower peninsula of Michigan—was concentrated in me. The others in my family were driven by feeble emotions like heartbreak, astonishment, and some happiness. My parents, after all, were peaceful people who lamented only in silence the forgotten pill, or the broken condom, or the ill-fitting diaphragm—whatever misadventure caused that one over-energized sperm to penetrate the defenses and pierce the shell of my mother's egg. Or perhaps the egg itself had kicked away the diaphragm, torn the condom, taken the dumb sperm by the tail and devoured it.

One evening while they ate supper in the kitchen, I sat with my TV tray in the living room. I usually watched the news in hopes of seeing fires or foreign brutalities, but today I had found *Dr. Jekyll and Mr. Hyde.* When good Dr. Jekyll turned into evil Mr. Hyde, hair sprouted from the backs of my hands in sympathy. "I am free!" shouted Mr. Hyde. "I am free!" He could whip that Irish girl like a horse now, just as I could whack Tommy Pederson with a lunch box while he wept and drooled. Laughter tinkled from the kitchen. My sister was on the middle school basketball team, and my family was celebrating some victory of hers with no idea what fate might await them. I twisted my mouth and imagined myself swaggering into the kitchen, knocking their microwaveable dishes to the floor and throttling their soft necks, one after another. I finished my dinner, imagining it was live bugs and amphibians instead of meat loaf and string beans, and then I chewed my thumb until it bled.

When my parents noticed my new form of self-mutilation, they bribed me with a promise of a *Dr. Jekyll and Mr. Hyde* book with over a hundred photo stills from the movie, and sent me to a real psychologist, Dr. Radcliff. Throughout several sessions, I growled in his office, halfheartedly willing my transformation to pit bull terrier at the reduced rate of sixty dollars an hour. He watched me, amused, arms crossed over his chest. He was a clean-cut man in his thirties, broad in the shoulders and not tall, apparently married to the rabbitlike blonde gritting her teeth in the photo on his desk. After a couple of weeks, when I finally deigned to sit in his patient's chair, he let loose with his twisted behaviorist theory. Whatever I felt, he said, was fine, just don't let on to anybody. Self-control was the key to survival.

"When you are older, eighteen or so," said Radcliff, "you can sleep in a doghouse, but for now, just pretend to be a civilized girl so they don't put you away or give you shock therapy. Humor your mother and eat your oatmeal instead of bugs, for God's sake." I did give up the bugs, but not for God's sake or my mother's. There was something about Radcliff's bulldog chest and forearms, his sweaty-cologne smell, and the Dracula green eyes. While the school psychologist had never stopped chattering and humoring me, Radcliff could sit silent for a full fifty minutes, waiting for me to answer a single question. I came to view him as a mentor, a man who refused to be shocked or seduced, a solid wall against which I could ram myself without fear of breaking it down.

Things went more smoothly for the next few years, until, as the school's brain-numbing health movies had promised, I began to menstruate. When I first discovered blood flowing from my nether regions, I was ecstatic. But by the third month, I realized there would never be more than a trickle. Why? I screamed at my mother.

Why all the goddamned fuss over this? To better express myself, I stomped into the backyard and pulled her rose bushes out of the ground with my bare hands, puncturing my palms, fingers and forearms with hundreds of thorns. I tossed the uprooted bushes at my mother and shook off those that stuck to me.

As I pounded bloody fists on the picture window and cursed her, my mother was on the phone arranging an emergency meeting with Radcliff. She cleaned me up before bringing me in, but I found a paper clip on Radcliff's carpet and toyed with it while he spoke. "You're really upsetting your mother," he said. I pushed the end of the paper clip deep into one after another of the thorn holes, so that each in turn began to dribble blood. When Radcliff realized what I was doing, he swooped like a bat and slapped me full across the face. "Jesus fucking Christ!" he said and grabbed my shoulders. "Do you want to be locked up? Because that's what's going to happen if you don't stop this shit. Am I getting through?" He throttled my shoulders and shook me, his thumbs digging into my chest. "Think tranquilizers. Think electrodes." The sting from his slap radiated outward until my whole body buzzed with calm.

"Tell your mother you're sorry," he said, loosening his grip.

I shook my head yes. He let go of me, but I still felt his fingers, and I hoped there'd be bruises.

PHYS ED had always been my favorite class, and in my sophomore year the gym teacher and track coach Ms. Heart cautiously invited me to join the track team. For months I had sensed her sizing up the wall of muscle beneath my skin, muscle as strong as chain mail, as tight as a straightjacket. After the first day of practice, she declared I was a mile runner. By the end of the season I would hold the school record for the mile, and in my junior year I would break the state record by more than a second. Each day Ms. Heart gave me a program written on an index card which took about three hours to complete. Sometimes before I could finish, I vomited behind the bleachers. The other girls slacked off, postured for the boys' track team, then lied to Heart about what they had done or else invented maladies. Heart was unsympathetic; running, she said, was the cure for cramps, headaches, and allergies. In her, as in Radcliff, I had an ally, a person who wouldn't turn soft, a constant force willing me to be stronger. When I jogged evenings in our neighborhood, it felt as though there were two of me: the person I saw in the mirror and that second creature with teeth like a pit bull, leashed and dragging a concrete block.

On a particularly warm spring day, after sprinting a quarter-mile around the track, I stood panting, hands on knees, near the high jump pit. A red-haired boy lay in the sun on the landing pad, one arm bent behind his head, the other absent-mindedly stroking his bare chest. He looked at me, as luxurious as a cat yawning, and let his thumb drift and then pause over his nipple. I became sensible of the wad between his legs. The heat from my own body was suddenly suffocating me, and I imagined that the boy's skin was cool. Only then did I realize how running and lifting weights had changed me. No longer was my muscle a single sheet beneath my skin, a rubbery exoskeleton holding me together. Each muscle in my arms and legs now felt like a separate creature, ready to chew through my skin and escape. When I was able to move, I sprinted around the school to the cross-country path where I ran six miles without stopping.

There's no sense pretending that I hadn't become good-looking. Though my father resembled a sea cow, my mother and siblings were handsome enough. If the monster Medusa had been the most beautiful creature in the ocean at one time, why not me? My black hair dangled in ropes to my shoulders—I hadn't the patience to brush it as my mother implored, and I cut it myself with blunt scissors, letting the ends fall to my bedroom floor. Often after a race, or even while I searched my hall locker, a circle of observers formed around me, at a safe distance, not close enough to touch me. In fact, nobody ever dared touch me until late one night when I was leg-pressing the maximum weight on the Universal machine, rhythmically pushing the pedals away with my bare feet, then easing them back with a clank. At the same time, I was planning a paper for my sociology class, shaping long, convincing sentences I could never compose while motionless.

Like a shaft of light, Heart's aroma of sweat, rubber, and cocoa butter spiked the room. Strong, small hands reached from behind and began to massage my shoulders and the back of my neck, speeding the flow of my blood. I closed my eyes and let my head fall to the side, moaning with each exhalation. But when she let her hands, dark veins erect on their backs, slide down over my biceps so they touched my breasts, the whole room began to throb. My vision blurred. I extended my legs to lift the stack of iron weights, tossed back my head, and roared like a jungle beast stuck with an arrow. Heart gasped, pulled away her hands, and ran from the room. I continued to howl, out of my mind with heat and confusion, wanting to stroke Heart's stringy, muscled limbs, and wanting to squeeze her leathery throat while she gasped for breath.

In the lobby of Radcliff's office, at my next regular appointment, I thumbed through issues of *National Geographic*, tapping my foot wildly, absent-mindedly stabbing myself with my house key, imprinting tiny, V-shaped wounds up and down my legs and arms. An article about big cats said they moved at speeds up to sixty miles per hour. Imagine the sting of the wind at such a velocity. An article about the great apes featured women researchers with gorillas. *King Kong* was one of my favorite movies, so these gorillas disappointed. Far from being bloodthirsty, they were gentle and strictly vegetarian. I had assumed they would eat grubs and insects at the very least. Hell, Kong had practically eaten people.

Radcliff seemed distracted, so I asked what he knew about the great apes, and he started up about how intelligent they were. King Kong had been plenty smart, I commented, and Radcliff laughed. He liked to think that I no longer wanted to be an animal, but at that very moment, I was concentrating on becoming a movie gorilla. As I felt the first pricklings of wild hair sprout from my pores, my insides began to quake. A tidal wave gained momentum. Floodgates threatened to burst. The big rock clogging the mouth of the volcano rattled in its niche.

Never had the transformation been like this. To stop myself, I told Radcliff about the incident with Heart. What had I felt? he asked. "I burned like a furnace," I said. "I roared like a lion."

Radcliff pushed his papers onto the floor. He dropped to his knees and laid his head on my lap. "I love you," he said, without warning or preamble. "I've loved you since you were eleven and you wanted to be a dog. God forgive me."

His head was heavy on my legs. I placed my open hand on the side of his face, which was bigger and more ghoulish up close. I pushed a strand of hair, gray and soft, behind his ear and slid the tips of my nail-bitten fingers between his beefy neck and the collar of his shirt. I leaned close to rub my cheek against his sandpaper face. As the musk of his sweat and aftershave seeped into my skin, my insides began to unfold and swell as though waves of flesh emanated from a hot liquid core. Radcliff's moist breath poured over my thigh, inflaming the skin. Though I wanted to caress him, I also foamed and bubbled like an angry cauldron.

A nervous seaweedy eye stared up from my lap. Was this pathetic swamp creature the man for whom I gave up the delicacies of the grasshopper family? Was this my champion of self-control? Was this the Frankenstein's chest against which I could hurl myself? My affections shriveled to a pea and fell to the floor of my stomach. He lifted a hand toward mine, but its pale fingers disgusted me, and I shoved him off my lap. "Asshole-bastard," I tried to say, but it came out as a snarl. "Son-of-aarrrrg," I growled, slamming the door behind me. The receptionist looked up through tiny eyes, alarmed, and I kicked her steel desk, making a sound that reverberated through the lobby. All the way home, I sputtered and spat, unable to form curses.

As I lay uncovered in the dark that night, tormented by thoughts of Radcliff, Heart, and the red-haired boy, I was driven to stroke my own naked chest. The blood rose to the surface of my skin, but I continued. My hands moved as if on a Ouija board across my stomach and between my legs, and once having given myself over to this adventure, I couldn't stop. The sensation I had felt in Radcliff's office now overwhelmed me, the unfolding away from some intense center—a dense flower whose lead-heavy petals grew from inside faster than I could tear them away. I rubbed myself until the muscles of my hands ached, bringing forth at least a dozen explosions of flesh, each one more excruciating than the last. My eyes rolled back so far I feared the muscles would snap. Once I screamed so loudly that my brother and father came running. I turned away and faked sleep, cupping my crotch until they left, pitiful stick figures.

Instead of relaxing or relieving, each climax further tormented me. My skin pumped sweat, and the flesh between my legs swelled and grew numb. I wept furiously into my pillow and bit it until feathers flew out. Finally I ripped the screen out of my window, jumped twelve feet to the grass, and filled my lungs with night air. Savoring the sting of the pavement on my bare feet, I ran naked through empty subdivision streets until I fell exhausted onto a manicured lawn a few miles away. I grasped some rose bushes and squeezed until the thorns punctured my hands. My blood had been altered, infused with sex. No longer would exercise suffice. I needed to be bled like a gypsy horse.

By entangling myself in the arms of something like a hundred men, I hoped to find one who would satisfy me, one who could give me a kind of pleasure which did not make me want to jump off a high building. The promise of each seemed great, but each failed me in turn. Once in a while, in the heated strangeness of passion, I felt the presence of my own male part, coexisting with my female organs. However, at this prompt, my mate's penis seemed to shrivel up inside of him and disappear. He became a receptacle, passive, small in proportion to me despite the physical facts to the contrary. However strong the men seemed, they longed, by the end, to be conquered. Fathers of neighborhood children, teachers, clerks at the grocery store, even Dr. Radcliff.

Radcliff was the biggest disappointment. Because of our years together, I thought he might be my match, but after an initial blaze, he fizzled and sank below the surface like the rest, and like the rest, he tried to drag me down with him. As he slept, I buzzed with energy and looked around his wood-paneled bedroom, overcome by the sensation that I had just given birth to him. Wasn't this the very picture of my rage? My strong body wrapped furiously around a limp and weakened man? His pale, spent penis touched his leg and rested upon the delicate and alien cushion of his scrotum. Tiny, raw, unprotected—here was the shape of the thing that infuriated me. His skin was cool, and I was on fire. I could crush those parts, first holding them lightly in my mouth and then biting down.

Radcliff was my second to last experiment. The following day, I bit the UPS delivery man so passionately that he went to the emergency room. Nights afterward, I lay alone in bed, grinding my teeth and trying to keep my hands at my sides but always, in the end, sacrificing myself to the horrible ecstasy.

In the last week of August, the fair came to town. On opening night I elbowed my way through the directionless mob. When I saw a girl from the track team, I spit at the ground. I got French fries with vinegar and ate them so hot they burned my mouth. Men lured me to play their coin games, their tossing and shooting games, but when I turned my Medusa gaze on them, they stopped cajoling. Their voices changed to whispers, their male parts shriveled.

At the far end of the midway, I paid two dollars to view "Samba of the Jungle: See Her Change Before Your Eyes." I handed the fat man my dollar and followed an anemic-looking kid into the tent. A blonde in a frayed, leopard-spotted wrap stood behind the bars of a cage on the dimly lit platform. Her eyes fluttered as if she were in a trance, but otherwise she remained still as patrons filtered in. When the overhead lights went out, a recorded circus voice scratched, "See Samba, a woman found in the jungles of Africa. A scientist studied her until they found him in his laboratory, torn to pieces by this she-beast."

The she-beast's skin was pasty; I wondered where in the jungle she'd found peroxide for her lousy bleach job. Varicose veins snaked down below her ratty dress. What had seemed at first a trance now looked like drunkenness. As the lights dimmed further, her face began to glow and change—her hair darkened, her features thickened, and then the tent went black. A spotlight flicked on, and a gorilla burst out of her cage and leapt into the audience. The other patrons screamed and ran for the exit. The ape jumped off the stage and roared into my face through rubber teeth. I fell to the grassy floor and pounded the earth as tears of pure joy streamed across my face. When the lights came on, the gorilla suit shook its head and humped back onto the stage and behind the curtain. I paid again and this time watched closely. As the woman's face lit up, I saw the pinpoint of light projecting from a spot above and behind the audience; a movie of the transformation was being shown on her face. The falseness of the act, however, didn't bother me—the poor woman simply hadn't learned to change herself yet. In the dark, at the back of the tent, hair sprouted sympathetically on my arms and legs.

Before I visited the Samba show the next morning, I saw the gorilla-blonde walking to the cinder-block public bathrooms. I ran to catch up with her. Here was a comrade, a fellow fury, a woman who yearned to be a beast.

"Hey, I saw your show."

"Leave me alone," she slurred and hastened her stumbly walk.

"But we're sisters, don't you see," I insisted, my voice unusually clear. "We both need to transform."

"Stay the hell away from me." Her bluish throat quivered.

I grabbed her frizzy hair and pulled her around to face me. She fluttered alcoholic eyes. Booze seeped from her glands, and the stale odor incensed me. I slapped her twice. She scratched at my face with her nails, but I grabbed her hands and squeezed her finger bones together until she fell to her knees. When I let go, she shook out her hands and started walking away, saying she would get the police, so I tackled her on the dirty lawn of flattened snow cone cups and cigarette butts and dragged her into the empty women's room. With my teeth I shredded the bottom of my shirt into ropes of cloth and tied her to the toilet seat. I held one hand over her mouth as I stripped her support hose from her hips and legs with the other, and then I gagged her with them. Now *I* was King Kong, only this dull-eyed bride wasn't coming with me. I locked the stall door and climbed out over the top. Samba of the jungle, my ass. She didn't deserve the distinction.

My plan crystallized as I walked, and the midway crowd opened for me at every turn. I bought French fries, but they were lukewarm, and I tossed them onto the ground in front of a policeman leaning against a temporary barrier. He looked into my eyes before deciding not to speak. I browsed the boutique trailers and then settled upon an oversized, tiger-striped shirt, which I put on as a dress behind a cotton candy stand. I returned to the Samba exhibit where I found the fat man who had taken my money sitting behind a sign, "Out-to-lunch." I informed him—his name was Mr. Boone—that his jungle girl was indisposed, and I would be taking her place.

"What the hell are you talking about?" His feet were crossed up on the entrance gate. His neck was red and bristly above an over-taxed pocket T-shirt. He paused to suck from a bottle of blackberry brandy. "Wait," he said, pointing a thick finger at me. "I've seen you hanging around."

"Fire her and give me her job."

"What's in it for me?" He had been staring at my legs, but when he leaned to look up my shirt-dress, I pushed his chair sideways with my foot as if flushing a public toilet. He barely caught himself. I stretched my lips around to display my whole set of teeth and growled.

Boone clutched his bottle to his stomach. "Are you threatening me, babe?" We stared at each other until he looked away. After taking another drink he stood, adjusted his suspenders, and studied me as though I were a prize beef heifer. "I've always had blondes," he said, lighting a cigarette. "But I can see you're well-muscled. If we put you in a bikini get up, guys might even pay to see you twice."

THE SIGNS advertising my act are absurd. They announce that I was retrieved from "Nairobi in South Africa." The blond hair on the old posters has been darkened. A picture labeled "The Experiment" shows me spread-eagle on a bed wearing electrodes, a geeky white scientist leaning over me. In the next frame, a gorilla stands with broken restraints dangling from its wrists. The scientist lies crumpled. It reads, "Something Terrible Happened."

This job gives me mornings free, so I work out, lifting weights with the guys who run the games of chance. Boone owns my favorite videos, which I watch in his trailer. At night I wander the 4-H barns, admiring insect collections and scaring ponies, and if I see a fat grasshopper I snap it into my mouth. Lately I have been paying one of the concessions women to braid my hair into thirty snakelike braids. Boone takes care of the money and arranges the gigs, and George, who wears the gorilla suit, handles the production. And every half-hour, noon to midnight, on cue, I wind my rage into a tighter and tighter ball behind my navel. When the pressure becomes too great, this ball explodes. The gates to the walled continent burst open, and the beast emerges.

Were the projector to switch off and the lights to click on, the audience would see a metamorphosis more shocking than they could imagine. My heart-shaped face sprouts hair, my skin darkens as though burned, male sex parts burst from my groin to complement my female ones, and my breasts harden into a muscular, leathery plate. The air becomes crisp, and every person in the tent feels connected to my Middle West gorilla, my mad-amorous crusher of households, my rampager of tidy rose gardens. Occasionally a woman rattles with laughter or else sobs in the dark—she has recognized, in my form, the monster of her own wasted strength.

Unlike my junky blond predecessor, I perform with eyes open. I search every audience for a gaze that doesn't shy from mine. I long for a whiff of animal yeast, a wildness outside myself—a mate, perhaps. I can hold the gorilla form for only a few seconds, and then I collapse. George enters my cage through the side, knocks down the barred door, and bursts into the audience. The spell is broken, and the audience is free to pretend the show is a hoax. As audience members shriek and stampede from the tent, I lie panting, exhausted and free of anger, alone for now, in the quiet eye of the carnival.

Old Dogs

A HUNTER'S moon watches over celery fields twenty years fallow. Wind from across the fields tears the last leaves off a front yard maple and rails against an asbestos-shingled house built on a concrete slab. Inside, three women whose long hair has turned all shades of gray lie on coming-unstuffed couches before a wood burning stove. As the season necessitates, the women have swathed themselves in sweaters and sweatshirts, no longer taking care to wear the cleanest ones on top. Overfilled ash trays sit beside each woman, and empty half-gallon vodka bottles litter the room. The three cola bottles will be walked to town tomorrow for the dime deposit. Two dogs are curled on the wall-length couch between two of the women, a third dog lies with Margrite on the smaller couch, and a fourth dog lies on a sweatshirt on the floor. Margrite hasn't ordered their number two oil yet, so the wood in the dwindling pile beside the back door provides their heat. Only one of the two bulbs in the overhead fixture glows; it has been glowing dimly for twenty years, while the other, when replaced, burns brightly and burns out in a few months.

Beneath the blankets, sweaters, and sweatpants, the women are thin, surprisingly so, considering that all of them battled extra weight for decades after they had children. The dogs, despite heartworms and fleas, are fat. Because the two bedrooms are cold, the women have taken to sleeping on these couches, falling quiet sometime after the sun sets and waking at the light of a sunrise fogged by the plastic Margrite stapled over the outside of the windows.

The other two women are already asleep when Margrite pulls the chain that switches off the light.

At the end of Margrite's couch lies King Lear, a collie, the biggest and oldest of the dogs, afflicted with a mange condition which is starting to make him smell bad. Margrite had King before either of the other women moved in with her. King has difficulty getting onto the couch now, but so far he has upheld his end of the domestic bargain—despite arthritis, he manages to get outside to relieve himself. If he stops being able to do that, he'll have to live outside, and the winter would probably kill him.

Lady Macbeth, a shiny black retriever mix, sleeps on her back on the other couch, her legs in the air. She is the cleverest of the dogs and a thief. Each morning she waits by the door to go out and make her rounds, and each noon she returns with loot. As well as her usual pizza boxes and bones left by poachers, she has brought home cast-iron pans, sandbox trucks, and, once, a gigantic pink bathing suit, big enough for a circus fat lady. She particularly likes shoes and occasionally has managed to get both of a pair, as she did the left and right beaded mocassins Margrite wears now. Lady's ancestors retrieved ducks for English aristocrats, so she has inherited the inclination not to puncture her finds. The time she dragged home a five-pound bag of dog food, she waited while Margrite opened it for her. Years ago an old friend brought Lady to Margrite, asked her if she would watch the dog for a few days. Margrite hasn't seen the old friend since.

Juliet, lying still beside Lady with her nose buried in blankets, might be the ugliest dog in the neighborhood. Somebody dropped her off as a puppy at the end of the road, and a neighbor girl took her home. The girl didn't care about Juliet's harelip and disproportionately short legs. Over the next few weeks, the harelip grew and the big head grew, and the legs stayed short. The dog's wiry hair clogged the girl's mother's vacuum cleaner, and the woman just couldn't stand the way the dog stared back at her, that guilty expression, then as now, a constant apology for her deformities. The neighbor girl, who had never before spoken to Margrite, showed up in tears at her door, begging Margrite to adopt the dog because her mother was taking it to animal control. The neighbor girl promised to visit and take care of the dog, but she'd only come once. That family later bought a cocker spaniel, which bit the girl.

Margrite awakens from her half-sleep coughing. At first she chokes quietly, but soon her chest and stomach convulse. She folds her body around her heaving lungs and around her raw, terrible throat. The other women awaken and shift, but they stifle their own coughs and breathe quietly as Margrite gags into her knees. Her left hand clutches the couch arm, and she presses her eyes shut. The other women's eyes glisten in the firelight. The dogs lift their ears and stare, their eyes glassy and alert. Margrite feels for her drink glass on the floor and swallows what's left, and although tears stream down her face and her hands shake, she sits very still and wills her cough to subside.

Hamlet, the best watchdog, has only three legs now. The fourth got caught at the knee in a fox trap two summers ago. When the trapper, a third-shift paper mill worker, checked his traps a couple days later, he considered shooting the dog, whose tibia and fibula had been snapped clean by the force of the trap jaws. He would have shot the dog, a lab mix with blue merle colors, if it had looked up at him and whimpered. But, once freed, the dog limped away without looking back, and the man figured he'd let the creature die in peace. Hamlet bled in the woods near the river for days, licking himself and dragging the half-attached leg from place to place. He finally caught the leg on some barbed wire and tore it the rest of the way off. He returned home across the celery field, thin and feverish, in order to heal or die. He licked his stump night and day, licked the busted bone and wound in a constant rhythm, never sleeping, working as though his infection produced an addictive liquor.

Though the stump has healed over, Hamlet has never stopped his vigil. All night, while the rest of the house sleeps, he licks the leg and his whole body in a continuous act of self-healing. He has long been able to stand and walk, but is unable to climb onto the high couches and so must accept the false humility of sleeping on the floor. Cushioned from the cold concrete by only a wafer of carpeting and whatever blankets or clothing falls to the floor, Hamlet remains alert long after people and other dogs are insensible.

Hamlet stops licking himself to watch Margrite light a cigarette and suck in a long draw. Hamlet watches her smoke the cigarette all the way down and then toss the filter into the fire. He watches her feed the fire another log from the stack drying beside the stove. He watches her gray head fall quiet against the couch arm with her mouth hanging open.

Hamlet smells the women's sweat and the sharp medicine from the bottom of glasses and bottles. He smells the cigarette tar on the women's breath as they exhale, and something of rotting meat, as well. He inhales the death smell of King's mange-ridden skin, and he resumes licking his own mottled coat.

Hamlet hears the breathing of Lady, whose head is tossed back in ecstatic dreaming of what she will steal tomorrow. Her limbs twitch and she growls at intervals. Hamlet listens to the women's quiet snoring, to the thinning crackles of a dying-down fire he can't feed, and to the rustle of unraked leaves beyond the house walls. The concrete beneath him grows colder as the fire fades, and the wind drums and rips at the window plastic outside until a milky corner tears loose and flaps, unsecured.

Eating Aunt Victoria

BESS rolled down the passenger-side window of her brother's Dodge Omni to let the night air fly into her face. She needed to be revived after the numbing dullness of her first evening working security at the Westland Mall.

"So, Bess," said her brother Hal. "Meet any bad guys?"

"Get this," she said. "They give me a walkie-talkie to carry on my belt, but when I try it there's nobody on the other end. Somebody causes trouble, I got to call 911 on the pay phone."

The downtown bank clock flashed 11:20 and 69 degrees alternately. They passed through Kalamazoo, then along a four-mile stretch of factories and warehouses where the air stank of paper processing, before entering Bangor Township. Bess lifted a cigarette from the pack of generics on the dashboard. She wondered idly what it would feel like if she and Hal were heading down the highway, toward Detroit or Chicago.

"There's a Navy recruiting office at the mall," she said.

"And there's a bridge over the Yangtze River," said Hal. "Doesn't mean you have to go there and jump off it." He flipped on his left blinker, and looked in both directions before steering over the tracks. The railroad crossing was unprotected, as were many of the private ones on the way out of town—no gates, no flashing lights, no warning. Two summers ago, a guy at the gravel pit had been hauling a backhoe across the tracks on a trailer when he was hit by the westbound Twilight Limited. The engine had plowed on, spewing chunks of yellow metal, sending half of the hydraulic arm of the backhoe into Hal's marijuana patch. Bess helped him pull the four-foot plants from around the twisted metal and carry them into the basement before the railroad police arrived.

The Omni shuddered up and over the tracks, and Hal cut the engine in the driveway beside their tarpapered, two-story house. Hal had been the one to insist that Bess finish high school. Now she was grateful, for it had delayed the monotony she felt tonight, the nagging feeling that the rest of her life stretched out empty before her, as desolate as the Westland Mall after hours. Hal had graduated a year ago and now was working at the Stop-n-Gas and attending classes at the community college.

They climbed the six steps onto the porch, where the soggy tongue-and-groove boards groaned beneath their weight. "You don't have to enlist," said Hal. "You already look like a military chick." Bess liked her security uniform, the tight belt around her middle and the rim of the hat pressing on the sides of her head. Hal would never listen to her when she mentioned joining the Navy. He didn't care about seeing the ocean or foreign countries, or anything else beyond his favorite Lake Michigan beach, forty miles due west.

They passed through the kitchen with its cracked plaster walls, worn cast-iron sink, and padlocked metal pantry where Aunt Victoria kept her personal food. The living room was dark except for the blue glow of the television lighting the split vinyl furniture and matted shag carpet. Hal walked right past Aunt Victoria in her reclining Naugahyde chair as though he wasn't going to speak to her.

"Where's my cards?" Victoria rumbled. Her speech had become almost indecipherable in the last few years. By this time of night, it sounded as though it came from a talking stomach without the aid of a throat or vocal cords.

"I'm still using them." Hal kept walking.

"I didn't give 'em to you to keep."

Bess met the woman's eyes briefly as she passed between her huge form and the television. Victoria's oily gaze slid back to the screen. Bess and Hal followed the basement stairs down to Hal's room, where they sat on the legless couch and put their feet up on the chipped veneer of the coffee table, next to Victoria's old Bakelite card caddy. Bess picked it up by the metal ring in the center and spun it around. It contained one deck of red cards and one of blue, both with soft, dirty edges. When their mother was alive, she and Victoria used to play poker three or four nights a week.

"Bitch," said Hal. "She told me again today I should be paying rent. I told her this house was half mine. Well, a quarter mine, a quarter yours. She says I need to learn responsibility, but she knows I'm in school and I've got no money. Once you get a couple full-time paychecks, she'll be after you."

"Why'd you borrow her cards?"

"Just to harass her."

"You got anything to eat?" Bess asked.

"I've got a Suzy-Q. You should've asked me to stop at the gas station."

"I don't get paid for two weeks. I wondered if you'd float me a loan."

"Tuition was due this week so twenty-two bucks has got to last me five days, and I got to get gas and cigarettes."

"Well, give me half that Suzy-Q and a cigarette, Brother. I promise I'll make it up to you. How was your hot date anyway?"

Hal tore open the package with his teeth and unwrapped the pair of cakes. "Bess," he said, holding one out to her, "I've been meaning to tell you something." He rolled the cellophane into a ball and crunched it in his hand. Usually by now he would have turned on the television or stereo or both.

"What?" asked Bess. "Just tell me."

"My date wasn't with a girl."

"What? You decided she was a real dog?"

"Listen, Bess," Hal paused. "I just might be gay."

"Huh?"

"Gay, like, you know, queer. I don't know." Hall was going on in a normal voice, as though he was at the Stop-n-Gas giving directions to the highway doughnut shop, as though he wasn't talking about ruining his entire life. Bess felt the furniture and posters of Metallica and Def Leppard grow large, then small, and then far away. Hal cleared his throat. "I never said anything to you, but I've been wondering for a while. And there's this guy from my algebra class."

"Stop!" said Bess. "Don't tell me any more."

"Why not?"

"Aw, shit, Hal, why do we all have to be so screwed up?"

"See, that's why I didn't tell you before," said Hal. "This does not make me screwed up, Bess."

"No, you're perfectly normal. And so was Mom. And Aunt Victoria. Damn it." Without realizing it, she had eaten the entire cream-filled cake. She looked down at her empty hand.

DURING her eight-hour shift the next night, Bess tried to ignore the smell of popcorn and melted butter from the Westland 4 Theater, but her stomach growled the whole time. Bess had felt hungry since she could remember, an endless, gnawing, empty feeling stretching in all directions. She leaned against the glass door, careful not to push the handle. A sign read: "Use other exits after 6:00 P.M." The north parking lot spread out before her, spaces for three hundred cars and nobody there. What about that succession of community college girls Hal had dragged around, one after another? Didn't they mean anything to him? Bess turned and walked back toward the theater. This used to be a popular shopping center, but now it was run down and half the stores had for-rent signs in their windows. New malls on the south side of town had pulled away the business. She shone her flashlight through the window of the Navy recruiting office. On the way into work, she had introduced herself to the officer in charge, a small solid man in uniform. One poster inside featured a massive gray battleship plunging through the ocean, cutting a track through the waves. On another, a group of uniformed, white-gloved men and women stood in sharp rows on the deck of an aircraft carrier. Each time she passed the recruiting office she straightened her shoulders.

When her mother died of lymphoid cancer almost seven years ago, Bess had somehow figured that a well-dressed man with a beautiful house would show up and say he was their father and take them home, but there was only the big, quiet woman who'd lived with them and slept with their mother. Every weekday morning of that first year without Mom, Aunt Victoria had grimly watched Bess cross the tracks and cross M-98 to get to the bus stop. Then Victoria stood there on the porch with her arms crossed until the bus came. Victoria's solemn expression had scared Bess, and Bess avoided looking back at her. Until that year, Hal had been a constant close presence, almost a twin, but he'd gone ahead of Bess to middle school.

The last movie in the Westland 4 Theater let out at 10:47, and the scattering of patrons left the building through the proper exits, without incident. Hal was waiting for Bess outside, but they didn't speak until they were nearly home. "Have you done it with a guy?" Bess asked, as they climbed the little hill.

"Not yet. No." The Omni rattled over the tracks.

"So how do you know you're gay?"

"I just feel like I am."

"Why, Hal?" she pleaded. "Why do you have to do this?"

"I don't know, Bess. Get used to it." Hal slammed the Omni door, took the porch stairs two at a time, and didn't hold the screen door for her. Bess paused outside to look down the tracks, to listen for a train whistle, a sound with no uncertainty, but she heard only the creaking of the porch boards. Bess had always wanted their lives to be simpler, and now Hal was moving in the exact opposite direction. Didn't he realize he was giving up the chance to be normal? And didn't he realize that he could end up as awful and miserable as Victoria?

As Bess passed through the blue-lit living room, she heard the purr of the vibrating Naugahyde chair in which Aunt Victoria was sleeping. Sometimes she spent the whole night in it. Bess stood silent, lulled by the chair's hum, and she wondered why her mother had died instead of Victoria. Her mother had enjoyed life, was always laughing and showing those big teeth like Hal's. Even back then Victoria never laughed—she had just watched Bess's mother and waited for her next cue, as though nothing mattered but pleasing her. Bess longed to hear her mother's loud, clear voice, to ride in the passenger's seat of the car while her mother drove, to sit with her on the couch under that needlepoint picture of Jesus, doing a thousand-piece jigsaw puzzle of a sky full of orange butterflies. The vinyl couch was torn, the shag rug matted and sticky. Aunt Victoria was a fat monster, turning to liquid in her vibrating recliner, and Hal was queer. How could you have let this happen? she silently asked the needlepoint Jesus, which was now so dusty you couldn't tell who it was. "Why?"

"I miss her too," said Victoria quietly in her rumbling stomach voice.

Bess hadn't realized she had spoken the last word aloud. She stood frozen.

"I told your mother I wanted to die with her." Victoria's watery eyes reflected blue from the television. "But she wouldn't let me."

"Oh." Bess's heart pounded fearfully.

"You need something to eat?" Victoria asked, her voice strange and soft. Victoria hadn't offered her anything to eat in years. Victoria just left food in the kitchen, and Bess either ate it or didn't.

"No." Bess wanted to run upstairs and hide her face in her own pillows. Instead she ascended slowly.

THE third night after work, Hal didn't show up. Bess could've tried him at home, but she decided to walk rather than risk getting Victoria on the phone. She didn't want Victoria to offer to come get her, because it was a long process for Victoria to get dressed and out to her car, and then what would she and Bess talk about for twenty minutes on the way home? Over the last year, since Victoria and Hal had been fighting, Bess had gotten to feel that any unnecessary communication with Victoria was a betrayal of Hal. Victoria and Hal had always argued, but they had practically been enemies since a year ago when Hal tried to get into her personal food cupboard with a screwdriver. He'd been smoking pot, and the metal was heavy gauge, so he hadn't done much damage by the time Victoria came home. She'd screamed at him, that he was an ungrateful bastard, that he had no respect. Hal had said calmly, "What are you going to do, sit on me?" and Victoria had erupted in a frenzy and thrown all the spoons and forks from the silverware drawer, sending Hal running outside into the driveway. The following day, Hal had taken the mashed potatoes from leftover dinners in the refrigerator and shaped ridges into the letters d-y-k-e on the counter beside the sink.

Victoria was half-owner and head cook at the Michigan Waffle House on Red Arrow Highway, and Bess used to eat what Victoria brought home—meat-loaf slices and chicken-fried steaks arranged on plates with mashed potatoes and a dab of overcooked vegetables. Ever since Hal had been about fifteen, he'd lived mostly on junk food and liked it, but Bess always craved meals. As Bess watched Victoria get fatter, however, Bess felt worse and worse about eating those Waffle House specials. Bess took to standing at the kitchen counter and eating the food from the take-away containers as quickly as she could, but after the mashed potato business, Bess just couldn't let herself anymore. Finally she'd left so many plates untouched, with the food beginning to mold beneath the plastic wrap, that Victoria quit bringing them, and now she only brought home loaves of white bread and hunks of sandwich meat or sometimes uncut American cheese.

Because there was no sidewalk, Bess tramped across the edges of the well-kept west side lawns, punctuated by streetlights every hundred yards. Before Hal had gotten a car, they used to slip out on warm June nights like this and prowl their township. They sat on the bench nearest the pond, smoking and tossing rocks into the water. They'd talked about missing their mom and about how bad Victoria was in comparison. Bess had always been more afraid of Victoria than hateful, and she wondered if Hal had really felt the hate he expressed back then. Bess wondered if she knew Hal at all. Were they ever as close as she thought they'd been?

After she'd walked about two miles, a red Camaro pulled alongside her. "Hey, baby, you need a ride?" the young driver yelled out the window. Bess put her hat back on her head and peered in.

"Um, uh," the guy stammered. "Excuse me, Officer."

"Jimmy Jukes? Is that you?" she asked. "It's Bess, from shop class. I helped you build your mom a bookshelf. What are you doing here?"

"Are you a cop now?" he asked.

"Security guard. My ride didn't pick me up. Can you give me a lift?"

"Sure." He had a well-fed look, plump arms, a nice hank of white-blond hair.

She lowered herself into the car, whose passenger seat tilted so far back she could barely see over the dashboard. The front of the car seemed to protrude from their hips. Operating the vehicle and flipping the radio stations absorbed Jimmy entirely as they raced through downtown, past the factories, through their township. The car effortlessly climbed the hill to Bess's house. Hal's Omni wasn't there.

"How can you live right on the tracks?" asked Jimmy. "Don't you get woken up by the trains?"

"I like train whistles."

"Last summer I took a train to Chicago," Jimmy said. "Me and my mom and my little sister went to the museums."

"What museums?" Bess turned to him.

"Science Museum, Natural History Museum, Aquarium, Planetarium," said Jimmy. "We slept downtown in a hotel, the Palmer House."

Bess imagined herself and Jimmy walking along a boulevard lined with museums, skyscrapers, and hotels. They'd share the sidewalk with people traveling briskly from their jobs to their homes, neatly dressed, confident that their lives made sense. Those people rode subways and read newspapers along the way, and they arranged their apartments with only a few pieces of simple, attractive, durable furniture. She'd never been to Chicago, but she knew Lake Michigan must glitter in every backdrop, decorated with sailboats and military ships. She leaned toward Jimmy and pressed her lips to his. Jimmy wrapped both arms around her and bent her against the passenger-side door, ending on his knees. He kissed with a stiff tongue and sloppy lips. Bess and Hal had taught each other to kiss when they were eleven and twelve. Remembering it now, Bess felt ashamed. She pulled away and mumbled the first part of thanks-for-the-ride, but before she finished Jimmy said, "Oh, yeah," and lunged across the seat for her again. Bess had been reaching for the door handle and the door sprang open. Her upper body fell outside, Jimmy on top of her, kissing toward her neck.

"Hey!" she shouted. "Cut it out. Let me straighten up."

"Sorry, man." When she sat back up, he put an arm over her shoulders, apparently content just to sit with her. She pulled the door closed. Where was Hal? The house looked emptier and dingier than usual. The fake-brick tarpaper had torn above Aunt Victoria's window and next to the porch door. Bess's mom used to enjoy working on the house, and Victoria had fetched tools for her and held window trim in place while Bess's mom nailed. Her mom used to plant flowers along the foundation in summer. Nobody had wielded a hammer or garden trowel in years.

Jimmy wasn't a bad-looking guy, and he did have this nice car. Bess leaned into him and kissed him, and again he jabbed his tongue toward the back of her throat. Maybe she wasn't going to like kissing men. Bess had kissed a few guys around school, and she especially had liked pressing against Derek Hill under the stairs last year, but Hal said he wasn't good enough for her, and anyway that memory felt distant and uncertain. Maybe she would end up like her mother, sharing a bed with some woman. Bess didn't want to face a life of being different, of being a lesbian. She felt the claustrophobic softness of that word pressing against her like another woman's breasts.

"Jimmy, have you ever had sex in this car?" she asked.

"Huh?"

"I mean, how could you with those bucket seats?" She hoped she was giving the impression she'd done this before. In fact, the few times she'd come close, either Hal had shown up, or she'd stopped herself by thinking about what Hal would say. How could it have been such a short time ago that Hal was always near her?

"Maybe the b-back?" suggested Jimmy.

"It's too small." Bess gestured at the abbreviated back seat. The house was out of the question because they'd have to pass Victoria in her chair. And anyway, Bess liked her bedroom to be all her own, and she didn't want anybody else in it, not even Hal, who made fun of her neatly made bed and carefully arranged and dusted dresser top. "Maybe on the hood there." She stepped around the wide door and sat herself on the car, facing the house, her back to the tracks. "This'll work," she said.

Jimmy got out and walked around to where she sat. "Here on the car?" he asked. "You want to do it here? With me?"

"Sure. Why not?"

"Cool." Jimmy was just about her height. He reached under her shirt, and stroked her breasts through her bra like a couple of puppies.

Bess found the sensation annoying, and after she unbuttoned her uniform shirt and unhooked her bra, it still didn't feel right. She pushed his hands around behind her, closed her eyes, and pretended she was with Derek under the stairs. Victoria's bedroom light switched on and then went out. Bess wrapped her legs around Jimmy and pulled him toward her. She wished Hal would pull into the driveway, even though she knew her future as a normal girl depended on going all the way. "You got a condom?" she asked.

"Yeah. Maybe." Jimmy opened the passenger door, and fumbled in the glove compartment while Bess unbuckled her belt and removed her shoes, pants, and panties, then perched on the hood again. Residual engine heat warmed her naked bottom. Jimmy managed to produce a condom, which he held between two fingers, away from himself. He stared at Bess's pubic hair open-mouthed. Bess grabbed the condom and tore the plastic package with her teeth.

"Come on," said Bess. "Let's hurry." She reached to unzip him.

"I have to go," he said.

"What do you mean, you have to go?"

"Um, this is my brother's car," he said. "I took it without permission." Jimmy walked around to the driver's side and got in like a robot.

"You're going to leave?" Bess asked. "Right now, you're going to leave?" She slid off the car, disentangled her underwear from the pile of clothes and pulled them on. She picked up her pants and shoes in one hand, while in the other she still held the condom. Before he closed his door, Bess glimpsed him in the dash light. His face was round and so soft he probably had never shaved. "Let's go get something to eat," she suggested through the window.

He revved the engine of the Camaro. "I have to go. I'll see you around." As he backed out of the driveway, Bess tossed the condom after him like a little frisbee; it bounced off the car's bumper and landed in the dirt. Jimmy screeched away over the tracks.

Bess dressed and dragged herself up the porch stairs and into the kitchen where she spread margarine across two slices of stale bread from a big restaurant loaf. She wrapped the bread around the last chunk of uncut bologna and leaned against the sink to eat, staring at Victoria's metal cupboard. The strange, sad way Victoria had talked last night made Bess think that all she'd have to do was ask and Victoria would open this cupboard and give her whatever food was in there. Bess felt relieved that Jimmy had taken off, but she knew she was going to have to do it sometime with some guy. Hal always said she should wait because the first time should be special. He'd done it with three girls, as far as Bess knew, but apparently none of them had been special enough.

BESS woke at ten the next morning to discover Hal still wasn't back. On Saturdays, Aunt Victoria was at the Waffle House until noon. Bess wandered outside, climbed up onto the tracks, and looked in both directions along the corridor of steel, stones, and railroad ties. Chicago was 150 miles west, and Detroit was the same distance to the east. Those were places where things happened, places to which people rode trains. Hal always said Chicago didn't have anything that mattered. The Sears Tower is there, Bess had said, and Hal said the Sears Tower was just another tall building. In the direction of Detroit, Bess spotted a brown bag, probably tossed from a passing car. She opened it to find six returnable Natural Lite cans. She balanced atop a straight, shining rail past the scrubby line of sumac and pricker bushes—just beyond which was hidden Hal's marijuana patch—past the septic-tank pumping company, past the gravel pit. Beyond that were two junkyards and the shredder where people sold truckloads of scrap metal. By then she'd found eight more ten-cent bottles.

She tightrope-walked back toward the township center, past her house, to the Beer Store, where she traded the cans for a single-serving carton of milk and an individual packet of cheese and cracker sticks. A car honked; she didn't recognize the driver, but in case he was honking at her, she waved back to let him know she liked guys. On the other side of the tracks, she stopped at the little pond where she and Hal used to sit when they snuck out at night. She thought of throwing her three pennies change into the water, but as she listened to the approaching whistle of a freight train, she changed her mind. She placed the pennies side by side on one rail and ran to safety. As she waited alongside, she saw, for just an instant, the engineer in a John Deere cap and wire-framed glasses shake his finger at her, scolding.

Bess counted forty-seven boxcars and no caboose, and afterwards she searched the tracks and found one of the pennies, still warm from the violence. She closed her hand around the coin and noticed that her fingernails were short and ragged—she must have chewed them in her sleep again last night. She didn't see either of the other pennies. Sometimes they were thrown clear or pulverized. Once home, she went upstairs and emptied a tin box of flattened pennies onto her dresser. She hadn't added to the collection in years. Her mother had shown her how to place them on the tracks when she was only five or six and had helped her find them afterwards. Where had Victoria been? Bess wondered. Had she watched them from a safe place? Each of those old pennies was wafer-thin with only a ghost of Lincoln's head on one side and the Lincoln Memorial on the other. In a split second each had suffered a century's worth of wear. Each coin represented a hundred-ton train speeding past, imparting a bit of energy and leaving Bess behind.

Bess sat on the porch to eat her crackers. Over the tracks she could see the tops of cars passing on M-98, and she saw right into the cab of a semi-truck, saw a man's fat belly pushing against a bright red T-shirt. In a flash he was gone. He was probably hauling that trailer from some other part of the country, the South maybe, or New England. Years ago, Bess and Hal used to pull down their pants and moon the passing Amtraks from this porch, then practically fall down laughing at the shock on the passengers' faces. All her life Bess had felt as though she was going to burst—out of her clothing, out of her desk at school, out of this town, out of her own skin. Maybe Victoria had felt this way once too, but instead she just swelled and stretched.

Finally she heard the sputtering of the Omni, climbing up and over the tracks, threatening to stall, then regaining its power at the top. Hal parked in his usual spot, close to the house. He jingled his keys as he sauntered up and stood before her, grinning, eyes bright. "Hi, Bess."

"Thanks a lot for picking me up from work last night."

"Oh, no, Bess. I'm sorry. I totally forgot."

"No shit." She stood up and went into the kitchen, letting the screen door snap behind her. Hal followed, closing the door carefully, and she felt his eyes on her back as she wiped margarine across a piece of bread. She tipped back her head to hold in the tears, and Hal reached around and handed her a lit cigarette. She took a long draw and released it. When she turned, Hal was still smiling as though he were the township idiot.

"What's that on your neck?" asked Bess.

"What?" Hal felt his neck with his hand.

"It's a hickey," she said, leaning closer. "You got a goddamn hickey."

Hal ran his fingers over his neck. Bess imagined the red-bellied truck driver kissing Hal's neck. She saw the scolding, wire-rimmed engineer with his green-capped head curled on Hal's chest. Bess stuffed some bread into her mouth. "Aren't you hungry?" she asked.

"Someone took me out to breakfast," said Hal.

"Someone a man?"

"Yes."

"So what did you have?"

Hal rolled his eyes, but then complied, counting the items on his fingers. "Scrambled eggs, bacon and sausage, toast, and hash browns."

"Were the eggs fluffy?" she asked.

"Sure, I guess."

"Link sausages or patties?"

"Links."

"Figures." She drew on her cigarette. "Smoky flavored?"

"Kind of smoky." He shrugged.

"I went out with a guy last night, too," said Bess. "He had a Camaro." Her vision blurred. She wasn't ready for Hal to leave her, not for a man or anybody.

The clock read 12:10, time for the westbound noon train, and neither spoke while the whistle sounded. They felt the usual rumbling in the floor. Hal would make a life for himself, thought Bess, and looking into those bright, laughing eyes, she knew it wouldn't be a sad life like Victoria's. Maybe it would be complicated, but it would be like their mother's life, full of love and fun. Bess didn't know why the thought made her want to cry. Her left hand went slack, and she dropped her half-slice of bread. Just about the time it hit the linoleum, a crash like a dull gray battleship shook their house; metal screamed and tore and gave way in the distance. Hal glanced at his watch, then back at Bess. The two stood dumb, sharing the same thought: Aunt Victoria was returning from work. Bess imagined Victoria's car wrenched in two, her gelatinous body ripped to bits across the tracks, bloody jowls and butt cheeks spread all over the township. They tore outside to see Aunt Victoria pulling safely into the driveway in her modified white Ford. The car tilted toward the driver's side and nearly lifted off the ground on the other. The driver's seat had been moved back to accommodate her size. Bess and Hal watched Victoria extricate herself from behind the steering wheel, her head still attached to her body. The car sprang miraculously to a level position.

"She must've gotten new shocks," whispered Hal.

"What the hell are you staring at?" Victoria growled.

"What do you think?" said Hal.

In the sunlight Victoria's skin was pale and delicate, straining to contain the sagging mass of her face. She had virtually no eyebrows and no visible neck. Her short reddish hair was cut the way Bess used to cut her dolls' hair, uneven and bristly. Bess ran her hand over her own neck and through her heavy shoulder-length hair, but she couldn't look away. Victoria took tiny steps, heaving side to side. Her arms stuck out from her body, and her thighs rubbed together like massive limbless lovers dry-humping through turquoise polyester. A paper bag clutched firmly in one hand, a purse the size of a roast beef in the other, she took the porch stairs one foot at a time, resting at each step, her breathing labored.

Sirens blew in the background as fire trucks and police rushed to the accident to the east. Bess yearned to run along the tracks, to discover broken glass and twisted metal scattered over the railroad stones, but her eyes were on Victoria and her awesome locomotion onto the top step.

"Come on, Bess," said Hal. "Let's go see what happened."

"There's an accident," said Bess, feeling, for the first time she could remember, a need to apologize to Victoria.

The woman stepped onto the middle of the porch. Bess realized Victoria had probably never intended to have children, had never meant to make herself the center of such a circle, and yet there she had been, left alone with two of somebody else's. The sirens overpowered the sounds of creaking boards, and without warning, Victoria was crashing through the porch floor.

Brother and sister stared at the hole and at the head which stuck out.

"Stop gawking and get me out of here!" Victoria's sleeve was torn, and a few scrapes on her shoulder began to color with blood. Bess hesitantly grabbed Victoria under one armpit, and Hal held the other. They tugged but couldn't budge her. Bess felt her hand being enveloped by folds of damp flesh. She had avoided touching Victoria for years, for fear that anything about her might be contagious.

"Help me!" Victoria roared.

"Can't you crawl underneath?" suggested Bess, but upon inspection she saw that the perimeter was concrete blocks cemented in place, even behind the stairs. "Can you move at all?"

"I can't move!" Victoria shrieked. "Who built this damn porch? There's bricks down here. My foot's twisted."

"Maybe you should sit?" suggested Bess.

"Didn't you hear me? I can't move!"

Bess looked to Hal, but now he was leaning against the wall, his arms folded, grinning. "Isn't this an interesting situation," he said. He picked up Victoria's grocery bag, pulled out a bag of chocolate-covered nuts and swung them back and forth. "Are you still hungry, Bess?" He produced a pint of Ben and Jerry's ice cream and held his hand in front of it as if he were a game show beauty. "Chocolate Fudge Brownie."

"That food's mine!" said Victoria.

"We're going to need energy to get you out of there." Hal ripped open the bag of nuts with his teeth and got a spoon from the kitchen. Sitting on the steps just five feet in front of Victoria, Hal tossed chocolate-coated nuts into the air, one at a time, and caught them in his mouth. Bess marveled that not a single nut fell on the ground. When Hal opened the ice cream and handed it to her, Bess couldn't stop herself from biting spoonful after spoonful.

"You little rats!" screamed Victoria, her voice deteriorating as she grew angrier. "Get me oud-ear! Ass my food!"

A red Camaro in pretty good shape pulled in the driveway, and out stepped Jimmy, carrying something blue.

"My hat!" shouted Bess, snatching it out of his hand.

"You left it in the car."

"Hi, Jimmy. This is my brother Hal." Bess pulled the security guard hat onto her head.

"Welcome to the carnival, kid. The fat lady is there behind us," said Hal, crinkling up the empty plastic bag. Bess nudged him with an elbow. She couldn't stay mad at Hal.

"Care for the last nut?" he asked, holding it up, offering it to Bess, then Jimmy.

Jimmy shook his head no. He looked mild and insignificant in his clean khaki pants, as rosy-cheeked as somebody's favorite grandson. Bess tried to puzzle out what she had seen in him before, but her concentration kept breaking down. She looked at Jimmy's plump arms and wondered what it would be like to bite into him.

"Jimmy," said Hal. "Meet Aunt Victoria."

"Hello, ma'am," said Jimmy hesitantly.

"Go to hell, all of you!" sputtered Aunt Victoria's head. She was working at the wood to get an arm out. "I saw you last night."

"Sorry ma'am." Jimmy looked down. "I didn't . . . I mean . . ."

"Get me oud ear!" Her face was growing red.

"Shouldn't we pull her out?" Jimmy asked.

"This is part of her exercise plan," said Hal.

"But she's screaming for help."

"We tried," said Bess. "We can't budge her."

"I've g-got to go," he said, putting his hands in and out of his pockets. "See you around, Bess." He hurried into his car and vroomed away.

"How old is he, Bess, about twelve?" asked Hal.

"I don't know what I saw in him." Bess shook her head. "I was even going to let him poke me."

"Maybe he'll poke me instead," said Hal, wiggling his eyebrows.

"God, Hal," she said. "You've only been queer for three days, and already you're a slut."

Hal slapped his leg and laughed, and Bess felt the last scraps of her anger dissolve into the background of sirens.

Victoria's shouts had gradually turned to whimpers. Bess wished Victoria would stay angry, because her sadness was like the fin of some lone surviving sea monster showing above the water's surface, terrifying but heartbreaking. Bess's mother would never believe how things had turned out. Wherever her mother was, she'd want to think of Bess and Hal playing poker with Victoria, the three of them sitting together enjoying each other's company, telling funny stories.

"I'm calling 911," Bess said. Nobody argued.

When she returned from the house, Bess was relieved to hear Hal and Victoria fighting in their usual manner about Hal's taking more responsibility.

"I'm not paying rent in my own house," said Hal.

"What if I'm gone? How are you going to pay the bills then?" she demanded. Probably nobody but Hal and Bess would have understood all her rumbling.

"Yeah, but I've seen your bank statements. You've got over thirty thousand dollars in the bank. I work part-time for minimum wage."

"You keep out of my papers."

"You going to lock those up too?"

"They're sending someone over," said Bess. "It'll be just a couple minutes."

"Hey, Bess," said Hal. "I'm still hungry. Think we could get into that cupboard?"

"Stay out of my food," said Victoria. Sweat had softened and flattened the hair around her face. "That's my private food."

"I don't think we should," said Bess.

"And look!" said Hal. He waved Victoria's purse. "I'll bet the key's in here."

"Give me my purse, you bastard!"

"Oh, no, Bess. The dyke is calling me a bastard." He fished through the purse, pausing to hand Bess some butterscotch candies, which she put in her front pocket. "Keys!" he shouted and made them jingle. Bess wrapped two arms around Hal in an attempt to hold him back, but when he pulled away she followed. She couldn't yet bear to separate from the Hal of her childhood, her dominant twin.

The doors to the cupboard fell open to reveal a whole body of food—bagged, canned, and boxed. A sealed glass jar of pickled beef tongue stared out at them from eye level, repulsive with taste buds; Bess pushed it behind a box of bacon-cheddar snacks. The bottom shelf held canned fruit and meat, and the middle shelf had breakfast cereals and six varieties of snack cakes. On the top were chips, cheese curls and salted nuts.

"The train!" shouted Bess. "I forgot all about the train."

"We'll go look in a few minutes." Hal was gnawing on a beef stick. Fat oozed out the end. Victoria resumed wailing, competing with the fire trucks and police cars rushing to the wreck. Bess watched through the screen door as Victoria got one arm out. At first she waved it as if to flag down a passing motorist but then laid it to rest on the porch boards. Before she could work her second arm out, an ambulance screeched into the driveway, and two EMTs, a man and a woman, were climbing onto the porch.

"Ma'am, just remain calm. We'll get you out of there." The man spoke to Victoria in a gentle way that made Bess feel ashamed.

Bess and Hal stepped onto the porch. Victoria's face had grown as purple as a beet root. She hissed a few quiet obscenities. "Sonfa . . ." and "Ssss . . ."

"Can we talk to you?" asked the woman, calling Bess and Hal out to the ambulance. "Is this your mom?"

"No," said Bess, glancing at Hal. "It's our aunt."

"How much does she weigh?"

"Five hundred, maybe five-fifty," suggested Hal, "no more than your average beef cow." Bess elbowed Hal in the ribs.

"This is a complicated situation," said the woman. She stood taller than Hal and wore a white uniform shirt.

"We tried to pull her out," said Bess. "We didn't know what to do."

"We'll wait for the fire department. We can get a sort of harness. It should fit . . . They'll saw away some of the wood around her, then we'll lift her out." The woman looked at her watch.

"What's the hurry," asked Hal.

"She can't move," said the woman. "A person that big, it's hard standing on her feet in one place like that. Her ankles are probably swelling. My partner's taking her vitals now. Do we have your cooperation?"

"Sure," said Hal. "Haul away."

"What medications is she on?"

Hal named three medications, and Bess wondered how in the world he knew what drugs Victoria took. Back in the kitchen Bess grabbed a box out of the cupboard and stood over the sink devouring handfuls of candy-coated popcorn with peanuts. Before now, Bess had tried not to know anything about Victoria, about what she took or ate or thought; but now she wished she knew everything, including why her mother had loved this woman. Hal appeared with some menthol cigarettes he must've taken from Victoria's purse. They each smoked one, tapping their ashes into the drain. A new siren wailed.

"Let's go," said Hal.

"Should we leave Victoria?" Bess asked.

"We'll be right back."

Bess kept her gaze away from Victoria who was now rumbling at the EMT man taking the blood pressure on her free arm. Bess recalled that her mother used to plant impatiens along the edge of the porch stairs, the only colorful thing that would grow in such dense shade, she'd said. Hal was already running, so Bess jumped off the side of the porch to catch him, holding her hat to her head. She was jumping out of a Navy plane, running behind enemy lines. They could train her to fight and swim in the Navy, and to operate radar.

She and Hal didn't need to go far before seeing the wreck and smelling it. The four-car Amtrak had ground to a halt and the front was covered with mud, or what looked like mud. Across the tracks lay a Stalwart's Septic pumping truck. The crushed chassis sprawled on its side like a smashed pop can, and septic waste continued to dribble out. The fluid had already coated everything—the stones, the rails, the engine, and part of the Amtrak club car. Translucent wads of toilet paper smudged the train and the ground, and flies buzzed over the whole sticky mess. Intercity travelers stared out through the brown-streaked windows of the club car like unredeemed spirits. Bess and Hal sidled alongside a dark-eyed man who was leaning against an ambulance. He wore a name tag which read "Robert" and "Kalamazoo Life Care."

"Was anybody hurt?" asked Bess.

"Truck stalled on the tracks," he said in a surprising Southern drawl. "Driver got out and ran. He's okay. Passengers are fine. The engineer refuses to go to the hospital. That's him with the fire chief, with the bandage on his head." The driver had glanced at Bess but addressed his comments to Hal. Hal raised his eyebrows at him. Bess stubbed the ground with her toe. "Hal, we'd better go back and check on Victoria."

"I'll be right behind you, Bess."

She stepped back over some pooled fluid in which an expired condom floated; another condom lay ghostly translucent over a railroad tie. Farther down the tracks, Bess misstepped and submerged her canvas shoe in a puddle of sludge. She worked the shoe off against the rail and left it behind. Hal was still talking with the driver. Bess kicked off the other shoe and went barefoot. Hal caught up with her as she reached the house, where they found a fire department tow truck, a second ambulance—this one a cube van—and a police car. The porch hole had been enlarged, and Aunt Victoria was fastened into a web of rope and canvas. The female technician squatted in the hole beside Victoria, easing her free from below, and Victoria was lifted slowly, like an ancient shipwreck rising from the depths into the corrupting air. She swayed slightly as the boom truck moved her forward, away from the porch, with the straps of the harness pressing into her flesh. The side of her shirt had ripped so that a monstrous breast threatened to burst over a strap, and Victoria seemed to be straining to hold herself together by force of will. Bess reached up, and grabbed Victoria's shirt and flesh in both hands and held the seam together as she walked beside her over sharp driveway stones. Though her chest and neck heaved, Victoria's eyes remained tightly shut and her white face was turned skyward. The harness held her arms and legs outspread so she now resembled a floating sea creature, reaching out in all directions at once.

Bess watched Aunt Victoria the way Victoria had watched her waiting for the school bus all that first year. Victoria must have been desperately frightened for Bess back then, terrified at sending her motherless and unprotected into the world each morning, into a world which would flatten a person, or pulverize her, or if she was lucky, throw her clear. While her mother was dying, Victoria had stayed with her in the hospital. Bess now imagined her mother's thinly covered bones as enveloped, awash, in Victoria's ample flesh. Night after night, Victoria had sat a silent watch on death, staring out through a tunnel with an intensity as foreign as the moon to twelve-year-old Bess. If anyone were a match for death, surely it would have been Victoria, but death had won.

Victoria was received into the attendants' hands, released from the harness, and laid on the oversized stretcher. Their hands fussed over her body, working in what looked like caresses. Victoria shook her head, rumbled that she didn't want to go to the hospital.

"It'll just be for a little while, to check you out," said the female technician.

"Arm comin ahhme anide?" asked Victoria. The technician looked confused.

Bess said, "She asked if she'll come home tonight." Hal stepped up and placed Victoria's purse near her hand.

"Sure you will, if nothing's wrong."

"She's probably going to have to rest for a few days," said the woman. "You two should tell the doctor if you'll be able to take care of her."

Victoria looked hungrily at Bess's and Hal's faces, as if to devour whatever resemblance she could find to their mother. Bess nodded yes, that they could take care of her. The two technicians, two firemen, and a cop slid the stretcher into the cube van, and drove

Victoria away. One by one, each of the remaining emergency vehicles departed, over little Jimmy's condom, then over the tracks. Bess and her brother sat on the porch side by side.

"Hal," she said. "Everything seems so different now." She felt the distance between them growing louder like drums, their separation as inevitable as the cleaving of Siamese twins.

Hal shrugged. "The sewage might be good for my pot plants."

"Do you hate Victoria?" asked Bess.

"Every family fights. We'll drive up and see her in a few minutes."

They heard the sounds of the crashed westbound train finally moving. In the midst of the chaos a new engine had backed up to the wreck, and now the train approached them with two engines, creeping along, gradually gaining speed. The sewer smell wafted over the house. Bess elbowed Hal, then stood, pulled down her cutoffs and aimed her hind end at the train. Hal stood alongside and made the same salute. As the whistle grew distant, the evening wind carried away the residual fragrance.

"I'm joining the Navy." Bess sat back down. "The recruiter said my grades were good enough." She expected Hal to argue, but he only nodded. Hal was releasing her into the universe. Bess shook a cigarette from his pack but didn't trust herself with the matches, for she was adrift, floating toward some new planet.

"Do you think you'll miss me?" asked Hal, looking toward Chicago.

"Don't you know?" Bess shook her head slowly. "I miss you already."

Shotgun Wedding

CLEARLY this groom is more accustomed to lugging hay bales and veal calves, but with those big hands he manages to lift my sister's veil and smooth it back prettily over her hair, revealing her face and shoulders. I feel vaguely shameful about this ritual undressing, though I myself have stripped naked in all sorts of places with men whom I've no intention of marrying. Now, as the groom bends toward my sister's face, the bought flowers vibrate in the vases, and my hands shake. My sister, who has a tiny waist and who is an honest-to-goodness virgin, absorbs the moment before the kiss and pulls all the energy from the room, leaving the rest of us feeling dull.

The softness of their kiss gives me the seasick feeling that I'm with my sister and the groom on the honeymoon bed. After all, I shared a room with her until I left for college. I look away, to the pastor who looms over this procedure with the gravity of a hangman, then up to the electric chandelier, which gleams motionless. No longer do I fear that my dress will come unzipped or that the brass fixture will fall and crack open my sister's skull; instead I fear that this kiss will not end, that time will freeze and abandon me in this orbit. My sister's eyes are closed, her lashes spread out over her cheeks. Even after they've opened again, her eyes remain in the sleep of that kiss as though covered with a milky effluent, something the fairies would make in their mouths and spit onto those they favor.

In the upholstered front-row pew, my parents' eyes seem covered with the milky substance as well. My mother dabs her face with a Kleenex; in the garden she wipes the sweat off her forehead with the bottom of her T-shirt. My father, who didn't even wear a suit to my aunt's funeral last year, is dressed like Fred Astaire and has got his legs crossed. The change in my parents frightens me more than walking on carpeting in three-inch heels, and I'm wishing that I had carried my own weedy bouquet of wild phlox or had neglected to shave my legs or had worn a necklace of stones, done anything that would make me feel more like myself. I'm letting my sister down by being sucked into her fairy tale. Someone should always remain vigilant.

My job now is to follow the bride and the groom down the aisle. My sister's gown is something out of a 1940s movie, sleeveless and crusted with embroidery, front and back—I wouldn't let her tell me what she paid for it. Her gloves extend past her elbows, to tiny biceps unbefitting a farm girl. Though we are not a touchy family, my father reaches out from the pew and squeezes my free hand with his calloused palm. He taught me to shoot, my father, by pressing his index finger over my own to squeeze the trigger the first time. As I shuffle behind the bride and groom, I let my father's hand drop and look away so he doesn't see that I've started to cry.

When my father taught me to shoot, I was ten. First I shot at a target placed against a side of the hill in the pasture, and then at raccoons who tried to get into the chicken house. My sister refused even to touch the shotgun; she did not want to be Annie Oakley or Laura on the prairie. She wanted to be Cinderella or Snow White, passive and pure at heart. Like the princess who couldn't bear the pea beneath the mattress, when my sister started her period, she spent three days in bed without speaking—she had seen the health movies in school, but she had honestly not believed that her own body would betray her in this way. My father always worried about my sister not learning to shoot; he told my mom that a girl like her especially needed to be able to defend herself.

From now on she has her husband to defend her, I suppose. And who knows? Maybe the two of them will have one of those lives of enduring bliss you hear about on the radio. I remain six feet behind my sister so I don't step on her train, and I take the hand of the flower girl, my cousin's daughter, who has emptied the basket of rose petals and is now fidgeting at having to walk so slowly. Suddenly, in the first unchoreographed move of this ceremony, just before passing through the double doors beneath the "Exit" sign, my sister turns and looks back toward the altar. Had I anticipated that she would then look at me, I'd have straightened out my face and smiled, but she catches my eyes full of tears and my mouth set grimly in the memory of shooting my first raccoon dead outside the chicken house, of the shot picking its body up off the ground and slamming it against the barn wall.

My sister wears all kinds of waterproof mascara and eye shadow, so her eyes appear especially white and alert; but the fairy milk clears the instant her gaze meets mine, leaving the naked look of a girl in the water who can't swim. She stares at me for one second, two seconds. Why doesn't the groom notice my sister's distress? He should turn her around and kiss her hard, crushing those flowers in his pocket if necessary. Kiss her, I want to yell. Instead, I collect myself into a half-smile which does not fool her. There's nothing I can do except reach down and straighten her embroidered train which I have almost just stepped on. The flower girl bends and helps, grateful for something to do. Through the back of my head I feel my parents watching.

When I was thirteen, my sister was nine. That was one of the winters both my father and my mother worked at the Halko plant making automotive armrests and glove boxes on third shift, leaving the house at ten-thirty at night. Though the area is starting to get built up, our house then was a half-mile from the next neighbor; the police might take half an hour to get to us, so my father told me to sleep with the shotgun against the wall beside my bed. He placed it there before he left each night. "If you hear anyone outside, you get that gun," he had instructed me. "If anyone comes into this house without your permission, you blow 'em away, honey."

My sister always slept soundly—Sleeping Beauty, my mother

called her because she was lost to our world for ten or twelve hours a night. I have never needed that much sleep, but I could read without disturbing her in the bed next to mine, or reorganize the shells and polished stones on the top of my dresser by shape or color or size. After my parents went to work, I sometimes got up and walked the floors of all the rooms, including what would have been my sister's room if she'd been willing to move into it. We'd cleared it out and painted it for her; she could have put up filmy curtains instead of living with the burlap ones Mom helped me make. Mom began to store boxes of our outgrown clothes in the room that my sister did not occupy, and eventually she put her sewing machine and ironing board back in.

One night just after Mom and Dad left for work, when the oil burner kicked off and left the house silent, I heard the crunching of driveway gravel, steps in a man's cadence, so that I thought it must be my father returning. I looked out from the window in the landing and did not see his truck, but saw a tall stranger walking toward our porch, glancing side to side, his hands in his pockets. He wore a quilted, red-checked flannel shirt without a jacket though it was below freezing out. I descended the stairs and moved toward the front door as the man ascended to the porch, so that we approached one another with trepidation, he with his laced-up workboots, and myself barefoot with the shotgun loaded and pointed forward, safety off. The man did not knock, but the doorknob turned halfway. I touched it to assure myself that my parents had locked the door on their way out. The brass conducted cold from outside. I stepped back and pointed the gun at the latch.

"Wait until an intruder's in the house," my father had said, "or else you'll have to drag him inside and tell the cops that's where you shot him." He had said this as if joking, but now I envisioned myself dragging that man's body across the threshold by one limp arm or a belt loop. My father had told me to shoot a man anywhere on the abdomen, because I couldn't miss at close range, and the twelve gauge at close range would tear a man apart. When I'd shot that first raccoon outside the chicken house its body turned inside out.

The man stood on the other side of the door, perhaps deciding which window to break, or deciding how much force it would take to destroy the front door hardware. It never occurred to me that the man might have come for warmth or merely to steal money or the television. My sister sleeping upstairs no longer seemed a regular flesh-and-blood girl, but had become a rare treasure like a unicorn or a living swan made of white gold, and it made sense that our house would be under siege.

The gun grew heavy against my shoulder, but the weight felt natural, and the metal of the barrel and the trigger gradually warmed to my body temperature. Whenever I'd actually pulled the trigger, I'd been bruised by the recoil; now I looked forward to that burst of pain again, the price I would pay for exploding this man's stomach or heart. One blast should take him down, but if he was still standing, I'd load and shoot again. After the first, there were four shots in the magazine, enough to kill a bull, or even a vampire. After I shot that raccoon, my father dug a hole and buried it right there; he said the other raccoons would smell it and stay away.

The man stepped to the side and looked in through the skinny single-paned window beside the door. Most likely he saw first the unidentifiable roundness of the end of the shotgun barrel, the size of a nickel, which I had moved to point straight at him. Then he cupped his hands against the glass and let his eyes adjust to the darkness, in which he gradually made out my face, my strawberry blond hair which has darkened in the years since, my freckles, my gray eyes. My face gave away nothing, and in the several seconds during which the man stared into my eyes, he might have seen his own self turned inside out.

His face seemed surprisingly delicate except for a day's growth of beard; his skin was pale and his eyes dark, quiet, and dilated. I had not expected an intruder to be beautiful. I let the gun slide forward slightly, so the tip of the barrel kissed the window, clinked against the glass like the turning of a key. The pretty gaze dissolved. His jaw fell loose. As the man's face disintegrated, I stood unearthly still, not even blinking, poised to fire. I felt no fear, standing in a flannel nightgown which was both too large and too short, whose pattern of galloping horses had faded, and whose frayed ruffle moved back and forth across my legs, brushing the bare skin just below my knees. I felt no fear, though my legs were thin, hardly bigger than the barrel of the gun, and my arms were strained. I felt no fear at the prospect of shooting this man, of watching his body crumple, then dragging the corpse inside, quickly so the heat didn't escape from the house.

I held the gun up long after the man turned and walked down the steps and ran across our frozen lawn toward the road. His hands were still in his pockets, but he held his arms tight against his sides now. When he looked back over his shoulder at the house, he tripped over an apple tree stump my father had been meaning to dig out with the backhoe. He briefly lay prone before he took his hands out of his pockets to push himself up and continue to the road at a jog. The electricity in the air dissipated, but still I held that gun up, even after my arms began to shake, pointing it at the front door where now only the ghost of the man remained. The house air seemed dusty and suffocating. A screech owl cried broken heartedly from the woods across the road. The furnace kicked on and kicked off twice before I lifted that gun off my shoulder and let my arms hang free. I would not sleep that night but would walk the rooms of the house until morning. Under my weight the floorboards creaked in a thousand places. I returned again and again to the room where my sister slept. Hour after hour, while I kept watch, her princess hair curled onto her pillow, and all night her long dark lashes rested against her cheeks, beneath eyes clenched firmly in dreams.

The Fishing Dog

AT first Gwen thought it was Jake coming downstream in the boat, but it turned out to be his brother Dan. At the noise of the boat engine, the yellow Labrador retriever across the river moved up the lawn toward its house, and a great blue heron who must have been fishing on the other side of the cabin launched itself into flight. Gwen watched it ascend, wishing she'd known the bird was nearby so she could have spied on it. There was another guy with Dan, but she could see he was about half as big as Jake. Maybe they'd brought food. She'd like to eat something besides fish that didn't come out of a can. She reeled in her line and grabbed Dan's prow as he idled alongside the dock.

"What do you think?" yelled Dan over the engine noise.

"You got a new boat, Dan."

He cut the motor. "She's pretty, ain't she? Got a steal on her from a guy getting divorced."

"Where's Jake?" Gwen didn't usually talk to Dan. Usually she stood by while Jake and Dan talked to each other.

"That's what I come to tell you, honey. Jake's in jail."

"For what?"

"For killing a man."

"You're lying."

"I ain't going to lie about a thing like that. Jake didn't mean for it to happen."

"If it's an accident, they'll let him go."

"Except this ain't the first time."

Gwen pointed at the five-gallon fish pail that Dan was lifting off the boat. "Give me that."

"Gwennie, are you crying?" He rested the bucket on the dock and put his arms around her. Dan was fatter than his brother, but he didn't feel all that different close up. Gwen thought of pulling away from him, of running in the woods until she fell into stinging nettles and poison ivy. She thought of smashing her fists into Dan's chest. If she'd had an axe in her hand, she'd have swung it into a tree.

She grabbed the bucket, sloshing water on herself and Dan. Two of the three catfish inside were longer than her forearms. Their seaweedy whiskers brushed against the sides as they slid over one another. "I've been waiting for a catfish," she said, holding her head up to let the tears drain through the backs of her eyes.

"These come from Willow Island," said Dan. He seemed even fatter suddenly, unsure of himself, waiting for a cue from Gwen, who wasn't accustomed to giving cues, especially not to men twice her age.

"Who you got with you?" she asked. The other man made no motions to disembark.

"That's just Charley. He works at the plant with me." Charley was skinny and had no teeth so his lips caved in.

Dan took the fish from the bucket one by one and held each carefully as he nailed its head to the nearest oak; the three tails strained and curled against the bark. The men stood by while Gwen stunned one with the hammer and began tearing off its skin with pliers.

"Tell me all of what happened." Though she knew better, Gwen brushed against the catfish fins and her fingers burned.

"Well, we left the Pub and was at the Tap in Roseville having a few beers, and Jake and this guy he's playing pool with gets to fighting, and Jake knocks him against a wall. But Jake don't seem to notice the guy is passed out so he picks him up and keeps hitting him."

Gwen could imagine Jake, crazy-eyed and drunk beyond talking to, slugging like a slugging machine gone haywire. When he was in that condition, he'd even pick a fight with Dan. Or Gwen if she didn't keep out of his way. Gwen's fingers trailed again across a catfish whisker. The pain was so sharp she was surprised not to see blood on her knuckle.

"Next thing you know, the son-of-a-bitch is dead. Brain hemorrhage or some shit like that. So the cops show up and they figure out right away about the other charge."

"What other charge?" asked Gwen.

"The manslaughter charge."

"What manslaughter charge?"

"Well, whatever the hell they're calling it. Up in the U.P. last winter. Jake must've told you about it. Why do you think he's been out here in the woods since February?"

The trees became thicker and taller around her. She tugged on the second catfish skin, trying not to let it split, but she stung her wrist and made a mess of it.

"Hey, Charley, toss me a beer," said Dan. Gwen looked up to see the can fly through the air. When Dan opened it, foam poured all over his hand. "How you coming there, Gwen?"

She worked slowly with the pliers on this last, smallest one, tugging around the sides evenly, removing the skin in one piece down to the tail. If what Jake had done in the U.P. was an accident, why hadn't he mentioned it to her?

"All the police had on that trouble up north was a description including them spaghetti scars on the back of his hand. It was the same deal, Jake drunk and not knowing when to quit."

"Can I see him?"

"It'd be better if you didn't, honey."

What else hadn't Jake told her about in the last five months? A wife, maybe?

Inside the cabin, Gwen fried the fish the way she would have for Jake, with cornmeal and flour in the last of the bacon grease. About the time they finished eating, Dan turned on his battery-powered fluorescent lantern. Gwen was surprised at how bug-stained the walls were, how ratty the rug looked in the cold light, and how grimy she had let her arms and legs become. She asked Dan to tell her more.

"There ain't nothing more to it."

"Does Jake own this cottage?" she asked.

"Me and Jake own it together. You can stay here as long as you want, Gwennie. Don't you worry your pretty head about that."

Dan and Charley drank beer while Gwen washed dishes with water she lugged in and heated on the propane stove. Gwen, who didn't usually drink, managed to get down three beers before she felt herself nodding off. She awoke with her forehead on the table, with Dan stroking her hair. Dan told Charley he could sleep in the rocking chair on the screen porch and threw him a sleeping bag from the boat. Then he half-carried Gwen into the tiny bedroom with him. She felt obliged, as though refusing to go to bed with him would've been inhospitable.

Early in the morning, she crawled out of bed and heated water for powdered coffee. There wasn't much propane left. When it ran out she'd have to take the boat to Confluence to get the tank filled, which would cost twenty dollars she didn't have. She walked past Charley slumped sideways in the porch chair—he'd have a terrible stiff neck when he woke up. From her dock she watched the green Jeep pull away from the house across the river. This evening when the man got home she could watch his yellow dog hunker down again at the river's edge. Since Jake had gone, she'd seen it catch a fish in its jaws five times.

After more than two weeks without Jake, Gwen had forgotten how a big man generated heat around him; the bedroom had been stifling last night. She'd never meant to sleep with Dan, but she'd let herself forget who he was when he rolled onto her. Guilt pricked her, as sharp as the catfish stingers. If Jake found out, he'd punch her like she was a man, and maybe she deserved it. She pushed those thoughts below the surface. The steam rose off her coffee as mist rose from the water.

Gwen found her siphon hose and sucked gas out of Dan's tank, enough for a trip up to Confluence, two maybe if she rowed back down without the motor. Or maybe she'd take a fishing trip to Willow Island where last time she'd seen a heron carry a little snake up to its tree nest. She rinsed the fuel taste from her mouth with coffee and spat it into the river. Back in the cottage, she lifted three beers out of Dan's cooler and hid them in the kitchen cupboard. Dan called her name, and she stepped into the tiny bedroom. He didn't look as much like Jake as he had yesterday; he looked more like a swollen possum washed up on her river bank.

"Come here, beautiful," he said. She hesitated, but the room was small enough that he was able to reach across, grab her arm, and drag her to the bed. He pulled off her loose jeans without unzipping them and pushed her T-shirt up around her shoulders. She bent her knees and tried to sit up, but he held her down with one hand and ran the other over her breasts and along her stomach. He pushed her knee out to the side and heaved himself onto her, then worked his hand beneath her buttock to tilt her, pushing deeper. He sighed her name in hot breath. She turned her head to look out the window but saw only empty sky. She wondered how she had let this happen. "Oh, Gwennie," he moaned again, and she felt his sickening heat over her face, through her hair, filling the room. She longed to see a heron fly across the sky framed by the window, its neck pressed into a tight S. She needed to feel that prehistoric swoop or hear the monster shriek of an angry male. A flash of blue-gray wing and she would survive this.

After Dan rolled off her, he fell asleep. Gwen pulled away from him and picked her clothes up off the floor with shaking hands. In the kitchen she sifted weevils out of the flour for pancakes—she needed to do something measured. Each time she let herself think of Dan lying in her bed, she had to sit and hold her head in her hands. She thought about grabbing the butcher knife with the burned handle and going back in there. She'd feel for a place between two ribs and sink the blade in. When Charley appeared in the kitchen with his gummy smile, holding his neck, she invited him to sit at the table. She opened a beer, poured half of it in her batter, then handed the open can to Charley. His company calmed her stomach. "Are you hungry, Charley?" she asked. "Did you sleep good?"

"You's got a toilet around here?" asked Charley. Gwen directed him to the outhouse.

WHEN Dan and Charley first powered away, Gwen was relieved. But as soon as the boat rounded the bend, she felt lonesome and nauseated. Dan had given her the food from his cooler—cheese, summer sausage, and sleeves of crackers—before pulling away to return to his wife. Later Gwen discovered two twenty-dollar bills on her pillow. She wished Dan had said something like, "Jake wanted me to give you this."

Hours later, after the Jeep returned, the fishing dog appeared in his place on the other side of the river. To lighten the boat for rowing, Gwen pulled off the outboard with shaking hands and placed it carefully on blocks so as not to bend the propeller, then rowed across. She had never touched the dog or seen him up close, but when she called him, he jumped into her boat. Gwen petted his head, which seemed to repel drops of water. "I'll call you King," she whispered, thinking of the big-headed kingfisher bird who lived across the river from her dad's trailer in Snow Pigeon. She didn't consider it stealing when she took the dog to her side and let him out to sniff the water's edge. If he wanted to stay and chase the raccoons up trees, that would be his choice. With a companion like him, Gwen wouldn't mind staying in the woods. But it wasn't long before she heard a man's voice shouting, "Ren-e-gade!" The dog plunged into the water and swam the fifty or so yards to the other side.

A WEEK of heavy rain made Gwen a prisoner in the cottage. When Jake was there, she hadn't minded so much being without a phone or a radio, but now she longed for voices. Back in Snow Pigeon, after years of pleading, she and her sister Paula had finally talked their dad into getting phone service. They'd been working on getting him to buy a television next. But even just bickering with Paula would have been entertainment enough now. The rain banged on the corrugated roof, making the same sound as rain hitting their trailer.

Years ago Gwen's father used to take her fishing; Paula was too fidgety, too noisy, Daddy said. Gwen used to practice sitting stone quiet sometimes so she could be a good girl in the boat. For the last couple years, though, when Daddy came in from work in the evenings, he just brooded and drank. For months before she left, Daddy, quiet in the best of times, hadn't spoken to her except to yell at her, and Paula was mad because Gwen upset Daddy by not staying away from boys. When Jake had started fishing in the river in front, talking sweet while Daddy was still at work, he had seemed like a knight to the rescue. When he asked her to come down the river with him, she'd hardly hesitated. And since she'd left in April, she'd never dared call Daddy or Paula, even to let them know she was alive. Gwen could still feel their anger flowing with the river's current all the way from Snow Pigeon.

THE first day the rains let up, Gwen crossed the river. She called the dog to her boat, and he jumped in. But before she could push off, the man who drove the Jeep appeared from behind the shed and stepped knee-deep into the water to grab the prow of her boat. He was thin and probably only a few inches taller than Gwen. "Evening," he said calmly. "Where are you taking my dog?"

"A-cr-cr-cross the river. I just . . . I live over there."

"I know where you live, but why are you taking Renegade?" His biceps strained against his bones. Tendons stood out on one side of his neck as Gwen continued rowing in place without speaking. He said, as much to himself as to her, "You're just plain not going to answer me."

Mosquitos lined up on Gwen's legs and arms, and she could feel them settling onto her face and sinking their stingers. She watched two, then three, then five mosquitos land on the man's forehead. His hair fell straight down from a center part; if it were any darker, it wouldn't have been blond. When he let go of her boat with one hand to swat at mosquitos, Gwen was able to break free. The man folded his arms and stood in the water watching her, looking more perplexed than angry as she rowed away. His jeans were soaked up past his knees, and his figure grew smaller as Gwen approached her own side. She parked at her dock, and King jumped out and swam to shallower water to sniff along the muskrat holes and mangled roots. The man across the river disappeared and returned with binoculars and walked the plank onto his oil-barrel float. Twenty minutes later he called, "Ren-e-gade!"

WHEN Gwen motored to Confluence to buy toilet paper and bottle gas, she didn't go near the Pub for fear of seeing Dan. Partway home, just above Willow Island, she cut the engine and floated downstream with the current, rowing only to fix her direction. The miles of dark, empty river belonged to her, but she'd have traded it all for one party, where music played and people danced under lanterns strung tree-to-tree. She'd drift near the bank or near a big island, and the people would motion her over to join them. Instead, she rounded the last bend above her hut and saw a speedboat there. A bright, cold light shone from inside the cabin—Dan's fluorescent lantern. She steered herself toward the opposite bank, soundlessly maneuvering to the downstream side of the fishing snag just below King's house. She watched her cottage until the light went out, and then she lay her head on a faded orange life vest. Over and over, she shrugged away the memory of Dan's hairy belly and crushing weight.

Gwen awoke shivering to barking and pale sunlight. King was licking her face. She pushed her fingers into the dog's fur, but when she saw a man standing over her, she jumped up and threw one foot into the boat. The Jeep driver looked into her face.

"I'm sorry," said Gwen. Her clothes were caked with mud.

"Sorry for what?"

"For taking your dog."

"Don't worry," he said. "Dogs are loyal. You feed them and they come back to you." He nodded toward her cabin. "If you're hiding from this guy, you can come to my house. He's going to see you if you stay here."

She checked the knot holding her boat to the fallen maple, then, unsure what else to do, followed the man along the river path. The dew that coated the weeds and grass would be slow to burn off. Where the poison ivy had climbed to the tops of trees, the triple leaves had already turned autumn red.

The side door opened into a kitchen with white-painted walls, yellow countertops, and a glossy wooden floor. But the baseboards were pulled away, revealing the uneven gap where the wallboards met the floorboards, and the table was piled with newspapers and books. "Do you want coffee?" the man asked. "Bathroom's through there if you need it."

She ventured onto a raw plywood floor, into what should have been a living room but contained a rumpled, queen-sized bed. Through the sliding glass door Gwen saw her dilapidated cabin on stilts, stained cottage green, Dan's boat still parked at its dock. The top drawer of a dresser was open a few inches, exposing a cache of pure white bras and underwear. Gwen hadn't seen a woman here since she'd been watching, since Jake had disappeared. She traced her finger along the scalloped lace edge of a bra. When the man appeared in the doorway, Gwen hurriedly shut the drawer.

"Oh, don't worry. She's long gone. I guess she left those for my next girlfriend."

"I'm sorry." A woman who wore those things was probably a great loss.

The man handed Gwen a mug of coffee almost white with cream. Jake had insisted she learn to drink coffee instant and black. She inhaled the aroma so deeply that she had to touch the dresser to steady herself. She had eaten French fries in Confluence yesterday, but nothing else.

"Do you want to take a shower?" he asked.

"No."

"You can't wear those clothes. Take something of Danielle's."

Gwen looked at the dresser and back at him.

"Why the hell not?" He laughed. "I was going to throw all her clothes in the river, anyway, let them float away with the current. Go ahead and take anything you want."

She took a long draw of the coffee, which tasted so good she didn't want to swallow. It didn't surprise Gwen that the man would want to take care of her; after Daddy, Jake had taken care of her, and Dan would now if she let him. She looked for a place to rest her cup, but the dresser top looked too clean, and she didn't want to leave a ring. In fact she didn't want to leave any trace that she had been here. In a lower dresser drawer she found and rejected the neatly folded blouses in pink, white, and mint green. The other dresser contained a tangle of the man's blue jeans, T-shirts, and sweatshirts. She put on one of each, and even the jeans weren't a bad fit when she cinched them at the waist with the most worn of three leather belts. She draped her muddy clothes over the side of the bathtub and wondered if this guy was accustomed to women who dressed as though every day was their wedding day and who never got smeared with creosote or fish guts.

She managed to retrieve her coffee from the plywood floor without spilling it. Another room opened off the living room and was probably supposed to be the bedroom, when it wasn't torn down to wall studs. In the middle of the room, balanced on sawhorses, was the curved wooden skeleton of what looked like a boat. Back in the kitchen, she found the man cooking. He placed items on the newspaper-covered table one at a time, and each thing glowed as it passed through a shaft of sunlight: plates, forks, two glistening jars of jelly, a stick of yellow-white butter on a cream-colored plate.

"You've got to be hungry." He held out his hand and shook hers. "I'm Michael. Mike Appel. I've lived here for a year, and other than the guy next door, you're the first person from the neighborhood who's been in my house. You'd think on a river, people'd always be socializing." He gestured with the spatula. "But look at you—you get house guests, you run off."

"I'm Gwen. Gwendolyn."

"That's a pretty name." He repeated it wistfully. "Gwen-do-lyn."

They way he laughed as he talked made Gwen want to say more, to add, "It was my mother's name too," but then she might end up trying to explain to a stranger that her mother left a husband and daughters, six and eight, and never even wrote. Michael pushed aside several books that lay open on top of each other and set a glass of orange juice and half an omelet in front of her. Gwen was careful not to put her glass down on the pages or the covers. One book with a library sticker was called *Building Bookshelves.* A paperback was called *More Greek Mythology.*

"What do you do over there at that little house?"

She shrugged. "I fish." Gwen thought the omelet, with mushrooms, onions, and peppers, was the best thing she'd ever tasted.

Next time she was in Confluence, if she had money, she'd buy eggs. She had only six dollars and some change left.

"I've never fished," he said. "Don't even know how to fish, but I'm building a boat."

"Fishing is easy," said Gwen.

"Maybe you can give me a lesson, tell me what tastes good out of this river. Hell, I don't even know how to bait a hook."

Gwen shrugged and lifted the edge of the omelet to look inside at tiny cubes of green pepper. There wasn't anything to teach, really.

"I should have put tomatoes in this," he said, "but I forgot to buy them. I work for the power company, so I know you've got no power over there. Have you got a generator? A phone?"

She shook her head no. The fishing dog lay under the table so Gwen worked her bare feet beneath him. She had left her shoes in the boat.

"It's incredible you live like that." He chewed, swallowed. "And you don't have a job?"

Gwen shook her head. A half-sheet of paper on the table read "Overdue book notice."

"Your house looks like a hideout, you know, like a place in a movie where criminals get away from the cops. Would you be the gangster's girlfriend?" He lifted his eyebrows. "Or his daughter maybe? You could be completely innocent, after all."

Did he know something? A sickly knot began to form in Gwen's stomach.

"You don't talk much. Now, Danielle, she could talk." He pointed a fork at Gwen. "And yet, she never thought to mention she was sleeping with my best friend. Funny. Of course, he didn't mention it either. But they're in love now, so everything's swell."

Gwen clung to silence. Why was he telling her this?

"I moved up here from Kalamazoo a year ago for my job. Where're you from?"

When she saw he was going to wait for an answer, she said, "Snow Pigeon."

"That's forty, fifty miles up the river. Did you grow up right on the water?"

She nodded yes and watched out the window. Dan was messing around on the dock.

"When Danielle was here, I hardly noticed the river. Now it's all I think about."

As Gwen finished her toast, Dan got into his boat and pulled away, and Gwen watched him grow smaller as he headed upstream. When he was out of sight, she took the last bite of her omelet and let her fork drop onto her plate. The clank startled her. "I've got to go," she said.

"Can't you stay a few minutes longer? I promise to stop complaining about women. Here, I'll make you another piece of toast."

She sat back down but kept her weight on the balls of her feet. She felt she was stretched across the river like a shock cord, ready to snap back.

"You act like a girl who was raised by wolves." He smiled. "They don't like to be in enclosed spaces."

"Thank you for the food." Gwen stood and hurried out the kitchen door, leaving the toast to pop up behind her. She broke into a run across the yard, and by the time she reached her boat she was panting. Out in the middle of the river, she felt a momentary sense of freedom, but upon reaching her dock the first thing she noticed were rotting catfish heads still nailed to the big oak. Then she remembered she had meant to buy matches. With her second to last match she started a fire in the wood burner, but she dozed off on the floor before it really got going. When she woke up, the sky was fully lit, so she moved to the dock for the sun's warmth. She looked down and was surprised to be wearing Michael's clothes. After his Jeep rolled away across the river, she pressed her face into the clean sweat shirt.

WHEN darkness muscled in again, she used her last match to light the kerosene lamp, but it only seemed to intensify the darkness outside. She heard a sampling of rain, and it occurred to her, as if for the first time, that Jake really wouldn't be coming back. She thought of her dad's trailer in Snow Pigeon and the shoulder-high stacks of wood her father must have already cut and split, which

Paula must have stacked by herself against the trailer for the winter. Her own winter supply was about two armloads of broken branches, and once the river iced up Gwen would have no transportation. She ought to cross while she could, walk to the road, and hitchhike someplace warm, Florida maybe. All evening she watched the lights in Michael's house: the kitchen, the hall, the bedroom that was supposed to be a living room. His silhouette sat hunched over the table where they'd eaten. She wondered, had girls really been raised by wolves?

Even though it was late, she had to get out of the cottage for a while. She pulled one of Jake's stretched wool sweaters over Michael's sweatshirt and carried her quilt to the boat in case it got really cold. Past Willow Island, almost to Confluence, her engine sputtered out of gas and died. She didn't protest, but let herself be pulled back down river. If she fell asleep out here, and slept long enough, she would wake up in Lake Michigan. The river was quiet and dark. The herons were asleep in their trees. Nobody danced on lawns, no stars shone, and cold rain began to pour down on the river. By the time her quilt became soaked through, she realized she should have kept rowing to reach Confluence to buy matches and boat gas for her next trip. And some food too, a burger and fries for starters. Instead she'd be stuck in a dark cabin with cans of beans and oily sardines. She reached into her pants pocket to feel her money and found nothing—she had left it in her jeans on Michael's bathtub. She drifted with a numbing sense of her own stupidity. Rainwater collected in the boat and pooled around her feet. Instead of going to her own side of the river when she rounded the last bend, she pulled up at Michael's oil-barrel float. Surely he'd loan her matches, and maybe he even had gasoline in his shed. She tied her boat and tucked the oars inside but found the shed locked. With the blanket around her, she approached the house and looked in through the sliding glass door. At first she could see only the glowing numbers on a digital clock. As her eyes adjusted, she saw King lift his head from the floor at the foot of the bed.

As quickly as King began to bark, Michael was standing on the other side of the glass in shorts. His chest was as hairless as the chests of schoolboys she had known before Jake. She had fooled around with boys back home and had always been afraid of her father finding out.

Michael switched on a blinding light and slid the door open. "Gwendolyn? Don't you ever sleep in a bed?"

"I'm sorry."

"Well, come on in. Be sorry inside."

She stepped up and puddles formed on the plywood.

"Damn, I've got to finish this floor. I'm going to put down oak like in the kitchen."

Gwen hadn't realized how cold she was until she stepped into the warm house.

"This blanket's soaked—let me put it in the dryer. I'll put your other clothes in there from this morning—I washed them. Talk to me, Gwen."

He looked at her until finally she said, "That omelet was good."

Michael laughed. "Take a shower now, and you can thank me for that tomorrow." Gwen closed her ears to his babbling and followed him to the bathroom. He started running the water, and she remembered only after she had peeled off her shirts that she shouldn't undress in front of a stranger. Michael looked away and abruptly left the room. Gwen hardly recognized the thin, dirty creature in the mirror. Her once dark, soft curls were matted, and her complexion was ruined with scratches and poison ivy scars. Three times she shampooed her hair before the water rinsed clean. She put on the dark terry cloth robe which hung on the back of the door, then padded across the hall to the room with the boat skeleton. It looked too big to fit through the doorway. The room didn't even have a view of the water, so it was no wonder he didn't sleep in there. She returned to the living room and lay with King on his rug. Michael came in and sat on the foot of the bed and looked amused. "Maybe you really are a wolf girl."

"I watch King fish from my house."

"Why do you call her King?"

"Her?"

"I never had a dog before Renegade." He stroked the dog's head. "It was the craziest thing. When I closed on this house the old owner asked if I'd keep her, because she loved the river." Mike tugged on the dog's ear and her mouth opened as if in a smile. "You sleep in my bed, and I'll sleep on the floor. I haven't got a couch."

"We can both sleep on the bed," said Gwen. "It's big." Still wearing the bathrobe, she climbed in on the river side. Michael got in the other.

"What's that mysterious light at your house?" he asked.

"A kerosene lamp. I used my last match so I had to leave it burning."

"Did you come here to teach me how to fish?"

"I need to borrow matches. And I ran out of gas on the way to Confluence."

"Did you see my boat in there?" Michael waited for her to nod. "When Danielle left, I decided to redo that room, but then I figured I'd rather have a boat. Then I could go to that island with the black willows. I'd like to live on that island."

"Why don't you *buy* a boat?"

"I want to build my own boat, the way I did this bed. I slept on mattresses on the floor for a month and a half until I finished this."

Gwen looked at the headboard, which was made of solid planks, nothing fancy. "How about a motor? You going to build that?" Her dad would have called her a smartass.

"Next door neighbor's got a two-and-a-half horsepower he'll sell me. I got my boat plan from a library-sale book from 1905. You have to bend the wood and use brass screws. You probably know all this stuff from living on the river. Maybe you can take me for a ride in your boat tomorrow."

Michael was propped on one elbow looking at her. Gwen had never driven a boat with a man in it, and it struck her as a fine idea that she'd take Michael up to Willow Island. Instead of offering, though, she leaned up and kissed Michael, and the kiss she got in return was so mild that she wasn't sure it had happened. When Jake kissed you, you knew you'd been kissed.

"Talk to me," he said. "I don't kiss just any girl who wanders in here. Who was that man at your house the other day?" When she didn't respond he said, "Tell me why you're out in the rain. What could a girl like you be afraid of out there?"

She couldn't tell if Michael was laughing at her, and she wasn't sure she minded if he was. She would've liked to tell him something—maybe that she'd seen the heron flying with a little snake—but then he'd want her to talk more. His arm lay above the blankets, small compared to Jake's or Dan's or her father's. This arm couldn't hold her down or put her any place she didn't want to be. A girl could even stand and fight against an arm like this, instead of running away. The light dimmed across the river, then flickered and went out. Michael started to talk several times, but stopped himself. Gwen felt sorry for him, for his being unable to overwhelm a woman. She turned to face him, then pulled him against her with what felt like somebody else's strength.

"I'm not afraid of anything," she whispered. Even if it was a lie, she liked saying it. She wrapped a hand around the back of Michael's neck and kissed him hard. She pushed her fingers through his hair, then felt along his bone-and-muscle shoulder with her hand, wanting suddenly to touch as much of his skin as possible. She leaned across him and felt the curve of his back and his buttock, then continued down his leg until she felt him shudder and move toward her. Fresh air trickled through a window not quite closed. King sighed on the floor. From the end of the hall she heard the clothes and blanket in the dryer turning around and around, softly falling on each other.

She woke alone to light pouring through the sliding glass door, luxurious on her clean skin. Her own cottage had no southern exposure, and she usually slept with her clothes on. Gwen pulled herself up and noticed her quilt and her jeans and red T-shirt folded on the end of the bed. Money was folded on top. Her heart thudded hotly before she realized that it was the bills and change that she'd left in her pants pocket. In the kitchen she found Michael wearing a tie and a name tag.

"Do you want to stay here while I'm at work?" He leaned against the sink counter. She tried to remember his warm, bare chest, but his body seemed stiff and small beneath the white shirt, and she couldn't imagine him naked.

"I'm going home," she said automatically.

He handed her a cup of coffee. "How old are you, Gwendolyn? I'm thirty-one."

"Eighteen." She pushed aside three clothbound books and an old *Mother Earth News* and rested her coffee on newspapers. King sat on the floor beside her.

"You wouldn't lie, would you?" he said. "If you're sixteen, I could be arrested for statutory rape. God, I had no intention of doing that last night. I don't even know you." He stared at Gwen in a way that seemed rude, so she refused to look up at him. He raping her—what a joke. She sipped her coffee and stroked King's head. The dog had the most glorious eyes, as warm as fire. As the silence expanded, Gwen let herself settle into it. Silence was a game that she felt comfortable with, the only game she knew she could win. She didn't even consider saying that she'd trade the whole river for coffee this good every morning. Instead, she pretended to be out in the boat with her father or Jake, pushing thoughts out of her mind so she wouldn't be tempted to express them.

"I'm sorry," Michael finally said, sitting across from her, giving in as suddenly as he had last night. "I just don't know anything about you. For all I know you're some lost heiress or a girl who just killed her whole family and buried them in the garden."

Through the window Gwen watched an old man in a limp fishing hat troll downstream.

"Or maybe I'm dreaming you." His voice grew quieter. "Because, believe me, if I dreamed a girl, she'd be just like you. She'd have beautiful shoulders like you. She'd be smart, and she'd even smell like you."

What could she smell like? Gwen wondered. She'd just had a shower.

"Except this girl would talk. She'd argue with me. And if I was lucky, she'd be an heiress with an island in the river."

Gwen still kept his words on the surface. She wasn't a wolf girl or a murderer or an heiress. Or a dream. She was Gwen, trying to figure out what to do next. Give her some matches and gas and she'd be fine for a while longer. King pushed her head beneath Gwen's hand until Gwen resumed petting her.

"But maybe that guy you live with will come back and cut me up and use me for bait."

Gwen thought that was the first sensible thing he'd said. "Don't worry about him."

"So he's gone for good?"

Gwen shrugged and tried not to think about Jake coming back. He could be found innocent. The judge could let him go.

"Are you going to live in that cottage year 'round? Keep warm with wood?"

"I'm thinking about going south this winter. Florida, maybe."

"The herons go to Florida. You'll fly south like the birds, eh?"

As if seeing through clear water, Gwen imagined Jake and Dan coming downstream in the boat, and her stomach knotted. The thought of Jake's body near hers made it hard to breathe. Suddenly she couldn't stand Michael's laughing talk. "I have to go."

"Will you come back tonight?" Michael's eyes were as brown and hopeful as King's. Jake's eyes were deep blue. "We can eat dinner or something. I could come get you in the Jeep."

"There's no road."

"And I don't have a boat yet, so I guess it's up to you, Gwendolyn." He folded his arms and watched her stand and drain her coffee and walk to the door, just as he'd watched her row away with his dog on the day they'd met.

Gwen sat cross-legged on her dock and watched Michael pull out of the driveway. She felt the tug of King and Michael and the house, solid even without its floors and walls and baseboards. Even the road onto which Michael turned pulled at her—it led to Confluence, Roseville, and Snow Pigeon, and all the towns on other rivers. Maybe she could go to Michael's house during the day to be with King or bring the dog over here. Or maybe, thought Gwen, she would just hitchhike away from here and find a new place, where people would let you start over again without asking a lot of questions. A heron dropped from the sky and settled out of sight downstream. Two female mallards drifted near shore, one not quite full-grown. Gwen wondered if this was all that remained of a dozen chicks that the momma hatched this June. Maybe this girl was the only one who survived the fat raccoons who hunted at the water's edge. Gwen lay back on her dock, her hands behind her head and her knees up, and fell asleep.

Late that afternoon, a pale car pulled into Michael's driveway, and Gwen knew immediately that the woman who stepped out of it was the owner of the white underthings. She disappeared behind the house and, shortly afterwards, King bounced down to the water. Was she intending to take the fishing dog away? As soon as Gwen considered the possibility, she reeled in her line, dragged the outboard motor off the boat without taking any care to protect the propeller, and rowed into the current, rowed so hard that she landed upstream. King ran to her, but bowed playfully and tossed her head instead of climbing into the boat. "King! Come!" Gwen barked. "King! Come!" As the dog jumped in, the woman appeared from inside the house. She wore a white sleeveless turtleneck. Gwen could imagine her holding a glass of champagne, looking over at Gwen and not inviting her to the party.

"What are you doing with Renegade?" the woman yelled. Her hair had the color and shine of caramel melted onto apples. Her bare arms were long and clean.

"She's not yours!" Gwen yelled. "You left her!"

"I'll call the police, you freaky little tramp."

King began to whimper, and as she rowed out into the river Gwen saw Michael stepping from his Jeep. The woman stomped toward him, yelling and pointing at Gwen, and Michael crossed his arms. Gwen looked away, but soon she heard Michael shout, "Ren-e-gade!" At the call, King jumped from her boat—nearly tipping it over—and swam back. Gwen stopped rowing and put her head in her hands. Upon reaching land, King followed Gwen's boat along the shoreline until Michael called her again. Then Michael shouted her own name, "Gwen-do-lyn!" She knew she should pick up her oars and row, if not to Michael then back to her own cottage, but she didn't have the will to fight the current. Instead, she let her boat be swept past Michael's house and everything that was familiar.

She glided past solitary black fishermen with bottles twisted in paper bags and the green heads of willows weeping beside them. Turtles and blue racers sunned themselves on fallen trees, sliding into the water at her approach. A heron fished silently at a tiny inlet, one bulging banded eye on her as she passed, wary, but not alarmed so long as she moved with the current. She was tempted to row and approach it, but decided instead to leave the bird in peace. The river widened. Men steered speedboats around her, and she tossed side to side in their wake. Her hands rested on the oar handles, but she dipped her oars only to right her downstream course. At times she let herself twirl in the current like a twig. She saw a tree which resembled first Jake and then, at closer range, her father, with her father's brooding face and big arms upraised.

After she'd floated for hours, houses began to appear more often on either side of the river, a sign that she must be approaching Lanakee and the harbor, but she didn't feel ready to see all those strangers and their houses and yards. She wished she could see her sister Paula, and maybe Michael, but they were both behind her. By finally taking hold of the oars she stopped herself, and tied the boat up at the ruined dock of an abandoned fishing cottage. She climbed onto the dock and lay carefully on the boards to soak in the last light before continuing. Downstream, after the river flowed under some traffic bridges and past boat slips, lay Lanakee Harbor and, beyond that, Lake Michigan—the coldest, darkest place she'd ever been. She knew what happened when the river met the lake, that the river emptied at a lighthouse which perched at the tip of a long tongue of concrete. The lighthouse winked red, then white, then red. Gwen found herself drifting beyond the lighthouse, dark water pressing on her from all directions. But from the heartless depths emerged the fishing dog, now paddling toward her boat, eyes as bright as fire. Upon hearing a splash beneath her, Gwen awoke.

As though part of her dream, a great blue heron flew up in front of her. Gwen held her breath as the bird spread its wings in slow motion, its feathers almost brushing her leg as it took off from under the dock and flew over the river, against the current. As the bird left her, Gwen felt herself shredding from the inside out. She wished she had been awake to see the heron close up, to stare into that clear, savage eye, to see the drops of water on his crest and witness the neck feathers roughen and smooth out. The motion of those wings reminded her of being with Michael in his bed—the feathery blankets, the night air through the window, his skin warm in her hands. She leaned back and let herself imagine the flush of wings again, the swoosh of air, as soft as her clothes turning in the dryer, falling upon themselves. She longed to hear the steady breathing of the fishing dog.

The sun was setting over houses where people were eating dinner. Paula was probably cooking Daddy macaroni and cheese. Paula had turned sixteen this summer without her, and maybe she'd finally learned to cook fish. If Gwen filled both gas tanks and had money to refuel in Confluence, she might be able to motor all the way to Snow Pigeon. She would sneak in and remind Paula not to feel bad, remind her that there was no pleasing Daddy. Jake was sitting in a jail cell, probably eating with a bunch of guys complaining about the food. Maybe Michael had cooked that woman dinner, or maybe he was eating alone or bending wood. Gwen's stomach hurt from hunger. She hadn't brought along fishing gear, and once she hit Lake Michigan the water would be empty and the tide would pull her out and away. She did not want to go. She did not want to starve to death in a cold, bottomless place. Somehow she would have to row back upstream.

To lessen the current, Gwen hugged the edge of the river as closely as she could without scraping bottom, dipping her left oar shallow. She faced backwards toward a fuming orange sunset, and as the color faded, her eyes adjusted. She rowed steadily, seeing the dark cottages and ancient trees only after she'd passed them. The hair stood up on her arms when she heard a whippoorwill cry. Farther upstream, a nighthawk made a crazy flutter as he stabbed the air for insects. Muskrats and other night hunters slid into the water and rose alongside her boat. When a quarter moon appeared, Gwen pulled herself up to a snag. Her arm muscles burned and her hands were raw from the oar handles. She felt the night pulling at her boat, luring her into the dark, easy current. If she gave up this time, it would carry her all the way to the blinking light at the entrance to Lake Michigan, where there were no herons, no dogs, nothing for her. She fell asleep leaning against her boat and awoke stiff and cold with no moon in the sky. The thought of working her muscles again brought tears stinging to her eyes, but resting wasn't helping, so she pushed off again and rowed. The river curved and narrowed until she could make out occasional irrigation pumps and boathouses on the opposite bank. She focused on a line of three bright stars until they disappeared behind trees. Blisters formed and ruptured on her hands, but she didn't let go of the oars, for fear she wouldn't be able to make herself grab hold again. To warm herself, she conjured up a picture of Michael's yellow-and-white kitchen, cluttered with books and jars of jelly.

She needed to stop rowing, to rest under her covers, even if there was sand in the bed. But when she finally caught sight of her dark place on stilts, she remembered that she had no matches, and she knew how the pockets of coldness would be trapped between her blankets long after she tried to curl up and sleep without a fire. And she'd left her warmest covering, her quilt, folded on Michael's bed. She headed instead across the river, to Michael's oil-barrel float. She misjudged the distance from shore and stepped out into thigh-deep water. Her fingers no longer worked well enough to make a knot, so she wound the rope as many times as she could around a crosswise support piece. As she worked, her aluminum prow clanged against the metal barrels. The noise must have woken King, because a light came on in the bedroom, and King jogged out into the yard and over the plank to watch Gwen at eye level. Gwen petted her, face to face.

When the kitchen light came on, Gwen suddenly noticed her legs were numb in the water, as though she'd fallen asleep standing. She staggered to shore. If that white underpants woman was gone, she and Michael could empty her dresser into the river. Gwen would like to drag out all of Jake's huge pants and flannel shirts and release them alongside the perfect brassieres. She and Michael could watch pieces of clothing twirl and dance on their way to Lake Michigan, sinking and resurfacing, grasping at each other before disappearing for good.

Michael opened the door before she knocked. King stayed beside her.

"Can I have some matches?" she asked. She thought deliriously of swallowing a box of wooden matches, having them fall to the bottom of her empty stomach.

"You're late for dinner." The clock behind him said 4:10. "Come in, though."

Gwen clenched her teeth, locking her jaw against the cold. She could survive in the cabin across the river, or in Florida, or anywhere. She asked, "Are you by yourself?"

"Don't worry about Danielle. I can defend myself against her."

"I brought King back. She came out to find me."

"Come in, Renegade," he said, stepping aside, but the dog didn't move. Michael looked into Gwen's face. "Did somebody do something to you? That guy with the speedboat?"

Gwen stopped her shivers by hunching her shoulders. Inside were coffee and butter and clean sheets. Food and hot water awaited, but she now wished she'd brought Michael something. She should have stopped at the cottage and gotten those three beers she'd taken from Dan. Or sardines. She was finally hungry enough to eat canned sardines. "That big island upstream," she said. "It's called Willow Island. I'll take you there if you want."

Michael leaned against the doorway. He crossed and uncrossed his arms, smiled, and said nothing.

Gwen felt drunk but blinked her eyes open. "What's your favorite bird?" she asked.

"My favorite bird? Let's see. How about the great blue heron?"

"There's herons on Willow Island." Gwen was dizzy from standing. "A campment of herons, living way up in the trees." She put one hand against the doorframe to steady herself. "Hundreds of them. One came so close it brushed me with a wing."

"I don't suppose you know the story about Leda and the swan?"

Gwen wondered if she'd get used to Michael.

"Your fingers are pure white." He took her free hand and held it up in the kitchen light. "They're so cold. And you've got blisters broken open. We should clean your hands with peroxide and bandage them." He tugged at her wrist but stopped when she resisted. "I forgot. You want to stand right here in the doorway. Well, I bought you a can of gas. Matches are right here on the stove. I'll hand you everything so you don't even have to come in."

"What if your boat doesn't fit through the doorway?" Gwen's teeth clacked together, breaking up her speech.

"Then I'll cut out the doorway with a Sawzall." Michael pulled her other hand off the doorframe and held both of them. In Gwen's blurred vision, it seemed that Michael's arms were fusing end-to-end with her goose-bumped and bruised arms, stretching into an impossible length of skin. "Come in, Gwen. Renegade's going to get cold out there waiting for you. I'll make you an omelet. This time I've got tomatoes."

Before she stepped through the doorway, Gwen looked behind her, across the river, toward the dark little house. She would row across tomorrow when her hands stopped hurting and close it against the raccoons. Beyond that, she didn't know yet what she'd do. King followed her inside.

The Perfect Lawn

FROM his hiding place in the backyard, Kevin could see into Madeline's bedroom window and into a basement living room with sliding glass doors. On the other side of her ruffled curtains, the beautiful Madeline lay with a science textbook propped on her knees. As usual, Mrs. Martin spent the evening on the couch with a paperback close to her face and the television glowing. She smoked nonstop, pressing a cigarette to her mouth and pulling it away as regular as a heartbeat. Several times this school year, Kevin had seen Madeline storm into the living room and stand before her mother, hands on hips, as if demanding an explanation or dishing out discipline, as though Madeline was the mother and Mrs. Martin was the daughter.

Madeline stood and pulled off her Red Devils sweatshirt to reveal a thick white bra. Kevin inhaled and held his breath, but Madeline undressed no further. She stepped into the hall and the bathroom light came on; through the frosted glass he could distinguish no shapes. He let out his breath, moved up the lawn closer to the house, near the burn barrel, and lay on his belly in the dry leaves.

The Martins' backyard was not just neglected—it was a travesty. Under the newly fallen leaves there were growths of moss, bare patches, and last year's decaying leaves and sticks. Kevin worked with his dad in the lawn care service when he wasn't in school, and he knew that with regular care this yard could be as nice as any in the township. The property abutted the neighbor's woods all the way down to the river, which afforded many landscaping options for this scraggly border in which he took cover. Kevin would suggest right off yanking these pricker bushes and planting some medium-sized shrubs, something that would flower in the spring—forsythia, maybe—and a couple of burning bushes for fall color. The other cheerleaders lived near the school in white-columned houses with manicured flower beds, or in the half-bricked ranch-style homes on Tiger Lake whose yards sloped toward little boathouses and docks. Though Madeline had every right to live on Tiger Lake and to have the best possible lawn, she and her mom lived instead in this small asbestos-shingled house on the river, not far from Kevin.

The night was unseasonably warm for November, so when Mrs. Martin got up from the couch and stepped outside with a grocery bag of trash, she didn't bother closing the sliding door behind her. She floated across the lawn, squinting against the smoke from the cigarette in her mouth, ashes and bits of paper falling away from her. Kevin flattened his body against the ground and cursed himself for choosing the new hiding spot. Mrs. Martin emptied the papers into the burn barrel and then held her disposable lighter inside until something ignited. The fire gradually lighted her face, neck, and chest. Her robe was fastened loosely, and Kevin wondered if it might slip open. Smoke spilled from her nose and mouth.

Kevin's dad smoked too, but he burned cigarettes right down to their butts, then smashed them out in big glass ashtrays, bending and twisting the filters. He exhaled smoke in long straight streams, while Mrs. Martin just let the smoke drift out of her. Up close, Kevin could see that Mrs. Martin looked sort of like Madeline, or at least she had the same long, reddish hair. Perhaps after Kevin and Madeline had gone together awhile, her mom and his dad would start dating. It gave Kevin a moment of relief to imagine the four playing cards or eating a Thanksgiving turkey, but Mrs. Martin was staring into the barrel as though conjuring a vision or reading a message from the dark side in the flames. Through the eye-sized air holes punched in the drum, Kevin watched the fire gaining fury.

She obviously wasn't wearing anything under that thin robe, not even a bra. She was standing too close over the fire, and he worried that her collar or the hair hanging in her face would ignite. He could almost see individual strands singe and shrivel toward her face.

Mrs. Martin took a step back and crossed her arms, holding her cigarette right in front of her face so she could drag on it without effort. Kevin could not see what was burning, but from the smells he imagined inserts from newspapers, a cereal box with a waxed-paper liner, a box of macaroni shells with a plastic window. Kevin didn't know what Madeline ate besides the pizza slices she carried away from the lunch line. Perhaps it was the thought of Madeline eating with her hands, or maybe he had been absentmindedly pushing himself into the ground. Whatever the reason, Kevin felt himself erect against the grass and leaves. He looked toward Madeline's window, but Mrs. Martin was blocking his view.

He contemplated scurrying away or else reaching under his body to adjust his personal part, despite the risk that Mrs. Martin might notice him. He could bring himself to do neither, and his whole body stiffened with indecision. Then with a tiny crackle, a piece of flaming something popped out of the barrel through one of the air holes and landed two feet away. Within minutes, Kevin smelled leaves smoldering. Mrs. Martin continued to gaze into the barrel, not noticing the new fire. Her nipple pushed against the fabric of her robe.

More leaves and some of the damp sticks began to smoke. Mrs. Martin's orange-lit face grew demonic in the rippling light. Her pale eyes shone wet, and the long shadows of her eyelashes reflected upward onto her forehead. She was some sort of thoughtless witch, unconcerned with what spells she was casting. Her snakelike fingers wrapped around each other and around her cigarette like an unholy tangling of limbs. He tried to remember Madeline's fingers. Certainly they were more respectable than this. The smoldering circle grew to the size of a fried egg.

He knew the longer he delayed, the worse it would be to reveal himself in all his tom-peepery. The smoldering orange-edged patch grew to the size of a small hubcap, but he would burn to death in silence rather than have Mrs. Martin tell his father that she'd found him skulking in her shrub bed. He pressed his groin into the lawn, rhythmically.

When Mrs. Martin finished her cigarette, she lit another from it and dropped the stub into the flames. She turned and headed toward the house, dragging her robe across overgrown grass, catching a stick and a couple of leaves in her hem. As soon as she slid the door shut behind her, Kevin stood and stomped out the smoking debris, breaking up the pile to make sure nothing was still burning. Then he collapsed on the ground, telling himself that if this fire had been let go, the woods next door could have caught. If Kevin had not been here watching, that big tree by the house eventually might have fallen in flames through Madeline's roof, pinning her in her bed. Kevin imagined the beautiful Madeline curled safely in the dark under blankets, wearing red cheerleader underpants and her bra.

ONE January afternoon, Madeline approached Kevin at school and stood with her arms crossed over those lush breasts, big and smooth like a couple of knolls built up for decorative annual plantings. Because there was a game tonight, she wore her cheerleader uniform.

"I'm sick of you following me," she said.

"Huh?" She was so close that Kevin smelled her powdery perfume.

"I purposely went out to the parking lot, then back to the gym so I could see for sure, and you definitely followed me." Madeline turned her face up and shook her hair against the cream-colored backdrop of the painted cinder-block hallway. She pushed her hand through her hair, front to back, pulling strands away from her face, giving the impression that possessing such a mane was a noble burden. Kevin never tired of this performance, and he couldn't help it that hair as thick and long as Madeline's gave a guy the idea that he'd like to have her head in his lap. Kevin's surveillance of Madeline Martin, however, had nothing to do with thoughts of initiating her into personal acts he might have seen in magazines his dad subscribed to. The burn-barrel fire had made Kevin aware that danger was always present and that he must continue to protect Madeline. He meant to come clean with her now, but he didn't know where to start. Instead he stared at her chest.

"And stop staring at my tits," said Madeline. "That is so rude."

"Sorry." His eyes traveled down to her pleated skirt, red and yellow, barely long enough. She would reveal the underpants during athletic maneuvers at tonight's game.

Many of his male classmates seemed to prefer the petite figure of Breanna Harding, head cheerleader and homecoming queen, but Kevin had studied them side by side, and Breanna's overmade face and blond hair looked as dull as a plastic mannequin's next to Madeline's natural glow. Little Breanna might posture on top of the pyramid with ease, but only because, at the bottom and center of the pile, with feet secure on the asphalt track or gymnasium floor, there was someone as solid as Madeline.

"If I catch you following me again, I'll tell the vice-principal." Her hands were propped on her hips and she looked him square in the face. Madeline was a forthright girl, no doubt about it, but her eyes were as cool green as the perfect lawn.

"I won't follow you anymore," Kevin mumbled, letting his vision fall farther toward her muscular legs and shapely feet.

"Good." She pivoted and walked away, her calf muscles clenching with each step, her thighs rubbing against one another, her hips swaying side to side, shifting her pleats so they flashed red-yellow-red-yellow like one of those plastic outdoor pinwheels.

Kevin was a man of his word, and not following her would probably be for the best, since he could stop being late to his classes. He might even graduate on time in May if he kept handing in his partially completed homework and didn't accumulate any more tardies. Attendance, rather than achievement, had always been his strong suit.

He hadn't made any promises about watching Madeline's house, of course, and to protect himself from the elements on cold winter evenings when his dad was at the Pub or sleeping, Kevin wore his dad's Carhartt coveralls with the snap-on hood. A piece of landscaping plastic kept him dry. Once he stuck one of his dad's business cards in their front door, but Mrs. Martin never called. By following her in his dad's truck one morning, Kevin discovered that she worked at the plastic-molding factory, which meant she probably couldn't afford a lawn service. The next time the snow melted, Kevin lugged a fifty-pound bag of lime through the woods, and by the light of a dull half-moon, he spread the grit over their half-frozen lawn. Lime dissolved slowly and would help bring the acidity in line by midsummer.

THE second fire started in the living room. Despite the cold, Kevin had fallen asleep near the pricker bushes, and when he awoke both bedroom lights were off and the downstairs was only dimly lit by the clock on the television. Something seemed odd inside, flickering and dimming. He walked to the sliding glass door, through which he saw thin streams of smoke. One tongue of flame rose from the couch, then disappeared. Another jabbed upward from the other side of the same cushion.

Kevin yanked open the glass door and took the carpeted stairs two at a time, then entered the first bedroom, which he knew to be Madeline's. He ran to her bed, pushed his arms under her, intending to scoop her up and carry her to safety. It had never occurred to Kevin that the beautiful Madeline would be heavy, heavier than him, and that she would scream and slap and punch him.

"Hey! Stop it! You! Stop it!" She continued to hit Kevin as he tried to work his arms out from underneath her. When he yanked himself free, Madeline toppled to the floor beside him. She grabbed her alarm clock and struck him in the head, momentarily stunning him.

Kevin held up his hands to protect himself from a second blow. "There's a fire, Madeline. I thought you had smoke absorption." Kevin had to admit, though, there was only a hint of smoke in the air.

"Who is that?" demanded Madeline. "I know that voice." She fumbled and switched on her ruffle-shaded bedside lamp. "Oh my God, it's you, Kevin, you gross thing. Get out! Get out of my bedroom now!" She stood and brushed off her T-shirt and pink-and-white boxer shorts as Kevin backed toward the hall, his eyes shocked by the light. Kevin would never see boxer shorts in the same way again.

"But there's a fire," he said from the doorway.

He had her attention.

"Downstairs," he said. He pushed his Carhartt hood off his head. "I think your couch is on fire."

She sniffed. "Oh shit! Damn you, Mom!" she shouted toward the wall.

Madeline pushed past Kevin, and he followed her down the stairs and into the living room. Flames shot up intermittently from the cushions and the air stank of burning foam rubber. "We've got to drag it outside," she said. She lifted one end of the couch apparently without effort; Kevin lifted the other end and pretended that he too found it effortless. Cigarette burns crusted the couch arm. Kevin's eyes watered from the smoke which had started to pour out of the cushions.

Once outside, Madeline pitched the cushions into the snow. Kevin could see through the clear patches of ice that crabgrass grew around the cracks in the cement. "Shouldn't we put water on it?" He felt odd about leaving the couch to smolder in the darkness, but he followed Madeline back inside. Kevin was warm in the coverall, which was a little too big around the middle and short in the legs, but Madeline's arms were covered with bumps, and the hair on them stood straight out. He willed himself not to look at her breasts.

"It won't do any good to pour water on it," said Madeline. "That padding burns for days. Nothing you can do. Believe me, I know." Then she threw back her head, shook her hair, and yelled up the stairs, "Damn you, Mom!"

Kevin considered sharing his secret about the burn-barrel fire, but it would mean letting on about watching her house. He looked up to see the smoke pooling at the ceiling.

"What the hell are you doing here, anyway?" she asked.

"I . . . just happened to be passing by." Kevin choked out a cough he'd been holding in.

"Through my backyard? You know I don't want you following me."

"I live farther down the river. This is a short cut."

"Well you shouldn't be shortcutting through people's yards." She ran a hand through her smoke-permeated hair. "I think you should leave now."

Just then, Mrs. Martin drifted into the stairway and turned to face Kevin with only one eye open. Her bathrobe hung so that her left breast was half visible. Kevin was struck by its softness, as compared with the firmness of Madeline's breasts.

"What is it, Madeline?" she asked sweetly, oblivious to the smoke.

"You just about burned the place down again, Mom. That's all."

"Where's our couch?" Mrs. Martin reached into her left-hand pocket and pulled a cigarette gently out of a pack.

"Mom, you aren't listening. The couch was on fire, from one of your stupid cigarettes."

Mrs. Martin's other eye finally opened, bloodshot. Her hair lay flat on one side of her head. She supported herself by the stairway railing.

"How much did you drink tonight, anyway, Mom?"

"Is this one of your boyfriends, dear?"

"Oh, God." Madeline rolled her eyes. "Look at him, Mom. He is not one of my boyfriends. This is Retardo-Kevin."

"What's that name?" Mrs. Martin's eye threatened to close again.

"Just Kevin, ma'am," he said.

"Oh, hello, Kevin."

"Nice to meet you, ma'am." Kevin stuck out his hand and shook hers, the way his father would shake a client's hand. She momentarily let go of the railing, but then took it up again.

"Did you two go out tonight?"

"Mom, get it through your head. I do not go out with Kevin." Madeline crossed her arms and looked up at the ceiling, which made an attractive gesture, Kevin thought, like certain flowers turning to face the sun.

Mrs. Martin lit her cigarette and let the match fall to the carpet.

"See, Mom, you're doing it again!" Madeline stomped as though she might lose her temper. "What did you just do with that match?"

"Don't worry, honey. I'll vacuum tomorrow." Then to Kevin, in slurred speech: "She's embarrassed for you to see the house when it's such a mess.

"No, Mom. I am not embarrassed for Kevin-the-Freak to see our messy house. I just want you not to burn it down. That's all."

"Did you want a beer, Kevin?" asked Mrs. Martin. Kevin wasn't sure he'd heard her correctly.

"He's not old enough to drink. He's in high school, Mom."

"You kids are so conservative these days." She laughed, lighter than air. Kevin couldn't imagine why he'd thought she was an evil witch out by the burn barrel. As Madeline and her mom bickered, Kevin watched the ash on the woman's cigarette grow long and yet defy gravity. Mrs. Martin seemed so light that if she let go of the bannister again, she might just float up. He felt an overwhelming desire to take care of Mrs. Martin, to get ashtrays for her, to check every hour whether or not her couch was on fire. He stared into Mrs. Martin's freckled chest.

"Mom, do yourself up," said Madeline tiredly. "Kevin, stop looking at her chest." Madeline adjusted the front of her mother's robe and cinched it tightly across her stomach, causing Mrs. Martin to lose her balance momentarily. Kevin felt a terrific pity for the woman; it must be difficult, he thought, to have a daughter as awesome as Madeline.

IN May, Kevin and Madeline graduated together, but the beautiful Madeline walked with a football player while Kevin walked with his cousin Crystal, who sniffed from allergies through the whole ceremony. After that, at least one afternoon a week, Kevin drove his father's mower along the shoulder of the road to the Martin house. He fertilized the lawn, spent hours dethatching and reseeding, and then he mowed it in straight lines. Having the river right there and the big trees at the side kept the grass lush without any watering. Mrs. Martin tried to pay him, but he would accept only supper and a beer. Kevin didn't like beer, but he figured he'd try to get used to it.

"Hi, weirdo," Madeline would say without even looking at him, and then she'd shake back her hair. "I'm not hungry for dinner today, Mom."

Mrs. Martin always asked Kevin what he wanted for dinner, and he'd say that, oh, anything would be fine. She'd make herself and him a grilled cheese sandwich, a burger, or macaroni and cheese from a package. She'd sit across the table from him as though she were his mom. He wished she'd offer him milk, but she never did. She read books even while she ate, read more than anyone he knew. His dad only read newspapers and the backs of fertilizer packages to see how much water to add.

"You should meet my dad," said Kevin one day, after the last bite of a cheese sandwich.

"Is he a nice person like you?"

"Oh, he's really nice. He has his own business, you know, and he's not married."

Mrs. Martin looked up from her book, kept looking at Kevin while she tugged a cigarette from her pack and lit it. The inside of her mouth looked dark compared to her cigarette and her teeth. Her skin looked pale, too, in the kitchen light. Kevin blushed, though he didn't know why. He tried to make conversation. "Do you like working at that plastics factory?"

Smoke poured out of her nose as she spoke. "It's kind of like dying and going to hell five days a week."

Beer went up into Kevin's nose, and he coughed until his throat cleared. Mrs. Martin went back to reading and Kevin looked out the kitchen window to where Madeline was finishing an entire bag of potato chips and sunning herself next to the driveway. She wore reflector glasses and a bikini cut so small and high over her hips that a person driving by could see almost every detail of her most personal body parts. Kevin excused himself and stepped out into the front yard.

"Why don't you lay in the backyard, by the river?" he asked.

"The river stinks. I don't go down there."

She was right; the river did stink, but you got used to it. "My dad and I used to fish on the river." Kevin put his hands in his pockets. "Before he started his own lawn business."

"My dad's an architect at a firm," said Madeline. Kevin couldn't see her eyes behind the glasses. "He's designing a shopping mall in Grand Rapids right now." The way she said it made Grand Rapids sound truly grand. "He lives outside Detroit with his wife."

"Do you like the way the lawn looks now?" asked Kevin.

"I'm leaving, so I don't care. I'm getting out of this hellhole and going to college in Ann Arbor. My dad is going to pay for what's left after my scholarship."

The revelation struck Kevin like an alarm clock to the head. Of course she would go to college, and of course she had too many talents to go to the community college like other kids.

"You won't know anybody there," said Kevin.

"That's right. And nobody will know I come from this place."

MRS. MARTIN invited Kevin to Madeline's small going-away party in the third week of August. Madeline was a vision of loveliness in a red-and-white-checkered miniskirt and matching halter top. Kevin hadn't thought an architect would look much different from a landscaper, but Mr. Martin turned out to be a tall, dark-haired, clean-shaven man with a distinct hairline—he looked to be of a different species altogether from Kevin's father. Kevin couldn't imagine Mr. Martin ever having been married to Mrs. Martin. Even now, Mr. Martin kept straightening his napkin and looking at Mrs. Martin as though she were overgrown limbs that someone needed to lop off and toss on the compost pile. Mrs. Martin had started out sober, but, upon the arrival of Mr. Martin, went into the kitchen and poured herself a half vodka, half orange juice in a tall glass. She grew unsteady and her mouth froze in a loopy smile, as though it was made out of play-dough and stuck there on her face. Madeline didn't treat her mother with her usual impatience; today Madeline ignored her entirely and hung at her father's side.

Mrs. Martin was going to be so alone without Madeline that Kevin felt like crying for her. He had to arrange a meeting soon between Mrs. Martin and his father. Perhaps they could speed up the dating process and get married right away. Madeline might take years to come around to Kevin, but Mrs. Martin seemed genuinely open-minded.

After everyone waved good-bye to Madeline and Mr. Martin, who was driving her to Ann Arbor, Kevin ran home to find his father—through the woods, through three other backyards, away from a German Shepherd that chased him, barking, to the end of a twenty-foot chain. When he got there, the truck was gone, so Kevin sprinted a half-mile to the Pub, where he found his dad at a table with Officer Harding and a guy in a postal uniform.

"Hi, son," said his father.

Kevin was too winded to speak right away.

"This your kid, Sam?" asked the postal man.

"Yep, this is Kevin. He's working with me full-time this summer." Kevin's dad clapped him on the back. After being outdoors in the sun, Kevin was blind in the dark bar, and he had to feel his way down into a captain's chair. The three men drank beer from draft glasses and expelled streams of smoke, tapping their cigarettes into a central glass ashtray. "Hey, Shirl, bring my boy a Coke."

"Diet or regular?" she shouted back, across the room.

"Hell, Shirl, do you think he's on a diet?"

"Last time you brought him in, he ordered Diet."

The men at the table glanced at Kevin, mildly alarmed.

Kevin had finally caught his breath. "Regular, please." He had ordered Diet last time because that's what Madeline drank. "Dad, I came over here because I want you to meet that lady I was telling you about."

"Boy's trying to fix me up," explained his dad, tapping his cigarette again on the ashtray, "with a lady named Martin, his girlfriend's mother."

"My daughter was in cheerleading with a Martin girl," said Officer Harding. "Same one?"

"Yes, sir," said Kevin. "She's going to the University of Michigan."

"Smart girl," said Officer Harding. "The mother's a little out there, though."

"No, sir," said Kevin.

"I picked her up once by the library," said Harding. "She was walking around in a bathrobe, drunk. Robe was hanging all the way open. So I give her a ride home." He leaned back from the table and raised his eyebrows. "I can tell you boys one thing—that broad's a natural born redhead."

The three men laughed, and it took Kevin a moment to catch on. His dad crushed out his cigarette, mashing and extinguishing the hot ash. How could an officer of the law talk about Mrs. Martin's personal parts that way? Didn't they see she was a struggling mother? Kevin felt an urgent need to check on Mrs. Martin, to see if she was okay, to make sure nothing was burning. He sucked down his Coke and excused himself. He walked halfway and then broke into a jog. When he got a cramp, he walked again.

Kevin entered through the back door and, out of habit, sniffed for smoke. He brought in some dirty paper cups from the picnic table and threw them away in the kitchen. A half-empty fifth of vodka sat on the counter. Kevin put the lid on the bottle, then climbed the stairs to Madeline's bedroom. Lace throw pillows and a ruffle-edged spread covered the bed. A scarf hung across her mirror, a scarf Madeline apparently could do without at college. The dresser top was arranged neatly with a jewelry box and a picture of herself in her cheerleader outfit. Her powdery smell lingered, but the room was only a shrine now. Kevin knew darn well Madeline wasn't coming back to these cracked plaster walls or to him. He sat on her bed, hands over his eyes, because he couldn't help himself—he'd started to cry.

An arm slipped around his shoulder. It was Mrs. Martin sitting beside him on the bed. Her eyes were red and teary; her hair fell limply around her face. She was the only one who would understand, the only one who loved Madeline as much as he did. She wrapped a second arm around him, pulling him toward her, as though she were an extensive lap upon which he could rest. To escape the stream of smoke from her cigarette, he let his face fall into her neck. She dropped the cigarette, still burning, onto Madeline's end table, and it rolled against a plastic-framed picture of Madeline and her father. Then Mrs. Martin's long fingers began to snake around Kevin; they reached inside his shirt, undressing him, pulling him apart. His desire for Mrs. Martin hit him unexpectedly, like an electric shock. She unzipped his jeans, and he kicked them the rest of the way off.

The softness of Mrs. Martin's breasts and skin made him want to swear allegiance to her, to say that he would protect her from fire and crabgrass and every other thing, but he was unable to form words or even to look into those eyes—not green like Madeline's, but orange. As Mrs. Martin opened her robe and laid her naked weight on him, Kevin struggled one last time to smell Madeline's perfume through the cigarette smoke and the scorching plastic of the picture frame. Long hair fell around his face and trailed in his mouth. Mrs. Martin's legs wrapped around him, and her body threatened to devour not just his personal part, but all the rest of him too. Invisible flames curled around him like a late summer heat that wilted flowers, singed grasses, and cracked bare earth. As his body combusted, he watched the backyard, through the window glass, and soothed his eyes upon the cool emerald expanse of the perfect lawn.

The Sudden Physical Development of Debra Dupuis

AFTER their first gym class, while the rest of the seventh-grade girls soaped and rinsed their poor bumps and swells, Debra tipped her head back and let the shower splash over her womanly bounty like a cleansing waterfall among serene and shapely volcanos. She dropped her towel in front of her gym locker and turned sideways to the mirror. An A-cup girl putting on mascara rolled her eyes, but Debra didn't care. Unfettered by gravity, Debra's breasts rose and floated above her rib cage, helium-filled flesh dirigibles, buoyant and blissful honeydew melons. Debra had been heartbroken this summer when her ex-best friend Nicole had invited another girl to go with her to Disney World, but it seemed God had taken pity on her, and as a consolation had sent her these sacred globes, these heavenly orbs, these twin suns around which the rest of her body now revolved.

"Debra!" called Miss Spartan as Debra was leaving the locker room. "Tell your mother to buy you a sports bra. Otherwise you're going to hurt yourself." Miss Spartan was tall, skinny and, Debra noticed for the first time, endowed with breasts like worn-down speed bumps.

That afternoon Mr. Chiccoine, the science teacher, could have chosen anyone, including her ex-best friend Nicole, but he asked

Debra to deliver a sealed envelope to the office. Debra descended the stairwell as elegantly as the cover model in her mother's current *Woman!* magazine containing the article "Wondering about Wonder Bras?" in which flat-chested women sang their laments and pinned hopes to a bit of fiber-fill padding. Envelope in one hand, neon-green laminated hall pass in the other, she kept her head straight and her chest thrust forward in a posture befitting a girl with such a blessing as hers. At the bottom, she opened the door into an empty hall.

In the school office, Debra handed the envelope to Mrs. Kraft, the secretary, whom everyone liked. Mrs. Kraft wore her hair in a neat French braid, and her lips were perfectly outlined and colored dark pink. She was married to Mr. Kraft, the math teacher, and her voice was quiet, which made everyone speak quietly around her. Last year Mrs. Kraft had told some girls that climbing stairs helped relieve menstrual cramps. For a month the stairs were thronged with girls traveling up and down—teachers even gave girls hall passes, which showed the strength of Mrs. Kraft's influence. That was, until Tamara Jenkins fell on her face, or was pushed, depending on who you asked, and broke her nose and loosened two front teeth.

The only other student in the office was Debra's classmate Southwell Banks, a thick-bodied boy who nobody talked to because his skin flaked off. Debra and Nicole used to speculate about the nature of Southwell's disease. They knew he bathed in oil—or had they made that up? They knew his parents looked gray and dusty, old enough to be great-grandparents. Focused on nothing before him, Southwell's eyes opened, reptilian, into a wet inner core, shielded beneath black brows and chafed eyelids.

"Debra," said Mrs. Kraft, and she touched the pearly button of her own pink crepe shirt just above and between her generous promontories. Debra looked down at her own chest and saw that the indicated button on her flowered shirt hung open. Her mother had inspected her this morning, but first thing at school Debra had undone that second button. Debra refastened it and glimpsed herself doing it in the reflection from the big window between the office and the hallway.

Josh Hines had left earlier to go to the dentist, and on her way back to class, Debra saw him pulling open the door into the stairwell.

"Hey, Josh!"

Josh turned and his eyes stuck to her chest like flies to fly-tape. "Hi," he squeaked like a pinned insect. He had grown probably six inches taller over the summer. He loomed over Debra, yet seemed less substantial than before. He cleared his throat and repeated "Hi" in a deeper voice. Last year he and Debra had worked together on a science project collecting fungus from the perimeter of the school grounds. In gym class, Debra had overheard that Josh's parents were divorcing and that his older brother just went to jail. Debra envisioned poor Josh in a cell with a bunk and a tiny metal sink. A poster-sized picture of herself, Debra Dupuis, would probably hang on the wall. In the picture, Debra would be wearing sheer red silk, like the July *Woman!* cover model, her nipples pressing against the translucent fabric like soft-cut rubies. The other inmates coveted the poster, of course, but Josh refused to trade it for any amount of money or cigarettes.

Perhaps for the poster, Debra would have let the silk garment slip down her arms. In a selfless gesture she might expose her immaculate form for a guy down on his luck the way Josh was. They entered the stairwell together, but Debra said, "Stay there," before Josh could begin to climb.

"Huh?"

Debra positioned herself several steps above him. Keeping an eye on the top of the stairwell, which was open to the second floor, Debra undid the cleavage button, then the other four. Josh moved his mouth but didn't speak. She peeled the sides of her blouse back, unwrapping herself as though she were a meal for a hungry belly, a Christmas gift for an orphan, medicine for the wounded. One after another, she unhooked the three clasps of her front-closing bra, and, as though bringing a surprise birthday cake lit with candles into a dark room, she presented Josh with the wonder of her divine endowments.

Josh fell sideways, and the wall caught him. He reached a hand toward Debra but let it drop. Debra bent forward to gather herself into her bra and fastened the clasps and shirt buttons, but Josh's mouth continued to move as if making bubbles. "Josh, come on, straighten up." Debra shook his arm. "Josh, come on." He followed, zombielike, up the stairs and to Mr. Chiccoine's class, his late excuse slip clutched in his fingers.

THAT night in her room, Debra lay propped in bed beside her reading light, staring out through the burglar bars. She couldn't sneak down the side of the house and wander through her dark neighborhood—her dad had caught her the one time she'd done it this summer, and he'd installed the bars the following weekend. He'd acted mad at her ever since. Now the bars imprisoned her in the same way a bra caged her. The stuffed tigers above her dresser frowned in sympathy—they had long ago suffered the loss of their tails at the hands of her idiot brother. Debra adjusted her crushed-velvet robe so that it was open in the front, and she assumed the same pose as the cover model in last year's Christmas Planning Issue of *Woman!* If a guy walked by on her street and looked up at the right angle, he would see her breasts pressed together like hands in prayer.

Debra had been surprised that Mrs. Kraft wanted her to cover herself. Her mother, small and drooping, Debra understood, but Mrs. Kraft was a young woman with her own bounteous attributes. Having shown her breasts to Josh made Debra want to show them to everyone, the way Nicole had displayed her dead grandmother's half-carat diamond ring last year, holding out her hand for inspection and admiration. Debra should not have to hide in the stairwell; she should pose in front of a chorus line of the rest of her girl classmates, on a stage, dressed in a loose blouse of chiffon through which her feminine outline was visible. After the audience had filled the room with anticipation, Debra would slowly unbutton to reveal her breasts like two full buckets of gold doubloons from a treasure cache. Everyone would be stunned at the wealth of which she was custodian. Debra would turn sideways and lift her arms so people could better admire the shape of her polished golden lamps with their magic spouts. Only after she had closed her shirt would the spell be broken, and the audience would begin to clap and cheer respectfully.

The other girls would overcome their jealousy and celebrate her, the way that runners-up in the Miss America Pageant all hug the winner. Even Mrs. Kraft would compliment her on her bravery, fully supportive. Debra's mother would realize how wrong she had been to demand Debra strap down and conceal her blessings with a bra and shirt buttons done up to her collarbone. Her father would call her "Princess" and promise to remove the window bars, saying he trusted her now. Nicole would apologize for not having asked her to Disney World and would want to be best friends again. And in the very back of the cafetorium, Southwell Banks, who never smiled, would be smiling slightly, experiencing, perhaps, a miraculous healing of his skin.

DEBRA, in her purple stretchy velveteen tee, leaned over Mr. Chiccoine's desk. She was supposed to be labeling the parts of a cell, but she had identified only the mitochondria, the powerhouse of the cell. Terry Orphid slipped behind Mr. Chiccoine and mimicked the movements of Mr. Chiccoine's upper body. "I have a headache," said Debra, leaning closer, pressing her arms together to make more cleavage. Mr. Chiccoine's sleeves were rolled up to just below his elbows, revealing tanned and muscled forearms tangled with dark arm hair.

"You're too young to have a headache," he said, looking past her breasts, into her face.

"I think it's my period," said Debra. "I get headaches at my period. I need some Tylenol. The counselor has a note from my mom."

Mr. Chiccoine squeezed his roller ball pen and tapped the desk blotter. Debra admired a blue vein stretching up the underside of his arm. "All right," he said. "Be back in six minutes or I'll mark you tardy." He pulled the hall pass from his left-hand desk drawer.

Debra was halfway down the stairs when she felt fingers digging into her sides, tickling her. She squirmed against them and turned to see Terry Orphid's face. "Hey! Stop it!" she whispered. "You snuck out of class."

"I needed a break, man," he said. "I'm having my pee-ree-yid."

"Shut up, Terry." Even though he was a pain, Debra had to admit that he was the funniest guy in class. Some of his wisecracks just cut you up. Mrs. Schultz sent him to the office without laughing, though, when he asked the other day if the first lady gave "head of state." Terry grabbed at Debra's sides again, and she pushed his hands down.

He said, "You have great mammaries."

She digested the word "mammaries." Like mammals, like whales, like cows with hairy, sagging milk sacs. She tried to think of soup for the hungry, of cures for diseases, but mostly she felt the nag of protest against sloppy udders and nipples like rubber glove fingers. Terry had no idea of the roundness of her breasts and the gravity they defied. He could not fathom her areolas like the salmon-colored centers of solar systems.

"You want to see them?"

"Sure." Terry's short bangs stuck straight out over a forehead newly afflicted by acne.

"Stand there." She pointed five stairs down. Debra stayed above him on the landing so she could see if anyone was coming. She hiked the velveteen fabric over her breasts, imagining herself on the cafetorium stage in breezy fabric, the audience holding its breath, waiting for her to uncover her middle school holy grail. She held her shirt under her chin as she unworked the bra hooks. The two sides snapped away from each other, but instead of being stunned into devotion, Terry lunged forward and grabbed a breast in each hand. He squeezed as though her breasts were not made of a person's flesh but were leather wrapped around hard rubber centers, oversize baseballs meant to be pitched and shagged and clobbered with bats.

In trying to pull away from him, Debra let herself be driven into the brick wall. She continued backing into the corner, snagging her shirt on the rough surface, slapping Terry, screaming "Stop it! Stop it!" When she was all the way in the corner, she looked into Terry's grimace. He was not laughing or grinning or enjoying himself—he seemed to be seriously engaged in pulling her treasures right off her chest. Adrenaline surged through Debra. "They're mine, damn it!" she screamed and kicked toward Terry's crotch. "Let go of me!" She knocked one of his arms loose and he backed away from her kicks but continued to hold with the other hand, stuck on her like a sea lamprey. Debra looked up past Terry and saw her classmates now standing at the railing, twenty faces staring down like pigeons from a bridge.

"Terry!" boomed Mr. Chiccoine. Terry's hands dropped automatically to his sides. Students gawked at Debra's red-streaked chest, but their shock and silence deteriorated quickly into giggles. Debra turned to face the brick corner as she worked to reconnect her bra, whose strap had twisted under both armpits. Though her anger started out solid, it liquefied in the fluorescent lights, and tears spilled onto her face. Vomit rose halfway up her throat and settled as she struggled with the clasps. Her breasts had been stretched and transformed into pulpy, veined appendages, sagging like fungus from trees. As she got them covered and adjusted her shirt, Mr. Chiccoine grabbed her neck with one hairy arm and Terry's neck with the other.

In the office, Debra couldn't look into Mrs. Kraft's face. The vice-principal positioned Debra and Terry on opposite sides of the office while he called Debra's mom and Terry's dad; Debra couldn't see Terry around the filing cabinet, but his reflection showed in the window. He was leaning back in his chair, a foot crossed over his knee, twitching. When the parents showed, the story came out sounding different, as though Debra had caused the problem. She defended herself: "Hey, I offered to show them to you, not have you tear them off." During the whole meeting, Debra's mother wore a face like a frozen chicken pie. The vice-principal sent both Debra and Terry home early.

The next time she saw Terry, Monday in homeroom, he acted all proud, huddling with a bunch of snickering boys. When he brushed her shoulder on the way to the pencil sharpener, Terry said, "I've seen better boobs than yours on my uncle's milk cows." Nicole's new best friend Becky flashed a fake smile, and Debra had to wonder how much Nicole had told her—everybody in school probably knew that Debra had started her period on the Tilt-o-Whirl and that she didn't notice until a lady carnival worker pointed it out to her. Nicole and Becky wore matching Minnie Mouse T-shirts and light pink lipstick. The color dulled Becky's brunette lips. Debra's throat stung. Crying over a girlfriend would be stupid. Girls in *Woman!* magazine didn't cry over other girls—they cried because of leaking silicone breast implants and turning forty. The outline of Nicole's trainer bra showed through her T-shirt, but otherwise her chest stretched as flat as a new canvas. Becky had breasts like anthills built at sidewalk cracks, the kind Debra would step on without hesitation.

Throughout the day, groups of guys radiated heat toward Debra, in the locker banks, in the cafetorium at lunch, their stares digging into her like the ends of fingers. Girls eyed her as though she were covered with flaking skin. A bathroom-smoking girl with a scar in her chin like a chip in a cocoa mug distinctly said "slut" at lunchtime even though Miss Spartan could have overheard. When Debra reached up into the top part of her locker, a short boy grabbed at her from behind, but missed her breast and squeezed her arm muscle instead. When Debra looked back, she saw only the blurred figures of four boys in high-top shoes running away. Later, somebody shot paper clips at her, and when one went down the front of her shirt she just left it there. She exited the school with her head high, keeping to the side of the cement path, but groups of people jostled her or whispered as she passed. On another sidewalk, heading in a different direction, Southwell Banks shuffled away from the school, his collar buttoned high onto his neck.

At dinner that night with her mother, father, and idiot fourth-grade brother, Debra ate her baked French fries, then picked at her drumstick. Her mother avoided looking at her, and every couple of minutes her dad shook his head for no reason.

"Why do you hate me?" asked Debra.

"We don't hate you," said her mother.

"You hate my breasts."

"How could we hate your breasts?" asked her mother. "They're just breasts, for Christ's sake. Why are you making such a big deal out of them? Believe me, Debra, women have grown breasts for millions of years."

Her father shook his head again.

Her idiot brother asked, "Are you a whore?"

Debra kicked him under the table and said, "No, but you're an idiot."

When Debra unhooked her bra in the upstairs bathroom, the paper clip from fifth hour fell out and chimed on the ceramic tile—

it had imprinted its shape into her skin. She showered for about the tenth time in four days and retired to her room. She didn't even care that she was grounded. Good thing for her parents there were bars on her window, because otherwise she might jump and end it all on the concrete patio. She tried to imagine her body lying there all perfect, her hair spread out around her head, shining like satin in the light from above the garage. But Debra knew she wouldn't tumble gracefully. She'd tangle herself into the patio furniture and land in a sickening twist of limbs and dangling boobs. Nicole and Becky would be there in matching outfits. "Gross," Nicole would say. Terry Orphid would say, "Sick, man," and if Mrs. Kraft didn't show up to stop him, Terry would poke at her chest. Mrs. Kraft *would* come, though, and in her quiet voice she'd send everyone away, and she'd rearrange the robe to cover Debra.

Debra opened her robe and looked in the mirror as she had not done since Friday. As much as she had imagined her breasts sagging and sinking, they did not. Despite all that had happened, her great pyramids jutted forward, temples still fully worthy of worship. She turned sideways and admired her cherry blossom peaks angled slightly upwards, as reverent as lips in prayer. In the bedroom light, her skin glowed all the way up her neck to her face, where a few pimples didn't really matter. As her hair dried, it began to shine with a halo like the base of a crown. Her mother was wrong about her breasts being like other breasts on millions of women. Debra had seen those other poor, regular tomatoes, small or plain or flattened. Jesus couldn't have breasts, but if he had them, they'd be like hers. And just as Jesus showed all men their holiness by his example, Debra's divine bestowal uplifted all the less than perfect bosoms around her. Held aloft by the hand of God, her oblate shrines offered salvation to all humanity, even if the humanity around here was not worthy of them. Terry Orphid said he'd seen better ones on milk cows. Well, he could go back to his uncle's farm because he was a heathen turd who didn't deserve to stand in the glow of their magnificence. Debra pulled her curtains closed, and the golden light of her incandescent lamp reflected against them, back to her. She curled on the bed, tucked the crushed-velvet robe around her, and hugged herself.

Sleeping Sickness

A CROCODILE. That's what I felt like. Hot, slow, and mean. But crocodiles live in Egypt, half-submerged in cool rivers, and I was frying like an egg outside of Alexander, Michigan, near the Indiana line. The humid air pressed on me from all sides, so I tried not to move, swatting at flies only when they buzzed in my ears or touched my face. I didn't bother to keep flies off the vegetables in front of me—people should know enough to wash them when they got home. For breakfast I'd had the last few pieces of my twelfth birthday cake, which I'd made and eaten almost entirely myself, and now the sticky yellow plate was covered with ants. When I put it on the grass, my orange tiger cat Ripley slid from the table to lick it clean. As I watched some crows picking at a road-hit possum, I was thinking that a person could forget to breathe on a day like this and then just pass out and die.

My vegetable table stood atop the hill, halfway between the house and the road, under two shagbark hickory trees, and ever since school had gotten out last week I was minding the stand full-time. I was sitting behind my perfectly arranged cucumbers, peppers, and jars of milk labeled "milk for cats" when John Blain first showed up. He drove by in a station wagon, knocking up dust which drifted and settled on me. He turned around and went by again slowly, then pulled into our dirt driveway and parked in front of my sign: "Cukes, Toms, Peps 6/$1." Ripley ran away toward the barn. John Blain got out of the driver's seat and left the door hanging open on its hinges. He was a white man about forty years old, wearing a Caterpillar cap. Dirty steam seemed to rise off him. "What do you want?" I asked.

The garden was behind me on my right, farther up the driveway, past the barn. The house was on the left, surrounded by the unruly bushes Mom called bridal wreath, whose white-flowered branches stretched out like octopus arms. The man took off his hat, wiped his forehead with it, ran a hand through forelocks as blond and rough as corn tassels, then put the hat back on. He had a pack of cigarettes in his T-shirt pocket. "Don't look like you got too much business, kiddo." He picked up a bell pepper, tossed it, and caught it, but he was looking beyond me, at the porch where Mom had just stepped.

"That your mom?"

"Maybe. What's it to you? She's got no money, so don't bother trying to sell her anything." I was telling the truth. In fact, she was needing all my vegetable money just to pay the power bill.

"I might want to buy something from her."

"She's got nothing to sell to you." I'd met enough men to know there wasn't any profit in being nice to ones like him. I was hoping for a breeze to blow in my shirt-sleeves. For my birthday Mom had given me a bra, but all it did was soak up sweat, and I needed to readjust it. "You're blocking my sign," I said, but the man wasn't listening, so I went around the stand and moved my piece of plywood to where it could be seen from the road. Not many cars were coming by, but I was making a point of not letting this guy interrupt my life. Mom was walking up the driveway toward us, wearing a flowered dress. Though it was about twelve-thirty, and I had been up for six and a half hours, she'd just gotten out of bed. I rearranged my cucumbers in order of their size, biggest to smallest.

"How you doing, Sunshine?" Mom talked sweet whenever she got around men. Sweat dripped from her temples, and she had to squint against the sun. She was talking to me, but looking at the man, smiling and blinking, her long, shiny hair dangling around her shoulders. Her skin was pale except for a few freckles because she hardly ever went outside.

"This guy is blocking my stand." I slumped in my chair.

"Don't be rude, Reg." Mom gave the man an apologetic smile.

"Merle at the service station in Alexander told me you got a Plymouth station wagon, same year as mine," said the man.

Mom said, "It was my father's. The engine's no good. It's been sitting out behind the house more than a year."

"If the body's good, I might be interested," he said. "And what's your name, ma'am?"

"Margie." Mom pushed her hair over her ear in a shy way.

"I'm John Blain. Pleased to meet you." He held out his hand, and she wiped hers on her dress before she shook it. "We sure got us a hot one today," he said, adjusting his hat. "We ought to be up in the U.P. where I just come from. Nice and cool up there."

"I've never been to the Upper Peninsula," said Mom, as though it was some dreamy place she'd been meaning to go. The next thing you know, she'd invited John Blain to have lunch with us, and he said sure, he'd love a cup of coffee. I left him and Mom talking and went into the barnyard for some privacy in adjusting my bra, I picked grass from along my garden fence and dropped the bits into the chicken yard; it fell like confetti around our four hens, who dashed to peck it up. I cooled my arms, legs and face with the hose by the side of the house, but by the time I went inside, I was hot again.

"This isn't a restaurant," I said, too quietly for Mom to hear. John Blain looked me in the eyes and growled. I made a sandwich and poured a glass of last night's milk from Jessie, our brown-and-white cow, wondering all the while what kind of man would growl at a person. For sure both he and Mom were out of their gourds. It was hot enough for blood to boil in your veins, and they were sipping coffee, and John Blain took long, hot draws from his cigarette. Mom laughed idiotically at everything he said.

After lunch I carried some crushed ice to my vegetables to revive them and to keep the milk-for-cats cold. I tied Jessie to a cement block nearby to graze. She had to get away from her calf for a few hours in order to have any milk by evening. There wasn't any reason people couldn't drink her milk—we did, after all—but, according to Mr. VanderVeen who sold us straw and cheap hay that had been rained on in the field, it was against the law to sell the milk for people. Jessie dragged her block behind her, tearing a line through the grass, and she swatted flies disinterestedly with her tail. I looked through my newspaper again, though I had already read it front to back. Then I used it to fan myself.

It was hard to concentrate in the new summer heat, hard to remember things, hard to make plans. I walked around to investigate John Blain's car, which was rusty and faded olive green. The back was folded down, and there was a mattress but no room for anyone to sleep with all that junk back there—cables and loose rusty tools, a chain saw, and even a bicycle with the wheels taken off. The front seat was full of food wrappers and Styrofoam cups, and across the passenger seat lay a green army sleeping bag. A freezer bag held a toothbrush, toothpaste, and a plastic razor. The least he could do, I thought, was move this rusted hulk away from my stand so I could earn a living.

I'd been cupping my hands at the passenger-side window to get a better view, and when I stepped back, the figure of a man towered behind me in the reflection. I screamed.

"Find anything interesting?" asked John Blain.

"You're a slob."

"And you're a nosey girl." John Blain walked around to the driver's side of the car and brushed his teeth in some water from a bottle, spitting foam onto the driveway. Then he grinned into his side-view mirror, showing all his teeth. "You take care of your teeth, kiddo, and they'll take care of you." I let him see me roll my eyes. He pulled a tool box out of the back of the car and carried it toward the house.

I yelled after him, "The price of the car is 250 bucks!"

SINCE my dad had left us, there'd been a river of no-good men running through our lives. I was glad when they didn't stay around, and they usually didn't. I knew Mom wasn't happy without a man, but she didn't have to go for whatever guy showed up in our driveway. That's what I told her that night at supper.

"How come every guy who comes around you're falling all over him?"

"I wasn't falling over him. He seemed like a nice man, didn't he? He stayed with his aunt in Alexander when he was a boy. That's why he came here. But his aunt's dead."

"Well, I hate him."

"Why don't you want me to be happy?" She asked the question with a heaving of her chest, as though exhausted and beleaguered by a long history of cruel treatment at my hands.

"Why can't you be happy without a stupid guy?"

"Reg, you're so young. You don't know how terrible it is to be alone."

"I'm alone all the time. I like being alone."

"Wait until you're grown up. Besides, this John Blain's not like the other men around here. I can tell." Mom lay on the couch, fitting herself into the imprint she'd made in the cushions over the years. We'd brought it with us from the trailer.

"Well, I hope he doesn't come back."

"You're so mean." She sounded tired and sad. "You're every bit as mean as your daddy."

"Maybe Daddy had a reason to be mean. Some day I'm going to find him and ask him all about it."

Mom turned away from me and fell asleep.

WHEN John Blain showed up the next evening with a pizza, Mom said he could stay the night, but he didn't end up sleeping on the couch like she'd suggested in front of me. That next morning, he got up early and drove out for a box of doughnuts from the highway stop, getting back just as I finished chores. I sat in the kitchen and ate a chocolate cake doughnut and a cruller without saying a word, even though John Blain kept going upstairs and returning and pacing. Finally, I overheard him in Mom's room saying her name louder and louder. I carried a frosted long john upstairs and watched from the hallway while he shook her. He turned, panic-stricken, his forehead strained.

"Oh, God! What's the matter with her? Why won't she wake up?"

"She's got the sleeping sickness," I said.

"Sleeping sickness? Encephalitis? She wasn't sick last night."

"She just sleeps a lot," I said. "Twelve hours a night. You can't wake her before eleven or even noon sometimes. And then she takes a nap in the afternoon."

John Blain collapsed in the chair by the bed. I noticed his blond hair was streaked with gray.

WE'D only lived on the farm two years, ever since my grandpa J.T. had died. Mom had gotten pregnant at age sixteen, and J.T. had told her that if she ran off with my dad, he'd never speak to her again, and because he was a man of his word, I never met him. Maybe the only reason he left her the farm was because he knew she hated it. If it had been up to her, she would have gotten rid of Jessie and the chickens, but I argued until she let me keep them so long as I took care of them. For weeks, then, Mrs. VanderVeen from next door had to come over and help me milk the cow until I could do it myself. When Mom was drunk, she'd say the house was "a goddamn jail." Whenever something went wrong, like a roof needed fixing, she'd say that she ought to sell the place. A few days before John Blain came, I told her I'd fix the roof over the porch, and she'd said accusingly, "You'd do anything to keep me here, wouldn't you?" That night I dreamed that we still lived in the trailer and that Mom's ex-boyfriends were all with us, drinking canned beer and sucking the oxygen out of the air. I woke up twisted in my sheets, sweating.

By the middle of tomato season, John Blain was well entrenched. He got a second-shift job, so I didn't see too much of him, except on the weekends, when I ignored him. One Saturday evening, though, I finished milking the cow and carried the bucket up to the porch, where John Blain was always squatting, his elbows on his knees, as still as a plant putting out roots. He stood when he saw me coming and made to open the door for me.

"I can open the door myself," I told him.

He let go of the door, wrapped a hand around my skinny biceps and clamped tight. "Why are you such a brat, Regina?" he asked. His breath smelled like whiskey, a bottle of which I'd seen him hide in the crotch of the apple tree next to the barn. "Your ma is so nice, and you're so damned mean."

My arm was starting to hurt, but when I twisted to free myself he tightened his grip. When I kicked him a dozen times hard enough to bruise his shins, he squeezed tighter still. I noticed white, dry salt around the edges of the sweat marks on the neck and armpits of his T-shirt. "What do you want?" I asked.

"A little respect. A kind word, maybe. For your ma's sake."

"I've got to strain the milk. Let me go."

"The milk'll wait. Life is too short to be so mean, Reg."

His grip exhausted me. He was only a half-foot taller than me, but I couldn't come near matching his strength. When tears threatened to drop over the edges of my eyes, I turned away and looked west, over my garden, toward the hot, dirty sun. I let out my breath in a tired sigh. John Blain leaned toward me and then kissed my mouth. His lips only just touched mine, then he pulled away with a look of surprise on his face. I sloshed milk onto the porch and on my shoes, and he followed me into the kitchen. "I'm sorry, Reg. I don't know what happened."

"Go to hell!" I screamed. He shook his head and went back out onto the porch, holding the door so it didn't slam. I set up my milk funnel and filter, but I could hardly see. I kept knocking the half-gallon bottle over, and finally I just left it all on the table. Ripley jumped up and started drinking right out of the bucket.

After that, John Blain kept a distance from me, as though we'd come to some kind of understanding. The next day he bought me the Detroit Sunday paper, and he continued to buy it every week, so I could spend Sunday afternoons reading and refolding each part. He wanted only the crossword puzzle. One Sunday, while I was reading at the kitchen table, Mom and John Blain were sitting in the living room where I could hear them.

"She's a beautiful girl, you know," he said, in just above a whisper.

"She's twelve," said Mom.

"But it happened just like that," he said and snapped his fingers. "All of a sudden, she's beautiful."

"I was beautiful, and where'd it get me?"

"What do you mean 'was'? Any man would trade his soul for a chance to gaze into that freckled face of yours. I'll die happy, woman, so long as I die with your hair twisted around me."

Mom laughed with pleasure. When I dared look at them from the kitchen, John Blain was back at his crossword, and Mom had fallen asleep on the couch.

After dinner, I usually worked in the garden, pulling weeds and picking vegetables to sell the next day. Mom did the dinner dishes. John Blain, when he wasn't working, would go out on the porch and squat down, and smoke cigarettes like a cowboy at a camp or a soldier staying low to avoid enemy fire. Both he and Mom looked west, Mom's face blurry through the window screen over the sink, John Blain's out in the open in clear focus. By the time I finished in the garden, Mom and John Blain would have started drinking jug wine, either sitting at the picnic table on the porch, or else in the kitchen if the mosquitos got bad. They'd be reading or playing cards or John Blain would be doing the crossword, and then after a while, for no reason, they'd start arguing and accusing each other. Sometimes Mom would tell him to get the hell out, but John Blain knew as well as I did that this was her way of testing whether or not he was going to stay. I took to going to bed even earlier so I wouldn't have to hear them. If they carried their argument up to the bedroom next to mine, I'd go out to the barn to sleep with Jessie. By the next day they always seemed to have forgotten whatever it was that had made them fight.

I didn't need an alarm clock to wake up each morning between five-thirty and six, and I'd do the chores first thing. Often I'd come across John Blain lying in a heap somewhere. Once I found him outside my room, and a few times he was on the kitchen floor, but more often I'd find him outside, as though he'd tried to leave us but collapsed from the effort. Most of the time he'd be north of the house, up the incline. The farthest he ever made it was into the pasture and to the row of white pines that made the property line. I'd say, "Get up, you," and if he didn't, I'd nudge him with my foot, then stand nearby until he slogged off.

The day he made it to the pine trees, I didn't find him until the afternoon. When I came in from the vegetable stand for lunch,

Mom was fidgeting, not drinking the coffee she'd poured. So I hunted around and found him lying awake on the moss, his hands locked across his belly. "I knew you'd find me if I waited," he said. "I'm glad you don't hate me anymore." We regarded each other, John Blain smiling, myself determined not to smile.

"Mom's worried. She thinks you left."

"She can see my car's still here," he said. "I'm not going to leave her, Reg, so you may as well get used to me." He supported himself on one elbow while he lit a cigarette. I probably looked skeptical, and maybe I rolled my eyes. "I swear, Reg, I'm not leaving your ma," he said, looking right at me. We walked back to the house, keeping a distance between us. Probably my dad had promised to stay too.

John Blain fixed the pasture fence during the last week of August. It'd been down in two places—one where a tree had fallen on it, the other where a corner post had rotted away. I'd tried propping it up using ropes and two-by-fours, but none held. The VanderVeens were mad because Jessie and the calf had gotten into their garden twice. John Blain found tools in the barn and restrung the whole thing, replacing parts of it, making it strong and tight, even better than the VanderVeen's fences. When I acted surprised that he knew how to put up fence, he said, "I can do just about everything, kiddo. And I'm going to teach it all to you."

The last fence post we reset was at the far corner of the pasture, out of sight of the house. Mom was most likely sleeping on the couch, and John Blain lay on the ground with a small log under his head. We'd already put the post into the hole and I was tamping the dirt with an axe handle.

"You're a hard worker, Reg. And you're strong for your age."

I shrugged and didn't look at him.

"You're a lot tougher than either me or your ma, and you're a lot smarter. You're not going to end up like us, a couple of drunks."

"You're not drunks," I said. I finished tamping and lay down beside him on the ground and propped my head up. "You're not a drunk." I was close enough that I could smell his cigarette breath and his sweat. I'd never noticed before that he had a tattoo on his forearm, a tiny eagle with wings folded, the size of a thumbprint.

Though I'd never before touched him on purpose, I pressed the tattoo through the hair on his arm. The pasture would be perfect now, after John Blain stretched this last corner. I opened my eyes and he was looking right at me, and for no reason I could fathom, I wanted him to wrap his fence-stretching arms around me and pull me to his chest and hold me there next to his heart. His chest expanded and deflated as he breathed, and my own breathing seemed loud. How could I live, I wondered, if he didn't put his arms around me? I moved closer, and he snubbed his cigarette in the dirt. He reached an arm around my shoulder, grabbed my bra strap through my T-shirt, pulled it out, and let it snap back.

"You creep!" I yelled.

He laughed and coughed, and reached for another cigarette. I stood and brushed myself off. "Why don't you just fix your stupid car and go back to the U.P.?" I picked up the mattock and lugged it down the incline, lifting and swinging it at every burdock plant.

That evening, I walked by the door to my mother's room and saw her sitting on the edge of her bed, looking into the adjoining bathroom, listening to John Blain. Her hair shone like a fresh penny in the light from the setting sun, and she wore a nylon slip that she used as a nightgown. She rested her bare feet on the wooden bed frame and wrapped her arms around her knees. John Blain was shaving with no shirt on, telling her about a Russian he knew in Copper Harbor. The humidity seemed to have softened the edges and the corners on everything in the room—the pictures in their frames, the furniture, and the steamy bathroom mirror all looked soft. Once I looked at John Blain, I couldn't look away. His nipples were like a girl's, like mine, his arms bronze below his shirt-sleeve line but as pale as Mom's above, and the tattoo like a bruise. As he shaved, I became afraid that he would cut himself with his razor, and I watched, concerned, until he caught my eye in the mirror. He smiled at me and winked.

"Jerk," I said to myself and returned to my room, but I couldn't clear my head. No longer did I want John Blain to hug me, but somehow I had tasted my mother's desperation, and I couldn't go back to not knowing it. When I found myself unable to sleep that night, I took out my photo album. On the first page was a picture of my father. His was a face I couldn't remember without reference, the hair as dark and curly as mine, the bloodshot eyes which looked angry. It was a handsome and peculiar face, but it wouldn't stick in my mind. Mom once said he was half Indian, but another time she said that was one of his lies. Daddy had always been full of jittery energy when we lived in the trailer, and about my only memory of him was wishing he'd be still so I could sit beside him. Now the vision in my head was just as restless, moving in and out of my memory even as I looked at his picture.

I flipped forward, then, to the pictures of our farm: the rust-colored barn, Jessie and newborn brown-and-white calf, the chickens, the bridal bushes. Mom had taken a photo of me standing in the soft muck outside the cow barn wearing rubber boots, holding my stainless steel milk bucket. I rubbed my cheek against the plastic which covered the picture of our rabbit Snoopy. I'd taken the picture right before he escaped from his cage and got killed by Ripley.

With my pillow and blanket under my arm, I slipped past Mom's room and outside. The barnyard was quiet at this time of night, chickens asleep on their perches, cows resting and ruminating. As my eyes adjusted to the darkness, the blue earth became brown, and the strange landscape became familiar. Fireflies sparkled in the bushes and around the apple tree outside the barn. I shook out some fresh straw in the cow stall and lay with my head on Jessie and my feet on her calf. Ripley stretched and yawned atop a bale of hay nearby. Crickets chirped intermittently. Jessie's giant belly moved rhythmically, and I fell asleep to the sweet smells of alfalfa and manure. But I was immediately jarred awake by what felt like sadness in the air around me. We'd sell the calf in a few months, and Jessie would be alone until she had another baby. My mother said she had no idea where my dad was—he could be lost and alone, maybe without a home. And now that John Blain was going to stay, he couldn't come back to us even if he wanted to. It occurred to me for the first time that my father must be sad when he thought of me.

IN September, my vegetable stand was covered with tomatoes, squash, and melons. Since John Blain had started paying the bills, I kept my vegetable profits in coffee cans in my closet—so far I had about $550. I was at school until three o'clock, so I left an empty metal box on the stand, and, as far as I could tell, most people were honest and put money in when they took something.

In October, I saved John Blain's life. Or that's what he told me. He finally got around to taking the engine out of his car and putting it in our station wagon. In the process, he cut the end of his thumb on the oil pan and had to explain to me how to pressure-bandage with gauze and duct tape while he bled all over the ground in front of the barn. He refused to go to the doctor, and, after that, he couldn't do much with his thumb.

In November, we sold the heifer to Mr. VanderVeen, which meant I had to milk twice a day, and Jessie gave way more milk than we could drink even though I convinced John Blain to drink his coffee half-full of hot milk.

Two nights before Christmas Eve, I woke to shouting in the next room. A wine bottle crashed to the floor but didn't break. "What's the matter with you?" yelled my mother. I got out of bed, put a coat over my pajamas, slipped into snowmobile boots, hat and gloves, and went outside. My garden was dead from frost, and my stand was shut down except for bottles of milk-for-cats that froze solid after a few hours. The air was crisp, and the sky was clear, with a zillion stars in sharp focus. Jessie was alone now, and each tree seemed alone without its leaves, and any creature who braved the winter night had to do so alone. There was no society of crickets or fireflies this time of year. I reached into the rotted crotch of the tree where John Blain kept his bad-tasting alcohol—whiskey or ginger brandy usually—and found instead a half-full pint-bottle of peppermint schnapps. With each sip, a warm shiver traveled into my legs. I leaned against the tree and looked back at the house. The light from their bedroom was on, a tiny bedside glow, reflecting the pinpricks up there in the heavens. My window was dark as I'd left it. Gradually the peppermint schnapps softened my vision. Though the roof sagged and the paint had all peeled off, our house looked beautiful surrounded by the leafless sticks of bridal bushes. Because I couldn't hear them, I imagined that Mom and John Blain had stopped arguing once and for all, that they had settled their disagreements and would live happily ever after. The stars changed from pricks to tiny blurs. I placed the empty bottle in the crotch of the tree and stumbled back to the house where it was warm.

The next morning I woke to a sky so bright it burned my eyes and to the sound of Jessie mooing crazily. The clock said quarter 'til nine. I hadn't slept this late in all the time we'd been on the farm. My mouth was dry and my head hurt, but I bundled up, grabbed my bucket, and ran out to the barn. On the way I saw John Blain crumpled up, sleeping on the ground near the apple tree, and I yelled, "Wake up, you!" and was surprised at the way my own voice hurt my head. Maybe he'd needed his schnapps last night and would be mad that I'd drunk it.

Jessie's bag was swollen as though it would burst, and a half-hour later, when I finished milking, John Blain was still lying there with his legs curled toward his chest and his hands between his knees. He wore a flannel shirt, wool socks, and jeans, but no boots and no jacket. "Come on, get up," I yelled. When I nudged him with my foot, his head fell back and he faced me. His lips were waxy white, and his unblinking eyelids opened onto dull, frosted-over marbles. When I screamed and dropped my milk bucket, Ripley came bounding across the frozen ground to lick up what milk he could.

I leaned against the wooden fence, unable to focus. A crow flew up out of the frozen garden with a startling "Caw! Caw! Caw!" Ripley, when his appetite was sated, padded over and rubbed himself from nose to tail against my leg. Cars rolled past on the road, somewhere far off a train whistle blew, and the sun rose a little higher in the sky. John Blain's hands remained locked between his knees. I knelt beside him and felt his neck for a pulse, but the skin was cold and silent. I pulled back his sleeve and touched the little eagle on his arm. I pushed his hair away from his forehead. The skin around his eyes was puffy as though he'd gone to sleep crying. I said, "I'm sorry, John Blain."

For a long time I stood beside Mom's bed. Her skin was creaseless. She reeked of wine, but her breathing was deep and regular, and she looked cozy under her blankets. I called to her over and over, raising my voice until I was screaming. I shook her violently. "John Blain's dead!" I yelled. "Dead! Dead!" She opened her eyes groggily, then closed them again. Never in my life had I felt so tired. I worked open the window beside her bed and propped it up with the lamp, and let icy air pour into the room. Then I tore the covers off and threw them on the floor. She shivered, curling smaller and smaller, into the same position as John Blain. I dragged her to the side of the bed, made her sit up, and turned her face toward the open window. "John Blain's dead, Mommy! Look!" Finally, she moaned in realization and leaned out the window toward the figure on the snow, knocking the lamp out so it hung by its cord, still burning, six feet down the side of the house. I pulled her back inside, reeled in the lamp, and closed the window.

Mom bolted and then appeared outside, leaning over the body, touching John Blain's face and then laying her head on his chest so her hair fell around him. I remembered him saying that was how he wanted to die, but Mom was a little late in getting to him. I went downstairs and met her as she stormed back into the house. She threw on her winter coat and boots over her slip, got a shovel from the utility room, and marched off past the body, into the pasture and up the incline. I was fastening my chore coat as I chased after her. She went near the spot where I had found John Blain lying the time he said he wouldn't leave us. "You son of a bitch!" she yelled. She was trying to dig, but the cold had made the ground hard.

"Mom, I think we'd better tell the police."

"The police don't give a damn about him."

"You can't just bury somebody. What if the police think we killed him?"

"Did I kill him, Reg? Did I kill the son of a bitch?"

"He didn't mean to die, Mom!" I yelled.

She dug furiously, her shovel making only tiny dents in the frozen ground, her hair flaming around her head. "I need the mattock, Reg. Go get it for me." And when I hesitated, she screamed, "Go get it!" Against my better judgment, I ran down the hill to the barn and returned dragging the mattock. By now Mom was on her knees, beating the ground with her fists, calling John Blain names and demanding, "How could you?" She grabbed the mattock and started chopping at the ground, her knuckles whitening as though fusing to the handle. With each stroke I worried she'd chop off her own foot, but she only went on like that for a minute or so before falling onto her knees again and dropping her face in her hands. She said, "Reg, it doesn't do any goddamned good to love a person."

If only I had not drunk his liquor, I would've woken at my regular time to milk Jessie, and John Blain would've lived. He depended on me to wake him up. He thought we had an understanding. Maybe he'd been out looking around for a bottle that wasn't empty. I could imagine him on the moss right here, sitting up to light a cigarette, asking why I drank his booze. I looked to the sky for a clue, but there wasn't even a cloud. Of course John Blain knew a lot, so maybe he'd known we lived in a world where all it took to kill a person was sleeping late.

"Mom, we're going down to the house now." I grabbed her cold hand and held it, though it didn't hold mine in return. She had become weak enough that I could boss her. I left the tools where they lay and led her down the frozen pasture, shutting the gate behind us so Jessie couldn't get out. I took her into the kitchen and started some coffee in the drip pot before calling the Alexander police. When they arrived, Mom was sitting as stiff as a fence post with a cup of coffee growing cold in front of her, her snow boots and parka still on. While we waited for the medical examiner, I told the two men that Mom wanted to bury John Blain on the hill, and they looked at each other as though we were crazy, and then Mom agreed to have the body taken to Peas Brothers Mortuary.

IN February, because the mortuary hadn't heard from any of John Blain's relations, they gave Mom the ashes in a metal box. That night she tried to drive his car drunk, but she crashed it into a tree before even getting out of the driveway. She didn't hurt herself, but the car wouldn't run anymore. One Saturday, after we'd had a week of thaws, Mom spent all day digging near the pines. She became a tiny silhouette of a woman, very far away. I didn't dare take my eyes off her, for fear she'd become smaller still and then disappear. She took the box of ashes up to where she had been digging, dumped them loose into the hole, and covered them with dirt, as though she expected him to grow again next year.

That night Mom cried and cried in the room next to mine, and since there was nothing I could do for her, I dressed warmly and dragged my quilt out to the barn. The moon was silent and half full beneath the blanket of sky. I curled beside Jessie and pulled the cover over both of us. Hopefully Mom was wrong about loving people, but I had never thought about John Blain in terms of love anyway. I just knew for sure that he didn't mean to leave us—he'd stayed as long as any of my tomato or squash plants, and in a way he was still there, if you counted his ashes. I was grateful his car was busted so Mom couldn't try to drive to the U.P. or the Alexander Bar & Grill. The smells of hay and manure mingled, and I held Jessie around the neck with both arms and breathed in the warmth from her body. Gazing out the barn window, I thought I could see the burning red tip of one of John Blain's cigarettes, a comforting little glow, but really it was only a star, or maybe Mars. As Jessie chewed beside me, rhythmically, peacefully, I thought about the garden I'd plant in May. Lush rows of beans and tomatoes curved through the barnyard and up the incline in my mind, and in my muscles I felt the pull of the young, strong plants toward the sun.

Celery Fields

THE police called as Georgina was swallowing her last bite of plain Cheerios with skim milk. "Ma'am, do you own a white Ford pickup?" Georgina didn't think of herself as a ma'am. "That's my husband's truck," she said. That's the truck that cost half as much as this house, she thought, the truck he'd bought without consulting her. Georgina stared into her empty bowl and clicked the clear-polished nails of her free hand on the polyurethane tabletop. As a kid she'd eaten at a varnished pine table that softened when anything wet spilled on it. "My husband's not here."

Andy was supposed to be out with his brother cutting firewood for their dad. On Saturdays, if he wasn't pouring cement, Andy usually did something with his brother. In late November they'd clip on their licenses and go deer hunting, which meant they hunkered in a dark field with a hundred other orange-clad men until the sun rose, and then they went to a chain restaurant near the game preserve and ate a lot of fried meat. At other times they'd go fishing or attend outdoors shows or gun shows at Wings Stadium. Georgina spread her fingers out on the table; for a moment she was surprised that her nails were clean.

"The truck's bogged down on some private property," said the cop, "and the owner called to complain. Your husband might want to tow it himself right away, save everybody else the trouble."

Andy had left some kind of caramel pastry here. Georgina pulled the box toward herself across the table until she could see through the plastic window. She didn't care what Andy ate during the day. Let him eat his deep-fried doughnuts and vending machine cashews. Let him pour maple-flavored corn syrup over his fucking Greek restaurant breakfast sausages. But he didn't have to bring this shit into the house to tempt her.

"Thank you, sir. I appreciate it," she said. According to the cop's directions, Andy's truck probably wasn't more than a half-mile from the house where Georgina had lived until she was fifteen. The old neighborhood had been run down, and the road along the river had always been littered with trash despite "No Dumping" signs. Kids there, including Georgina, had earned nickels from the bait shop by digging nightcrawlers out of the soft muck.

Georgina hung up the phone and resisted an urge to take out her file and further clean and smooth her nails. She had been planning to get her hair trimmed today, to buy a red blazer, and to visit her sister-in-law who wanted her to host a party to sell candles or lingerie or some shit. She thought about pretending she'd never gotten that call about the truck, but she'd become curious about the old neighborhood, and besides she'd like to see just how stuck Andy had gotten himself. Andy had eaten a corner piece out of the pastry, a rectangle no bigger than a folded-up paycheck. Why would a person who was going to eat only that much buy a whole goddamn box?

Georgina hadn't eaten pastry in years. Dieting had changed her body into an efficient machine, one which needed surprisingly few calories to sustain itself. When she had originally cut her rations, her stomach radioed her primitive brain—the oldest, grayest part, at the base of her skull—and sent the message that she was a woman lost from her tribe, banished from her native lands, scavenging on hillsides in years of drought, scratching for the sustenance of wildflower seeds, berries, and weed roots.

With the handle of her cereal spoon, she cut a piece of pastry about the same size as the missing piece. She held it between two fingers and moved it toward her mouth and almost bit down, but instead she returned it to the box and wiped her hands on her jeans. Stop it, she told herself. But she wondered if biting into that sweet stuff would open up an alternative universe, one she'd entirely forgotten. Maybe it would be a universe of surrender. Vegetables and rice cakes never surrendered. Cheerios always stood up to her in the white china bowl, which sat before her now looking very empty, as though it had never contained cereal or anything. She rinsed the bowl and the spoon and put them both in the drainer. Eat me, the pastry cried from the table, bite me, as boys used to say in the neighborhood.

She could probably eat more if she exercised, but she couldn't imagine herself bouncing around the way women did. Maybe martial arts. Gardening would have worked, but Andy didn't want her tearing up any part of the lawn. He claimed it would interfere with his underground sprinkler system. She went into the attached garage and started up her Volkswagen Golf. Georgina had thought she, not Andy, would be the first to get a new vehicle, since hers was ten years old with some rust on the rear body panels, and yet, something stopped her from giving up a car that still ran well. In another year or two, her car would look at home in the old neighborhood, parked in a dirt driveway, next to a sagging front porch on which an unshaven man in a sleeveless undershirt lounged on a torn and disheveled couch.

As she backed into the street, away from her vinyl-sided, white-trimmed white house, the perfect blackness of tarred and curbed driveway poured out in front of her. Covering the land between house and driveway was Andy's sacred green, uninterrupted by bush, flower, or weed. The garage door rolled toward the ground. From somewhere out of sight Georgina heard the buzz of chain saws and diesel motors; she smelled the burning oil of two-stroke engines, of men clearing the way for another house like hers, of bulldozers shoving felled trees to the back of one hundred-by-two hundred foot building lots. There was so much development around here; everybody wanted to live in these gently curving rows of tidy and respectable prefabricated homes.

IN a field near the river, Mexicans with machetes trudged north along the rows, the muck closing around their feet with each step so their rubber boots became as weighted as balls and chains. The men hacked with knives as long as their forearms and tossed heads of celery, half as thick as they were high, into the wagon that rolled beside them. The sweet peppery fragrance of celery leaves and seeds poured into Georgina's car through open windows and became so strong that she had to stop and park. Her granny used to grow a patch of celery behind the barn and she'd told Georgina about the old days, when the farmers grew acres and acres of the best celery in the world right here. Georgina wished Granny could see this. Along with the other old neighbor ladies, her granny had worked most of her springs planting seeds, and her summers placing bleach-boards against each plant to block the sun and make the celery grow anemic pale, the way people liked it in New York and Chicago. The black-haired men in boots, jeans, and straw cowboy hats moved steadily away, abreast one another, shouting in Spanish, slashing and tossing, synchronized in a harvest line dance.

When Georgina no longer could hear the men's voices or make out their hands and necks, she shifted into first. For half a mile, celery heads grew on either side of the road, green columns which, after all these years, had somehow thrust upward from their roots with enough force to displace the heavy soil. After her granny died, Georgina, who was ten, had asked her mother why nobody grew celery anymore. Georgina's mother told her that the soil was finally used up, once and for all, and that was why the fields lay weedy and uncultivated, including the little garden plot behind their barn.

The houses beyond the fields were exactly as Georgina remembered—simple, small, peeling-paint houses built on concrete block foundations or on slabs poured atop mounds of slag landfill, above yards low enough to flood after a big rain. Georgina slowed to pass a driveway where four children with dirt-smeared legs played a game of running and hand-slapping. Even with Andy's sprinkler system and fertilizer, her new west side lawn didn't stay lush like these yards, fed by a watertable not more than a foot below the surface. That watertable explained everything about this place, why the celery grew, why the earth used to heave behind her old house, where one month there might be a valley a foot deep and the next month there'd be a little hill, and why Andy's truck, when she reached it, was mired nearly to its axles. If he couldn't live without the new truck as he'd insisted, then why had he risked the thing by coming to the river, of all places, to get firewood? Andy's truck was as white as a wedding cake, a pure color that seemed wrong here. She'd expect green-whites like the celery her granny once protected from the sun, and she'd expect red-whites like the crazy eyes of that pony that had been trapped in the mud a decade ago.

God, she hadn't thought of that pony in ages. As a kid, Georgina had seen cars stuck when older kids unfamiliar with the area would park and make out, and then they'd have to call their parents or a tow truck to winch them. The girl who lived up on the ridge must have known she was pushing her luck riding her pony into that part of the woods after spring rains. When Georgina and other kids on the street heard the commotion, they came tearing through their patched screen doors and out of their weedy backyards. The pony, purply-brown and sweating, had sunk past its knees. It screamed and tossed its neck in the air as if trying to throw off its head. Its eyes rolled back in its sockets and grass-colored foam poured out of its mouth and coated the leather bridle and reins which whipped around like swamp snakes.

Though visions of the pony used to keep her awake nights, she had managed not to think of the animal since she'd moved with her mom out of the neighborhood. If they'd given Georgina a chance, she might have been able to free that pony, but back then she hadn't done anything but watch it thrash and listen to its screams, half-animal, half-machine. The girl had run up the ridge in her cowboy boots and leather fringe and returned with her father who dangled a shotgun. He made the girl stand back as he raised the gun to his shoulder. "No, Daddy! No!" screamed the girl. Georgina woke into the nightmare that the man wasn't even trying to save the creature, and that people up the ridge were cruel and stupid. The girl in fringe covered her eyes, and Georgina watched the ash-faced hill farmer buck at the force with which the shot left the gun. Later he and some other men shoveled a mound of dirt over the pony. A year later the ground was level again.

Undoubtedly the animal had gone a little mad—but what greater madness drove that man to bring his gun down the hill? Was it the same thing that made Andy drive his thirty-five thousand dollar truck into the mud? Nights after the hill farmer shot the pony, Georgina had devised plans for pulling it out alive, using ropes and winches, block-and-tackles, devices which could lift that pony straight into the air, maybe in a hammock made of her bed sheets. The muck would have released the pony if they'd worked it. Why had the man been so anxious to sacrifice the creature that he didn't even ask the river people for help?

Georgina pulled off the road alongside a drainage ditch and the car tilted sideways. She wished she had brought Andy's pastry and given it to the dirty children back there—if they were like her, they'd have torn it apart with their hands and chewed it with their mouths open as they shouted to one another. When she got out of the car, she saw that if she'd pulled a few inches farther off the road, the car might have fallen into the ditch. She crossed the road toward the woods and the truck. If this were March instead of September, the rigid, spiked cradles of skunk cabbage flowers would be poking up from the mud. Were this May, the leaves of the skunk cabbage would have unfurled as fresh and green as that celery. Georgina used to bend down and smell the skunk cabbage each spring, and now she remembered it like the stink of her own sweat before she'd ever used deodorant. In the summer she had roamed the cool woods, gnawing wild onion and the roots of wild ginger. Andy's double rear tires had crushed a stand of jewel weed blossoming at the edge of the road. If this were late September instead of late August, she would touch the orange pods of the jewel weed, and they would explode against her fingers. In addition to celery, Georgina's granny used to grow tomatoes, cucumbers, and muskmelons in the black dirt behind their old house.

Four-wheel drive had apparently done Andy no good with all four wheels buried. Maybe that's why the cops called the house—if the truck had been easy to tow, somebody would have towed it already. Andy deserved to be stuck if he was here trying to steal from somebody else's land; he deserved to be stuck for thinking these people wouldn't stop him from taking their wood. And yet Georgina couldn't help but think she should at least try to free the truck, to make up for not rescuing the pony.

On the other side of the truck, three men stood in the driveway of an asbestos-shingled house painted the color of lime sherbet. One was old and bald and small-headed and two were about Georgina's age and wore baseball caps. Their property was built up unevenly, several feet higher at one side of the concrete block foundation. A full-length crack in the front picture window was held steady with duct tape. Beside the driveway sat a trailer made out of the back end of a pickup, rusted and filled with split wood, one of its tires flat. Andy's truck with its clean white panels and black wheels looked like a spaceship in contrast. It had sunk low enough that Georgina hardly had to step up to get inside.

Everybody Georgina remembered from this neighborhood had been a mutant of some kind, malformed or marked, as if nature loved each so much she couldn't let him look like anybody else. Look at that old man standing in the driveway with the tiny head, hardly enough room in that head for a regular brain. Georgina's mother, a pale-haired mammoth of a woman, used to have a mole on the side of her neck, a great protuberance that looked as though it might grow into a second illegitimate child, a sister for Georgina. When they'd moved away, the first thing Georgina's mother had done was get that mole removed. Delbert, a boy with whom Georgina waited for the school bus, had a raspberry-colored birthmark covering half his face. The woman next door was confined to a wheelchair; a long, unpainted ramp led to the front door, its boards coming loose, regularly stranding the woman partway so she had to holler for help from her six children. After her granny died, Georgina's whole body had become a mutation, round and soft as a tumor from eating any food she could get hold of. Without Granny's yellow cakes and date cakes cooked with coffee, Georgina spent all her nightcrawler money on cream-filled cookies and honey buns and ate them right outside the store, standing next to the electric meters. In the morning she filled her cereal bowl again and again, with sugar-flavored cereal, then milk, then more cereal.

Out of habit, Georgina pulled the seat belt around her. Andy's truck, which cost more than the houses in this neighborhood, started easily with a turn of her own key, vrooming at first, then slowing and idling into a low growl. Maybe Georgina could drive to her old house by cutting a new trail through the woods, swerving through trees along the river, then turning back south. She felt an inclination toward the old place, a pull verging on homesickness for the solid feel of its carpeted concrete floors, the lumpy and changing landscape of its backyard, her granny's garden, sodden and weedy after a night of rains—some weeds grew a foot a day in this soil, Granny had complained, mud smeared to her elbows. Some previous owner had cut away a curved doorway between their kitchen and the living room but had never smoothed it out or plastered its edges. Spiders had built webs there in the spaces between the pieces of sheetrock. Granny said spiders helped control the flies, but after her granny became too sick to argue, her mother used to spray insecticide into the cracks.

But now that the celery was growing here again, folks didn't have to leave this neighborhood the way she and her mother had. People could plant and tend huge gardens that watered themselves from below, and if they canned and froze, the vegetables could feed them half the winter. People's houses could be cleaned and painted, and windows could be thrown open to let in the sweet peppery smell. Plaster and drywall could be patched so that spiders were relegated to attics, and people's lives could be made lush the way they once were, as fertile as when her granny worked the celery.

Georgina adjusted the rearview mirror and in it saw Andy walking toward her from the road. Andy had grown up far from the river, in the neighborhood Georgina and her mother moved to when Georgina was fifteen, a neighborhood like the one she lived in now, where the ranch houses had decorative shutters, aluminum or vinyl siding, and attached garages. Georgina first had made out with Andy in his father's car, and then they'd had furious sex at every opportunity in his parents' paneled basement. Once he had torn her shirt in his hurry to undress her. She'd told herself he was passionate, but she knew now that he was devouring her the way she used to eat those cheap pastries she bought with her nightcrawler money, without even tasting them.

She turned to watch Andy lumber toward her, his boots sinking with each step. Georgina's white tennis shoes were still clean as they stretched for the pedals. She hadn't bogged down as she walked, partly because she was lighter than Andy, but also because she knew how to place her feet on this kind of mud. Andy saw nothing in this neighborhood but wood to steal and, in November, deer to shoot at. Outside Georgina's bedroom window, the deer used to travel through the morning fog like the starved ghosts of ponies, alone or in families, on their way to drink at the river. The deer were the food of last resort. In or out of season, a person shot one if he needed the meat and dressed it out on his own kitchen table. For Andy's ignorant selfishness, the mud would swallow him.

The truck windows were rolled up, and Georgina locked the doors with the automatic button as Andy reached her. He pulled on the door handle, but Georgina looked away and fiddled with the radio, turning channels until she found a female voice wailing on a country station. Georgina turned up the volume loud enough that she couldn't hear Andy, and she put her finger on top of the door lock button each time he inserted his key and tried to turn it. Georgina watched the mouth she had not been able to stop kissing in that basement rec room and on a honeymoon hotel bed in Mexico. The mouth shouted, barely audible above the radio, "Let me in the goddamn truck. You're gonna get it stuck worse."

At their wedding reception, she and Andy had fed each other mouthfuls of a three-tiered wedding cake that Georgina had chosen from among a hundred nearly identical designs. Then they'd returned to their table, each with a single tower of pure white cake. Georgina ate her own piece, scraped the plate and licked the fork, while Andy ate about half of his and ignored the rest. When he later clunked the plate with a beer glass, his remaining cake toppled and lay collapsed.

Georgina looked straight ahead toward the river as she shifted into first, what Andy called "crawl," what the men from this neighborhood called "swamp gear." The wheels all began to spin beneath her.

Andy's face grew red outside the window. Georgina jammed the big knob into second gear. The wheels spun faster, and Georgina felt the truck sink. As she shifted into third, Andy began pounding on the glass with both fists. In his crybaby desperation he looked like an even bigger man than he was. Just over a year ago, in his rented tuxedo, he had picked up Georgina in her dolly lace and, to the cheers of his brother and friends, carried her squealing out to the parking lot, slung over his shoulder like something he'd shot up north. Now mud from the front tires flew all over him, up his big left arm, onto his cheek, like cake raining on him, a crazy chocolate cake tossed handful after handful by some dirty, bad-ass bride.

Georgina looked over her shoulder and saw a policeman at the edge of the road, slim-hipped with his arms crossed over his chest, probably the guy who'd called her "ma'am." Andy's little brother appeared beside the cop, his mouth hanging open as usual, his monkey arms dangling. No doubt Andy's brother intended to pull this truck out with his own truck. They'd had it all figured out, except they hadn't counted on Georgina showing up. She shifted into fourth at four thousand revolutions per minute. She thought of the apple cake her granny used to make every fall, "plain apple cake" she used to call it, and Georgina's salivary glands shot spit through her mouth.

Andy fell away from the side of the truck and leaned against a tree, an immense swamp oak thrusting upward like the world's biggest celery stalk, a tree that had somehow defeated the chain saws of a thousand men like Andy who couldn't grow anything but grass. On the other side of the truck, the small-headed man watched patiently with no expression, as if he saw this sort of thing all the time, as if just yesterday he'd seen the farmer march down from the hill and shoot his daughter's pony, as if Georgina, the cop, Andy, and his brother were just another collection of fools. Georgina closed her eyes and floored the accelerator pedal. As the wheels beneath her tore at the ground, she felt herself easing that pony free. She saw herself smashing layer after layer of her wedding cake with both fists. With the big wheels of the truck, she imagined she was cultivating, at last, the heavy black river earth that a generation had neglected.

Running

THE path behind my house joins a dirt road leading to Turtle Lake, and on that road my next-door neighbor's fifteen-year-old daughter, Amber, is parked with a guy in a Camaro. The nine hundred acres including Turtle Lake was willed to the Audubon Society by a detergent king who had no descendants, and it is now preserved as a bird sanctuary and wetland. Most evenings I jog the path around the lake, about three miles. Days I work as a biologist in the company founded by the detergent king, now a pharmaceuticals research firm, and I live in a house that the company located for my husband and me in order to lure us to Michigan. My husband is a chemist, and my own current research involves the animal-testing phase of a drug which shows promise in preventing breast cancer.

When I cross the dirt road, I pass within ten feet of the Camaro, but neither Amber nor the boy notices me. Teenagers ignore married women in their thirties who are not their teachers or their mothers or their friends' mothers. Teenagers make out in cars here all the time and sometimes brave the muck to swim, but with the exception of Amber, the birds interest me far more. Amber has long, straight, lemon-colored hair, a vibrant hue she conjured up recently, perhaps to distress her mother. Presently, the back of her head is pressed against the passenger-side window and her face and fingers are obscured by the boy whose back and hair she is grasping. Just last night I saw her stubbed fingernails with their dark, chipped polish, and I've listened to her mother Jackie repeatedly on the subject of nail-biting. Amber's mother has offered her thirty dollars if she'll stop chewing her nails for a month.

For the last few weeks, male red-winged blackbirds have been staking out territories as they're doing now, perching on sumacs and last year's cattails, scrawking at one another across the marsh, exposing their red epaulettes and rippling their shoulders to make the marks throb. Brown-streaked females peck seeds nearby. They seem disinterested, but soon they'll perk up and choose mates. The females build their nests close to the ground.

My husband and I are not inclined toward having children, though lately I haven't felt entirely settled in this decision. When my husband takes a position, he tends to embrace it wholeheartedly. ("Think of all that college tuition we're going to save!" he told his sister on the phone recently, giving a cheerful response to one of her critical comments. "Be happy. This way we can leave our fortune to *your* kids.") But I worry that if I express my doubts, he might suddenly change his mind and want children as much as he doesn't want them now.

Amber's mom Jackie has one child and no husband. I've only gotten to know Jackie because she is bursting to talk about Amber the minute the girl goes off to school, and in all but the worst weather I'm sitting outside drinking coffee at that time, watching the feeders from a bench my husband built for me. This morning, from opposite sides of the split-rail fence, Jackie and I watched Amber get on the bus.

"Two weeks until school's out," said Jackie. "One more absence and she fails the semester."

Jackie was wearing her terry-cloth robe, and I noticed the rectangle of her crush-proof cigarette pack in the pocket. After Amber leaves for school, Jackie usually goes back to bed.

"They've got a strict policy at that school," said Jackie. "Ten absences, you flunk."

"That is strict," I said. I approve of strict policies.

"I found cigarettes in her backpack last night."

I could have told Jackie that children of parents who smoke tend to smoke. I could have told her that rifling through her daughter's belongings will destroy whatever trust they have between them. As a non-parent, however, I nodded and sipped coffee.

"She told me they were her friend's cigarettes, that she was carrying them for a friend."

Before I quit smoking, the best cigarette of the day was always the first one, the one I used to have at this time with my coffee, after my lungs had cleaned themselves during sleep.

"She expects me to believe that," said Jackie. "Does she think I'm stupid?"

I shook my head in sympathy. Parenting and growing up both seem like overwhelming prospects, far more difficult than quitting smoking and maintaining a program of exercise.

AT the stream which feeds Turtle Lake, I clatter over a wood and metal bridge. Before it empties, the stream meanders over a marsh, where I sometimes see great blue herons and, on a good day, less common species such as green herons and loons. During the spring migration bird-count, my husband and I sighted a wood duck perched on a dead branch above the water. His harlequin pattern of green, blue, burgundy, and white looked like a map of the world. And why shouldn't the world be drawn on a duck? And why not on a duck that was hunted nearly to extinction at the turn of the century, probably by the very people who admired it most, the people who should have been taking care of the population. If a particular female of this species builds a safe-looking nest twelve feet above the ground in a good tree, other females will drop by and lay their eggs in it, which is why one female may be seen herding as many as forty tiny, fluffy ducklings toward the water. With so many predators about, however, many of them don't survive the trip.

When I am as far from my house and Amber's boyfriend's car as this path takes me, I spy a male and female mallard in the grass. The female shakes her tail feathers. The male nudges closer, not quite touching her. As I pass, the ducks shift nervously and pause in their ritual. A few days ago, in this same spot, two male mallards were jumping on a female, almost crushing her. The female kept slipping out from under and waddling forward, but before she could get the momentum to take flight, one or the other would jump on her again.

My neighbor Jackie's face always looks tired, but she has beautiful dark eyes and straight teeth, very white against her bronzed skin. Perhaps she doesn't know that the artificial light in tanning salons can do nearly as much damage as sunlight. She has the slim-hipped figure that until recently I thought exercise might give me. Earlier this week I asked her, "How do you stay in shape?" Jackie's nails are longish and always red; mine are clipped short and unpolished.

"I'm a waitress, remember. I run my ass off eight hours a shift." She crushed out a cigarette on the top fence-rail and snapped the butt into her own grass. "Pretty birds, those yellow ones." She motioned with a nod. I have read that when food is hard to find, some overstressed parent birds feed their screaming young bits of plastic and cigarette butts.

A half-dozen male goldfinches have appeared on and around the thistle feeder this week, their winter gray-green exchanged for brilliant yellow. Goldfinches breed late into the season, either raising several broods a year or waiting until August or even September to make a nest. Last year we had a surprise ice storm in October that killed a particularly late batch of goldfinch chicks in our side yard. Because the leaves had not yet fallen, the weight from the ice bent trees and bushes to the ground, and from the woods behind our house we heard the gunshots of breaking limbs. My husband and I shoveled through the slush the next morning and buried the chicks, nest and all. For a week I didn't walk in the woods for fear of what other dead birds and animals I might find.

Jackie has given Amber a nine o'clock curfew on school nights, but because of her work hours she is often not there to enforce it. When I first met Jackie, I figured she was older than me, but she is only thirty-two, which means she had Amber when she was seventeen. Premature wrinkling is another good reason not to smoke.

Running is something, like smoking, that I've left and come back to dozens of times, but I haven't smoked since we moved into this house, and I've been a more dedicated runner as well. In high school, I belonged to the debate club and the science club, but I should have joined the cross-country team, because it took me a decade to learn what the coach and gym teacher would have taught me in a season about running and my body. When I was Amber's age, I was not pretty, and my real concern was getting a scholarship at a good college, so maybe it's not surprising that I didn't have any boyfriends.

Excepting the occasional detention, Amber evidently doesn't participate in any sanctioned after-school activities.

"Amber isn't in anything?" I asked, surprised.

Her mother gave me a puzzled look and exhaled smoke. "What would she be in?"

I shrugged and watched the cigarette travel to the fence. Smoking was the only bad habit I'd ever had, and I just couldn't stop missing it. "A sports team?" I suggested. "Debate? Drama?" Even as I spoke, I knew how stupid I sounded to Jackie. Though smart enough to achieve, Jackie had no doubt been bored with high school and saw no reason to pretend otherwise. She probably had older boyfriends, and had sex, and smoked pot. Had I known her then, I would have felt both superior to her and jealous of her, which is more or less how I feel now.

Where the path nears the water again, I see another mallard pair floating. The difference between the sexes in some birds is stunning. Compare the iridescent-green head of this male with the female's plain browns. The male needs that coloring for females to notice him, and the female relies on her camouflage—she'll pull out her own feathers to line her nest, which she will then be unable to protect from raccoons, crows, and snakes. Above and to the east, a turkey vulture circles; vulture numbers are increasing in Michigan, in part because they eat roadkill, which at this time of year they partially digest and throw up for their young. The sexes look alike. Ornithologists say that vulture nests are hot and smelly.

A filmy white grocery bag lies half drowned at the lake's edge, probably blown here by the wind. Back there, near the wood and metal bridge, I saw the stiff plastic from a cheese and crackers lunch package, the kind that consumer groups recently determined did not have the nutrition a kid needs from a meal. When I have time on the weekends, I come out here and pick up the fast-food wrappers and drink cups and occasionally, used condoms. A small effort on my part keeps the place fairly clean, which may well be preventing more people from leaving trash. Coming around the final stretch, I see Amber get out of the car and run up the path that leads to our houses. The sun is setting, so it must be almost nine o'clock. Jackie will either be home or she'll call home from the bar to check on Amber. Last night Jackie called my house.

"I'm sorry for bothering you," she said. Behind her surprisingly clear voice was music, shouting, and the clanking of glasses and pool balls.

"It's no bother. What can I do for you?" My husband had fallen asleep on the couch with the new issue of *Science* over his face.

"I know it's late, but could you go over to my house and look in on Amber?" When she paused to draw on her cigarette, I could almost taste the smoke. "The phone has been busy for forty minutes, and I'm wondering if she took it off the hook."

"I'll go check. Call me back in ten minutes."

The living room next door was dimly lit, and the curtains were closed. As I knocked at the front, I would almost swear I heard the back door open and close, and someone might have been running behind the house, toward the dirt path.

"Mom's at work," said Amber. It had taken her more than a minute to answer the door.

"I know. She called and asked me to check on you. Your phone's been busy."

"Mom doesn't trust me." Amber spoke matter-of-factly. Her black fingernail polish was chewed most of the way off her short, ragged nails. Her cuticles were ripped, and on some fingers that cuticle skin was red and slightly swollen as though infected. Weren't there ointments a person applied that tasted like grapefruit rind? Wasn't there a school psychologist she could see? Was there an amount of money that would induce her to stop mauling herself? Somebody had to do something! I wanted to shake her shoulders and scream into her face, "Stop it, you stupid girl, or you're going to end up pregnant!"

Instead I said, "Your mom was worried."

Amber shrugged and bit once at a hangnail on her middle finger, then stopped herself. As the clenched hand fell to her side, she stiffened and stood waiting for me to leave. She was as tall as I am, but she looked muscular and fertile, and, despite her mutilated fingertips, confident. She reminded me of girls from high school sports teams, girls with springy footsteps who walked right down the middle of hallways, girls who, even at fifteen and sixteen, thought they had mastery over their bodies.

"I must have knocked the phone off the hook," she said.

"Your mother said you were having trouble with math," I said. My heart beat as though I were presenting findings to my superiors, results which called into question my own earlier research. "I can help you with math. Or any other schoolwork. I'd be glad to help. Really, Amber."

"Thanks. I'll let you know." She sounded both condescending and suspicious of me, and on the way home, I told myself I was glad she didn't want help, because tutoring would cut into what little time I had in the evenings with my husband. We don't go out to movies or plays nearly as often as we'd like. Amber doesn't know I'm behind her now as she runs.

The Camaro boyfriend backs out of his parking place—too quickly, I think. If he loved Amber, he would sit for a minute and watch her figure disappear down the woods path. Instead, he screeches toward the asphalt, spitting up gravel without looking back to see either me or Amber, whose bright hair rises and falls, whose arms flail. Her leather sandals are heavy and loose—I wore similar sandals at one time, made from actual tire treads. Today I wear the best technical running shoes I've ever owned, with an adjustment for pronation.

Amber wears hip-hugger bell-bottoms which she hikes up as she runs, and this, along with the clunky sandals, slows her. The clumsiness of youth surprises me, for certainly Amber is stronger than me. Though her running is loose-jointed and effortless, she has no idea how to run.

I could show her how to breathe and stride, how to hold her arms so as not to waste energy, how to dress to move easily. If she wanted to join the debate club, I could help her construct solid arguments and do the necessary research. At this moment, I want to share with the girl everything I've learned—about men, about algebra, about breast cancer—but she is not interested, and in any case she would break my heart with her crazy hair and chewed-up nails, and with the way she goes with boys who don't appreciate her. I speed up slightly to narrow the distance between us, though not enough to catch up with her. She doesn't hear me behind her as together we travel the path that leads to our separate houses.

Taking Care of the O'Learys

THE two-story monstrosity rose in the distance before them, its roof a bright and humiliating blue—Barb had sewn together four overlapping vinyl tarps to keep the weather out of their rooms until she and Martin could buy the materials to finish shingling. The house disappeared behind trees as they neared the driveway. Couldn't they just keep going, Barb wondered, drive right past that godforsaken ruin? Steer the pickup into a field? As the sky darkened, she'd strip and lie naked on the cool metal truck bed and pull Martin down onto her. What if she threw herself across the truck seat right now and pressed Martin against the driver's side door? The steering wheel would whip around, and the truck would swerve into the trees or crash through a wall into somebody's living room.

But the godforsaken ruin to which they were returning was their home, and thirteen-year-old Rebecca was waiting for them. Gravel flew up as they turned into the quarter-mile dirt driveway. Barb thought of the creatures—opossums, squirrels, cats, and dogs—that might dash beneath their wheels. As he maneuvered through potholes, Martin wrapped his hand around Barb's leg and squeezed. Though a moment ago Barb had wanted to mash her body into his, she now stiffened against his hand.

"What's the matter, Barbie?"

"Aren't you going a little fast?"

"Do you want to drive?" he asked, taking his hands off the wheel.

"Just be careful." She hated the way she sounded, but she wished he'd slow down and watch what was in front of him.

"You worry too much." He slowed slightly. "Hey, you haven't seen any bats around here, have you?"

Barb hadn't. They bounced over the gravel to the house that used to belong to Martin's parents, and to Martin's father's parents before that. Barb hoped that Rebecca hadn't let Muffin outside—it was a miracle Martin hadn't yet run over their dog. At their old house, the dog had stayed inside a fenced backyard. Barb had liked their small brick house next to the post office, within walking distance of the dentist's office where she worked nine to three. Rebecca had a half-dozen friends within a few blocks, and Martin had walked to the library after dinner most evenings. Living across from the mortuary had made Barb uneasy at first, but Peas Brothers turned out to be nice, quiet neighbors. Then Martin's poor crazy mother had died, and Martin's father offered them the big family house, along with its ridiculous tax delinquency—ridiculous because Mr. O'Leary could have paid the taxes for the last four years but hadn't bothered. Martin had refused to let the dilapidated place go, so the only choice had been to lose the house in town with the window boxes and wall-to-wall carpeting. Barb wondered every day if she'd given in too easily.

Their headlights lit a pair of red metallic eyes beside the driveway. Too close to the ground to be Muffin, it was probably a rabbit, as likely to dart in front of the car as not. When they had some extra money and time, Barb would figure out how to run some kind of barrier, chicken wire maybe, along the driveway—after they finished shingling the roof and about ten other projects, that is. Martin searched the trees as he flew down the driveway, watching for bats. He'd build bat boxes, he said. The nature center would give him a pamphlet showing him how.

A car was parked in Martin's spot, and though Barb said, "Somebody's here," Martin only pulled his attention from the trees and swerved to avoid it at the last second. It was an old Toyota with California plates and a smashed rear bumper.

"Who the heck's that?" He screeched to a stop.

Barb got out and rolled her shoulders. "Maybe it's a friend of Becky's," she said, not that she'd like the idea of Rebecca having friends whose cars were registered two thousand miles away. She and Martin walked along the stone path leading up to the house. Martin had hardly changed since they'd made out in the back of his first pickup. He worked at the same small-engine sales and repair shop halfway between here and town, though now he was the manager. "Bat boxes," Martin said again, taking Barb's hand and swinging it. Barb was continually surprised at his competence each time they took on a new house project, but getting him to finish the old job before starting a new one could be a problem.

They entered the kitchen to see two girls with chairs pulled up to the kitchen counter. When the girls simultaneously turned their round faces toward her, Barb felt the ground give way. Two pretty noses, two heads of blonde hair cut blunt at the earlobes. Two Rebeccas? Martin burst past Barb and held out his arms.

"Martha-Marmalade! Where'd you come from?"

"Los Angeles," Martha squeaked as Martin squeezed the breath from her.

"Why didn't you call?" Martin let loose, then bear-hugged his little sister again.

Martha grinned at Barb over Martin's shoulder and waved. Barb's surprise turned to shame at having a guest see her kitchen, even if it was only her sister-in-law. Not that Barb had stained the floor tile or neglected to paint the window frames for fifty years, nor had she worn the porcelain of the sink through to the cast iron. Barb would never have let a grease fire burn long enough to inflict those marks on the ceiling.

Barb thought for a moment that her daughter was holding a cigarette between two fingers with chipped red nail polish, but she traced the hand to Martha. The smoke fretted toward the twelve-foot ceilings to hang like cobwebs. Martha had not even come back for her mother's funeral—no one had been able to contact her. At close range, Martha's age showed in the lines around her eyes. Rebecca's complexion was perfect and clear.

"Did the two of you get something to eat?" Barb asked.

"We're fine, Mom."

Martin clasped his sister a third time. "How long are you here?" he asked.

"I'm not sure." Martha looked at Barb.

"Well, stay as long as you like," said Martin. "We've got plenty of room, all right. Don't we, Barbie?" He spread out his arms as if to fill in some of the space. "Hey, let's have a nightcap."

"I can't believe you guys are living here," said Martha.

"Mom can't either," said Rebecca.

FOUR months ago, in January, when Barb, Martin, and Rebecca first moved into their cold, crumbling bedrooms, Martin kept pacing the hallway shouting "All this space!" and stretching out his arms. Rebecca had followed his lead, singing "Give me space!" and then the two had started dancing around, waving their arms, celebrating the surrounding decay like members of some demented tribe. Barb had liked the size of their old house; there, she knew at all times which rooms her daughter and husband occupied. Whenever they had visited Martin's parents in this house, she'd felt uneasy about the big rooms filled with cobwebs and the dirty walls, not to mention the way Mr. O'Leary flirted with her, as though she were not his daughter-in-law, but some bar waitress. After he buried his wife, Mr. O'Leary packed up what he wanted, left everything else, and moved to Florida, where, he said, he'd be chasing rich widows.

After they got Martha settled into the cleanest of the empty rooms, Barb lay in bed and stared at some moonlit lathe showing through the wall. If she were to push it with her hand, the plaster would crumble, and she would see right into the bathroom. On the other side she could break through above the stairway. She smelled mold—tomorrow she'd spray again with disinfectant. Martin rolled over in his sleep, cupped his body around hers, and placed an arm across her. She adjusted to be closer to him, then lay awake, feeling his body pressing all around her like a warm, small dwelling.

When she next awoke, Martin had turned away and spread himself across two-thirds of the bed, snoring in a private bliss. Barb heard creaking throughout the house. When they'd first moved in, there had been families of red squirrels living in the attic, but Barb thought sleepily that these other noises were probably just the ghosts of O'Leary's, too loud to be contained in the nether world: drunken, back-clapping, overemotional ghosts, howling at their own jokes the way Martin's father did, their skeletons' elbows clacking as they nudged each other.

Martin's mother, poor Mrs. O'Leary, had been drugged half-numb as long as Barb had known her, wandering in and out of rooms like a thick-limbed, badly-wired Stepford wife. Barb had once seen Mrs. O'Leary carry an ashtray into the kitchen and dump it into the pot of beef stew instead of the garbage pail beside the stove. Barb fished the cigarette filters out of the pot and never said a word. And for years Mrs. O'Leary had saved potato water, first in quart-jars, and then in five-gallon pails. It was full of vitamins, she explained to Barb through badly-applied orangish lipstick that did not suit her complexion.

"Why don't you dump them out?" Barb asked her father-in-law before Mrs. O'Leary died. Marrying into this family might well have been Mrs. O'Leary's downfall. Barb had seen the pictures of Mrs. O'Leary as a young woman, looking as normal as Barb herself.

"That's her thing," Martin's father had said. "Let her do her thing." As Barb had turned away from him, he reached out and pinched her bottom. "Hee-hee," he said, like some retarded demon.

When Mrs. O'Leary died, there had been twenty-two buckets of potato water molding in the big kitchen. Barb had mopped every day since they moved in, trying to remove those sunken bucket rings from the kitchen's fake-brick white linoleum. Replacing the tile in the huge room was a job they couldn't yet afford when more pressing concerns, such as shingling the roof, lay before them. Now Barb had to make sure that Martin didn't get distracted and start building bat boxes instead. She closed her eyes and listened to his sweet, easy breathing.

Barb was up by six-thirty, and she had French toast ready by the time Rebecca ambled to the table. That smooth skin, those nearly-red lips, that thin, elegant nose. How had such an exquisite creature sprung from her? Rebecca was taller than her, as tall as Martha already, which made Barb feel vaguely guilty, as though she had allowed the girl to grow up too quickly.

"Mom, stop staring at me. I'm trying to eat."

Barb thought she could still see Martha's smoke drifting around from last night. She stared up at the ceiling, willing the paint chips—almost certainly lead—not to fall.

"Where's Dad?" asked Rebecca.

"He's getting up."

Rebecca turned and screamed, "Da-ad, hurry up!"

"Don't yell," said Barb. She envisioned a storm-colored paint chip shaking loose at the vibration from Rebecca's voice, falling in slow motion toward a bite of French toast en route to the girl's mouth.

"Coming!" floated down the stairway.

Then from the same direction, a woman's voice: "It's only four A.M. California time."

"Get up, Martha-Marmalade!" yelled Martin. "Rise and shine. Men are out searching for wives today."

"Then I guess I'd better stay in bed!"

"Aunt Martha!" yelled Rebecca. "Come on. Get up!"

Barb had been trained by her own mother to speak quietly, but in this house, people yelled from room to room, as though they wanted to fill all the excess space with sound.

Martin appeared at the table ten minutes later in green uniform Dickies. Martha appeared shortly after, draped in a ratty flannel bathrobe.

"Martha, do you want some French toast?" asked Barb.

"Oh, no, just coffee. Let me get it myself." In this light, Barb noticed Martha had dark half-circles like faded bruises beneath her blue eyes.

When Rebecca finished eating, she plopped onto her Dad's lap and sat sideways, talking to Martha. Martin forked French toast into his mouth around Rebecca's back, holding her hair out of the way of the syrup. Martha blinked her eyes against falling back to sleep. Her robe was missing its belt and she repeatedly pulled the garment together across her cleavage. It would have been unkind of Barb to wish that her daughter hadn't inherited those fine bones, almost too feminine for Martin really, but on Martha, spectacular. Martha had married and divorced a drug-abusing bully, and now she was thirty-three and didn't even have an address. The older sister, Suzanne, was five years dead by suicide. Had their fates been cooked into the marrow of those graceful bones?

AFTER work and before supper, Barb mopped the kitchen floor, and when she looked up the clock read 5:02. She searched for Rebecca outside the back door and in the dining room. She inhaled as if to yell, but instead parked her mop and walked up the stairs. Rebecca's bedroom door hung open, and she wasn't there. Barb knocked on the room Martha was using.

"Come in," shouted Martha. "You don't have to knock."

Martha sat cross-legged on the floor beside Rebecca, who handled a stack of envelopes.

"Look, Mom, love letters from Grandma's boyfriends. We found them in the wall."

"From Grandpa?" asked Barb.

"No. Other men," said Rebecca. "One was a soldier."

Martha looked on approvingly, as if letters from other lovers affirmed, or perhaps increased, the value of their common pedigree.

"Rebecca," said Barb. "Muffin's been outside for two hours, and your dad's going to be home in a few minutes."

"Dad is not going to run him over."

"Rebecca, I shouldn't have to remind you. If anything happened to Muffin, you'd feel terrible."

Barb returned to the kitchen and took a few last swipes at the floor. She'd done wonders in the beginning, but no matter how much she worked now, the improvement was only minuscule. The same with the wood floors in the rest of the house. She'd scrubbed and polished them, but they needed to be sanded and refinished. The downstairs walls and ceilings needed to be scraped and plaster-patched. Most of the bedrooms upstairs would have to be gutted and reconstructed with drywall. And all this on their regular paychecks. Barb stood frozen, mop in hand. A good solid rain, and water would run under those blue roof tarps and flood their bedrooms.

When she looked up, Rebecca stood in the kitchen doorway with

Muffin on a leash. "Mom?" she asked. "You've got love letters, don't you?"

"YOU are so lucky," said Martha at supper. Barb had insisted they eat in the dining room instead of the kitchen. Martin had brought home a bottle of wine.

"To have the house, you mean?" asked Martin.

"And to have a daughter like Becky. I wish I could have a daughter like this without having to have a baby. I wish I could give birth and then, boom, she'd be this age. None of that crying and breast-feeding—although maybe the breast-feeding part would be okay." Martha winked at Barb. "This is the daughter I want. Smart. Can take care of herself. Look at that face. She looks like you, Barb."

Had Martha meant that as a joke?

"You don't usually get brown eyes with blond hair. I used to have blond hair, but now it grows with these dark roots." Martha put her hands on either side of the part in her hair and bent her head for inspection. Then she put her arm around Becky's neck and squeezed her. "Don't be embarrassed about being beautiful, kid."

"She is a beauty, isn't she?" said Martin. "Just like her ma." Martin winked at Barb.

Barb smiled back. As always she was grateful for Martin's compliments but couldn't help thinking they came too easily to him.

"Cut it out," said Rebecca, blushing.

"You guys are like a real family," said Martha. "You're like Mom and Dad now." She gulped from her wineglass. "Only you're totally sane."

"You haven't seen Mom scrubbing the kitchen floor," said Rebecca.

Barb looked at Rebecca, but the girl wouldn't meet her gaze.

"It's like she's possessed." Rebecca laid down her fork and moved her hands in a scrubbing motion. "Scrubbing and scrubbing."

"A regular Lady Macbeth, aren't you, Barb?" added Martin, grinning.

Barb felt the stab of betrayal twice. "We need new tile," she said apologetically. "That floor is ruined."

"Did Mom leave all those buckets?" asked Martha. "You know,

once she read how healthy potato water was, she wouldn't throw it out anymore." Martin joined in laughing.

How could they laugh about it? Why hadn't Martha dumped the buckets? Barb wanted to scream. Why had everyone let that poor woman keep all that stinking, molding potato water? Hadn't anyone cared about her?

"It is sad, isn't it?" said Martha. "Four of us kids, Martin, and the next generation is down to one, little Becky." Martha reached for the wine bottle and filled her glass halfway again. "It's all up to you, Becky, to carry on the O'Leary name."

Rebecca asked: "Aren't you going to have any kids, Martha?"

"I don't think so."

"Weren't you married?"

"Sure, but O'Leary women aren't much good at picking husbands."

"I might not ever get married."

"Good girl."

Martha emptied her wine glass, then worked at her pork chop in silence.

"What's the matter, Martha?" asked Martin.

"It just makes me sentimental to be here. I miss them so much." Martha was suddenly wiping away tears. "I miss Mom and Jack and Suzanne." Barb hadn't known Jack, the oldest, who'd died at seventeen in a car wreck.

"I do too, kid," said Martin. This was a pain in which Barb wasn't a full partner.

Rebecca watched her aunt in admiration, as if laughing one minute, crying the next, changing emotions without warning, was a marvelous feat.

"Stay with us, Martha," said Martin. "I miss you when you're gone."

Martha pushed herself away from the table. "I'll be right back. I just need to go outside." She pulled the door closed behind her, but it didn't latch, and with ghostly slowness it swung open again. Barb knew that Martin would have loved having lots of kids, a big, loud family like the one he grew up in. They heard Martha's car start up and pull out of the driveway.

Later, after deciding not to wait up for Martha, Barb closed the bedroom door tightly and climbed into bed beside Martin. "Aren't you worried about your sister?"

"She's a big girl. She can take care of herself."

"You think everybody's fine all the time."

"They're not?" He laid his hand over Barb's stomach and moved it across her rib cage. She put her hand on his to push it harder against her small breasts. She didn't mind him a little drunk. He negotiated his hand under her nightgown, and desire for him struck her like heat lightning, at once uncontained, unrestricted. She pushed his hand between her legs and wrung its electricity. When he slid a finger in her, she cupped his wrist and tried to push his whole hand after it. She twisted around him, until her face was in his lap, and she took him so deeply into her throat that she had to fight not to gag. The whole house swirled around them, blue vinyl tarps flapping like skirts in the night wind, doors banging open on their hinges, plaster walls crumbling.

Barb had been sleeping for several hours when she awoke to laughing and footsteps. She recognized Martha's giggle and a lower voice, a man's voice. She heard them enter Martha's room, their gritty shoes scraping the raw pine floors that had never been properly finished. There had never been a strange man in the house in town. The clock beside her ticked incessantly.

Barb extracted her nightgown from the tangle of sheets and put it on. The floor groaned beneath her with each step. At night, this long hall felt like a public place, the hall of a boardinghouse. She tiptoed to her daughter's room and pushed the door open slowly. Through the top of the six-foot-tall window, she saw a three-quarters moon. Her daughter's skin shone both pale and bright, except where branches outside the window projected moon-shadows onto her, jungle-bird shapes with wings flapping. Rebecca had covered some of the ruined plaster with a poster of a messy-haired guitar player. Through a few holes in the wall, one could view the empty bedroom next door, and the girl had painted around these disturbances with red and gold. Barb picked up two shirts and a pair of jeans and underpants from beside the bed and dropped them in the hamper. Like Martin, Rebecca slept soundly. Rebecca's shoulders seemed small in the sheets. Her bones pressed outward against her veneer of skin. Barb wished she could baby-powder and swaddle the girl and keep her safe from every crazy thing. Something thudded. If only she could lock Rebecca's room from the outside, thought Barb, and carry the key herself.

"Stop it!" said Martha, from her room.

"Just relax, baby," said a man's voice.

Martha's door was cracked, and when Barb peered through, she saw Martha with both arms handcuffed together to the metal-frame headboard. A man with a dark pony tail sat beside her, fending off halfhearted kicks. Vomit rose in Barb's throat. She didn't even want to know people like this.

"These are too tight," complained Martha.

"So stop pulling on them," the man said, slurring his speech.

"Take them off. I'll handcuff you instead."

The man grabbed both of Martha's bare legs and held them affectionately. "Are you sure, baby?"

Martha tucked back her legs, then with full force kicked the man off the end of the bed. His head clunked against the heavy glass dresser top, and he slid down and lay sprawled on his back.

"Martha, are you okay?" Barb whispered through the door.

"Barb, is that you?" Martha threw back her head and laughed.

Barb hesitantly entered, the floor creaking beneath her. She smelled the mildew from the stained and yellowed walls. Martha's forehead was scraped and some blood had crusted on one side.

"Martha, please don't wake Rebecca."

"Barb, I need your help." Martha slurred as much as the man had. "I'm locked to this damned bed."

"Let me get Martin," said Barb.

"Let's just keep this between us women," Martha said. "Get his key. Isss in his front pocket. Hurry, before he wakes up."

"But," said Barb, but she didn't know how to finish her sentence. But I'm not a member of your family? But I can't help crazy people? But I don't want to be here at all? I want to be in my small brick house in town with the fenced-in backyard.

"Please, Barb," laughed Martha, "or I might panic and start yelling."

Damn her. Barb would get the key so that this man would leave, and eventually Martha would leave, and nobody would wake Rebecca. Barb knelt beside the man, who lay on his back in the dark, his head curled against the dresser. His breath was woody like bourbon, and his body smelled faintly skunky. The muscles of his arms and chest pressed against the Harley Davidson T-shirt, and his jeans were shiny with grease. A bulge of keys showed at his right front hip. Barb looked up at Martha before pushing her hand into the pocket. His skin emanated heat through the thin cotton. When the man groaned and shifted, a shiver passed across Barb's back. She grasped the keys, but hesitated before withdrawing her hand. The man's eyes fluttered once, and Barb closed her own eyes. In fifteen years she hadn't touched another man as intimately as this. When she opened her eyes, Martha was staring at her from the bed, half-smiling, one eye squinted. Barb slid the keys from the man's pocket, controlling her breathing.

"It's a small key," said Martha. "He showed it to me."

Barb flipped through the keys, her hands shaking. She held Martha's wrists, which were warm against the cold metal of the handcuffs. The skin on Martha's wrists seemed impossibly thin and delicate. The older sister Suzanne had made three-inch lengthwise slits in wrists like these. The key clicked, and Barb reluctantly let go. The veins of her own wrists were obscured by a layer of fat and muscle from housework. Martha rubbed her wrists where the cuffs had imprinted red rings around them.

Martha worked the handcuff key off the key chain before tossing the rest at the man's limp body. When the man didn't stir, she tossed a footstool at him, one leg of which stabbed him in the crotch. Barb flinched. The man groaned and sat up.

"What's the matter with you, asshole?" said Martha.

"What the hell's . . . ?" he moaned. "You crazy bitch."

"Why don't you leave, now," said Barb.

"Sure," he said. "Get me the hell out of here."

"I'll walk you to the door," said Martha, picking his keys off the floor and pressing them into his hand. She buttoned his shirt, adjusted her cutoffs, tucked her hair behind her ears—despite her drunkenness, she was as cool as a newscaster. Barb noticed that a leather jacket hung over the back of a chair in Martha's room, and the handcuffs and key lay on the bedside table.

Martha supported the man as they stepped out into the hall and down the stairs. Barb followed, fearing that Rebecca would appear and ask what was happening. Barb couldn't help but notice how pretty Martha's legs were, as long and tan as a teenager's. No hint of cellulite or varicosities. Martha released the man to stumble out into the night.

"Does my face look O.K.?" asked Martha.

Barb felt a breathless panic. But this was Martha, not Rebecca. And she reeked of beer.

"He hurt you. You're bleeding a little."

"I fell off his motorcycle. Am I bad?" She reached up as if to touch the wound, but instead stuck her finger in her eye.

"It's not that bad. I'll clean you up in the kitchen."

Martha sat at the table while Barb boiled water, made chamomile tea, gathered first-aid supplies and then placed two mugs between them. The steam from their cups and the smoke from Martha's cigarette mingled on the way to the ceiling.

"Where'd that guy come from?" asked Barb.

"The Eastside Tavern."

"You just picked up a guy and brought him here?"

"I think I used to know him." She wrinkled her forehead as if actively thinking.

"So you just brought him here?" asked Barb. "To this house?"

"Hey, don't pull that shit on me," she slurred. "This is my house too." Barb felt her own anger seep like greenish chlorine gas out from under kitchen cabinets and doors. Had Martha paid any taxes on this house? Had she ever caulked a window? Nailed sheathing? Instead, Barb said, "You don't have a daughter to worry about."

"You're right, Barb. I'm sorry. But you shouldn't try to protect Becky so much. Or else one day, boom! she'll figure it all out, and . . ." Martha trailed off, as though she had forgotten what she was going to say.

Barb sponged the blood from around Martha's temple. The skin at her eyebrow was abraded; there was one cut above her eyebrow which Barb thought might leave a tiny scar.

"You know, you're the best thing that ever happened to this family," said Martha, clanging her tea mug on the table. "All the rest of us are crazy. You're a fool of sanity, I mean a pool." Barb waited to hear more, but Martha changed the subject as quickly as she'd started it. "You should've met my husband. Fucking worthless son-of-a-bitch."

Before long Martha's eyelids drooped, and she said good night and stumbled up to bed for some of that undisturbed O'Leary sleep. Barb didn't follow but sat motionless at the table for more than an hour, until golden patches of light formed along the length of the countertops. As the sun grew brighter, the fibers of the house began to rustle and sparkle as though awakening, and Barb's own body came alive with it, her skin first, then the muscles and bones of her arms. She ran a bucket of water and knelt on the floor in a broad patch of light. She meant to scrub with the stiff-bristled brush, but instead just sat in the warmth. Last week when she had washed those windows she had cursed them for being too big, for letting in too much weather. She looked into the dining room where three bright rectangles shone on the wood floor. She closed her eyes and faced the sun.

A LITTLE after six, Barb made coffee, and Rebecca's noisy arrival in the kitchen at seven jarred her nerves. Rebecca plopped into a chair. "Hi, Mom. Somebody was in my room."

"What?" Barb's heart pounded out of rhythm.

"Somebody put my dirty clothes in the hamper. I figured it was you."

What if Martha's guest had accidentally gone into Rebecca's room? Would the man have noticed that this girl was not Martha but only a baby?

Martin appeared, poured himself a cup of coffee, and sat at the kitchen table. Barb couldn't shake an image of Rebecca handcuffed to her twin headboard, and though she had turned on the water only to rinse her cup, she let it run over her hands. When she pulled them out of the stream, they were ice cold.

Rebecca finished her cereal, then climbed onto her father's lap. Martin wrapped both arms around her. The way Martin touched

Rebecca suddenly bothered Barb. When Barb had been on top of him in bed last night, hadn't he pulled her to him the same way? With those same hands, those fingers that had been inside of her. Rebecca squealed as Martin began to tickle her. Dear God, had he even washed his hands? Barb stared at the worst of the gray bucket rings on the kitchen floor. Would they never go away?

She hustled Rebecca to school and kissed Martin off to work, but still got a late start to the office herself, and then halfway out the driveway she saw something dead. Barb rested her forehead on the steering wheel before getting out to go look, and when she finally approached it, three tiny rabbits scampered away. They didn't go far, but stopped in the nearest patch of weed cover, their tiny hearts beating, bright eyes wet, bodies small enough to fold into her hand. She picked up the mother rabbit by one foot and tossed her toward the woods. She didn't have time to bury her. The three babies stood perfectly still. Barb felt their terror and confusion move across the brush in little waves.

AT 5:12 that evening, according to the kitchen clock, Barb dropped her potato peeler in the sink. The dog. Where was the dog?

She yelled upstairs for Rebecca, but there was no answer. Martin would be home any second. Barb ran down the flagstone path into the middle of the driveway. Martin's truck approached her, going too fast. She put her hand to her mouth, but the rest of her muscles froze. Martin screeched to a halt and jumped out of the pickup. "What's wrong, Barb?"

"Where's Muffin?" she asked, panicked.

"I don't know," he said.

"You didn't hit him, did you?"

"Why do you think I would kill our dog?" demanded Martin. "Tell me. Do you think I'm some kind of monster?"

"You're just so damned careless!" said Barb. She didn't want to fight, but she needed to be heard. "You and your whole family! You don't see what's happening around you! You live like drunken cavalry."

"You want me to live like you, Barb? Scared of everything?" Color flowed into his cheeks.

"The buckets, Martin! The buckets!" Barb's hands formed fists, as though she were clutching bucket handles. "You let your poor mother keep all those buckets of water! Those rotting, stinking, moldy buckets of potato water!"

Martin stared at her, eyebrows screwed up. His flush of color had disappeared.

Then into the curve of the driveway, from a path through the trees, stepped Rebecca, as fresh as a wood sprite, leading Muffin on a leash. "What's the matter?" Rebecca asked.

"See, Barb, Muffin's fine. Everything's fine." Martin's expression showed concern. It occurred to Barb that Martin thought she was going insane. An O'Leary worried that *she* was crazy. Barb looked down at the driveway gravel and shook her head, feeling the distance growing huge between herself and her husband and daughter.

Martin walked with Rebecca up the stone path toward the house, one arm draped over the girl's shoulder. Barb followed. "Let's build a bonfire tonight," said Martin. "We've got to burn that rotten wood your ma and I took off the roof."

"Cool, Dad."

"Where's your aunt?"

"In her room," said Rebecca. "She won't come out."

"Oh, I'll get her out," said Martin. "Hung over still, is she?"

"Please don't bother her," said Barb. "She had a rough night."

"Oh, I'll bother her, all right." Martin let go of Rebecca and rubbed his hands together. "Martha's a girl who needs to be bothered."

Martin had already freed himself from his anger, dropped it like a bundle of shingles, but Barb's stuck in her esophagus and her bronchial tubes. She didn't want to yell anymore. She wanted to arrange her thoughts, phrase them intelligently, so sanely that Martin would have to agree with her.

"What should I do for the fire, Dad?" asked Rebecca.

"Collect all the sticks you can find, and logs, kitchen chairs, whatever. Pull stuff out of the woods. I'll pour kerosene over it, and we'll eat supper while it soaks in, then light it. Boom!"

"Boom!" repeated Rebecca and threw her arms out in an explosion, inadvertently yanking the dog up short. Muffin yelped.

AFTER supper, Barb said she had to go to the store but instead drove to town and parked beside the mortuary, across the street from her old house. It was a family house, with well-defined rooms, one for eating, one for cooking, two for sleeping. No crazy, disintegrating rooms where love letters reeking of infidelity fell like paint chips and plaster dust, where rain could pour down on people in their beds, where dirty, muscular strangers entered without warning.

A car pulled into the driveway of the brick house, and a tall man in a white shirt and gray pants stepped out of it, jacket over his arm. She'd met him at the closing, but she'd felt no connection to him then. He glanced in Barb's direction as he made his way up the front steps, then took out his key and unlocked the door. Before entering, he turned and looked again through wire-framed glasses. His jaw was dark with the day's growth of beard. He slept in the room where she used to sleep. He hung his pants over the back of a chair beside the bed. She remembered the feel of her naked feet on the padded bedroom carpet.

Barb let herself fall back against the headrest. She thought of one afternoon two weeks ago when she and Martin had been working on the roof, driving nails into opposite sides of a four-by-eight piece of plywood. Barb had stopped and watched him pound. She feared he would miss and smash his thumb. More than that, though, she feared she wouldn't stop herself from reaching for him, climbing on top of him on the sloping roof. Rebecca was twenty-five feet below them with the dogs and rabbits and opossums. Barb imagined herself and Martin rolling and sliding toward the edge of the roof, plywood splinters driving into their skin. She had awakened from this thought when she noticed Martin had stopped nailing and was watching her. "You look worried," he'd said. "What's the matter?" Barb had answered, "Nothing."

Barb unclenched the steering wheel, and when she looked back at the house, she saw it differently. The kitchen, she remembered, had almost no counter space, and the windows didn't let in much light, especially since the southern exposure was entirely blocked by the house next door. The roof hung so close to the ground. Rebecca's bedroom had been tiny, perfect for her as a baby, but maybe she couldn't have grown up if they'd stayed there. Barb had a strange feeling that even her own body had grown larger since they'd moved out, that this house couldn't fit her any more, that she'd have to duck as she passed through doorways. But if she didn't belong in the big O'Leary house, and she couldn't return to this place, then she was on her own. Barb put the car in gear and headed along the secondary highway and then slowly up their dirt drive, watching out for innocent creatures. She couldn't change the O'Learys, but tomorrow, when it was light, she would find and bury that poor mother rabbit. And when she got her paycheck this Friday, she would not buy shingles as she ought to. Instead she'd buy chicken wire, and she'd nail it to trees and string it along the driveway herself, even if it took all night. As she approached the house, she saw a great blaze.

Barb got out of the car and walked in darkness along the path toward the bonfire where the three O'Learys moved in strange relief against the flames. Martha held Rebecca's hand, and Rebecca held her father's as they traveled around the fire in a line. Rebecca hesitated once and stumbled over her feet, and Barb couldn't help but think of her flying into the fire. Barb imagined she saw not only the three, but the rest of the family as well, moving among the flames: Martin's mother, sluggish and thick, doped up on Thorazine; Martin's sister Suzanne waving her long thin limbs, her wrists transparent and scarred; the lost brother, forever seventeen, with pretty gray eyes and wild curls like a woman's. The rest of the family swayed and grasped, ancients with round faces, small noses, and wide-set eyes. She imagined the howls of O'Leary men tied to medieval racks or chained to dungeon walls, their arms and legs stretched obscenely. Pear-shaped women wore their make-up skewed, lips blurred into noses and chins. The flames were hot blankets beneath which the figures clinched and writhed. The fizzing and popping and creosote-stink were messages from one generation to the next.

Martin, Rebecca and Martha disappeared around the far side and then reappeared. Martha wore the leather jacket the man had left in her room. It flapped too-big around her and the zipper glinted, its wide teeth grinning into the fire. As Barb stepped into the light, Rebecca and Martin spun off and fell onto the ground beside each other, laughing, with Muffin licking at them. Their faces were turned toward the sky, open to whatever enlightenment might fall down from the heavens or waft out of the fire. Their wrists were joined by a bright steel chain.

"Martin," said Barb. She wanted Martin to acknowledge the handcuffs. Then maybe she could explain about the potato water, and tell him she intended to buy chicken wire. But Martin's forehead glowed in the firelight, and she knew she'd never be able to explain. He bent down to kiss Barb, and his shirt front was hot. One of his plastic buttons singed her neck, but instead of pulling away she pressed harder against it. When Martha grabbed Martin's hand, Martin tried to pull Barb along as well, but she resisted and stepped back. When Rebecca began baying like a wolf, Martin and Martha joined in, moaning, "Ow-ow-owoooo," to the moon.

Barb was surprised how cold the air became just a few yards from the fire. Lights shone from the house, from the kitchen and Martha's bedroom, but beyond that everything was dark. Barb wrapped her arms around herself, then felt the warmth of other arms. The three flesh-and-blood O'Learys closed around her, their limbs and breath like those of a hundred people. "Ring-around-the-rosie," they chanted. The musky smell of sweat rose off them. At first Barb stood stiff against their bodies, but when she looked into those faces, all like her daughter's, she felt a surge of love too large for her chest to contain.

"Ash-es, ash-es," the three said in unison, and Barb prepared to fall with them into the cool grass.

Shifting Gears

THE sun glowed red in the gloss finish of Tommy's three-quarter ton F-250 four-wheel drive long-box pickup. The paint glistened like fresh blood, as clean and smooth as something just born, something whose outer layers had been peeled away. The truck's beauty still overwhelmed Tommy though he'd been driving it for a couple weeks now, since the end of September. He'd traded in the old blue bomb which now sat in the Ford dealer's bargain lot. Tommy would not be lying on the cold ground under that hunk of junk this winter. He stood in the driveway with one hand on the hood, soaking in the warmth of the engine. Though he was home, he was in no hurry to go into his house.

Ever since his wife had left him, the house seemed reptilian, as lifeless as a snake cage at the zoo. He took all the overtime he could get these days, and he drove the truck everywhere he could think of, but eventually he had to come home each night. When his neighbors Bob and Sharon stepped out of their house into the late sunshine, Tommy waved. He unlocked the front door of the house only to let his dog out, then headed over to Bob's. Sharon was nine months pregnant with her first child, so what was she doing? She had picked up a fan rake and was dragging it across the lawn. She seemed angry and impatient, as usual.

"Ought she to be doing that?" Tommy asked Bob.

"Her sister told her it'll make her have the baby."

Even though he was getting fat, Bob had those blond, athletic looks women seemed to like. He didn't have any problems talking to women. Tommy was smaller by about eighty pounds with a thin moustache that he worried between his thumb and forefinger. Bob worked at a paper converting plant, first shift, Sharon worked at the Harding's grocery, and Tommy worked at Taggert Plumbing Supply, filling orders and making deliveries.

Bob went into his house and brought out two beers. He walked on the balls of his feet like the football player he used to be in high school. Bob could surprise you with his abilities, like this Labor Day weekend when he put up vinyl siding on his house. He started it on Friday evening and finished on Monday, the trim around the windows and everything. A perimeter of paint chips surrounded Tommy's house—blue gray and green patches showed through the latest coat of white paint. The two men sat on the picnic table, which afforded them a good view of both Sharon's raking and Tommy's truck.

"You ought to get a new truck, Bob," said Tommy. "That '83 is dying."

"It's an '84."

"It needs an exhaust. I heard you clear down to M-98 this morning."

Bob's dog, a female beagle some guy had sold him because she wouldn't hunt, walked across Bob's yard and lay down on Sharon's pile of leaves.

"Stupid bitch!" screamed Sharon and whacked the dog with the rake.

The Bitch—that's what Bob named the dog—picked herself up and followed a zigzag path of scents, then lay under the picnic table.

Tommy's dog Moe rolled on his back and crunched leaves. Moe was a black lab who until six months ago spent a good part of his time chasing females in heat. Six months ago, Tommy's wife had gotten Moe neutered. Tommy had to admit that now, with his wife gone, it was a comfort to have his dog sticking close to home. And bailing him out of the pound had been getting expensive.

Tommy produced a second pair of beers from his house and gave one to Bob. As they were cracking open the beers, Sharon turned and pitched her rake through the air at the picnic table. It fell way short of them.

"What's the matter, honey?" yelled Bob.

"Why don't you two just stay out here all night and drink beer. I'm sick of your faces. You make me want to scream." She went inside and slammed the door.

"I wonder if she's going to make supper," said Bob.

The yellow leaves on Tommy's front yard maple flickered like gas jets. Tommy imagined Sharon inside peeling potatoes, gouging out the eyes with the end of the peeler. Tommy and Bob sat outside until after the sun set, nursing the beers until Sharon appeared in the doorway barefoot, wearing only a thin bathrobe. The light from indoors was shining right through it, outlining her swollen shape. Tommy watched her without turning to face her. He knew that Sharon had never much liked him, and because she was close with his wife she liked him even less since the divorce. Sharon didn't ever talk to Tommy, but spoke to the air around him or to anybody else who happened to be in the vicinity. Lately, Sharon didn't seem to like Bob all that much either. Even so, Tommy took comfort in seeing Sharon every day, at home or in the Harding's checkout line. Standing there in the doorway, with her hair hanging in her face, she looked different than usual, frail. Tommy thought of a storm traveling east across the sky. He wanted to go to Sharon, to fall down and wrap his arms around her legs and feet, confess that he'd do anything for her. He pushed these thoughts out of his head, on the off chance that Bob could read his mind.

"Bob, I think Sharon wants you," he said.

Bob drained his beer and crushed the can in his hand. He stood up and called the Bitch. When she didn't come, he pulled her out from under the picnic table by her front legs, and carried her home in his big arms. She laid a shiny cord of drool all along the sleeve of his flannel shirt.

Tommy dragged Moe inside by the collar and poured some nuggets into his bowl. Suppers always caused Tommy trouble. Breakfast was coffee and a doughnut at work. Lunch he could eat at the

Greek's with all the other working guys. But supper never felt right now that he was alone. He imagined that next door Bob was sitting across the table from Sharon, eating some fresh squash and mashing butter into a potato alongside a hunk of New York strip or a T-bone. Maybe tomorrow Tommy'd pick up a piece of meat on the way home. He could see his truck sitting in the Harding's parking lot, as pretty as a picture beside all those other beat-up trucks like Bob's. He'd stand in Sharon's check-out lane if she was there. Tommy settled on a Salisbury steak frozen dinner that he microwaved and ate in front of the television.

When Tommy heard noises next door, he pressed the mute button on his remote control, put on his hunting jacket, and stepped out into the leaves. The sharp coldness of the air made him think about his wife again. He'd liked being married, liked his wife's roundness and the shampoo smell of her hair. He'd looked forward to coming home after work so much he'd turned down overtime. But after about a year, his wife was always mad at him. She'd said he wasn't capable of really caring about anybody, not even himself. Tommy's maple swayed above, spilling leaves over him. As he brushed a leaf out of his hair, painful thoughts of his wife began to fade, to be replaced by disconcerting visions of Sharon waddling pregnant out to the mailbox or scanning the items he'd bought at the grocery store, one by one, without looking up at him.

The sky was dark and metallic, punctured by a crescent moon and some sharp stars, just the kind of weather for a first hard freeze, the kind of weather that made you think of pumpkins carved with ghouls' faces. In the moonlight Tommy's truck looked almost black, lacquer black like his wife's mirrored dresser, of which there was nothing left but imprints in the carpet. On top, she'd had hundreds of pairs of earrings in neat rows, some scarves, and a wooden inlaid jewelry box lined with velvet. Tommy's dresser, then as now, had a heap of clothes on the top. His wife used to beg him to put his clothes away. A few times he'd cleared off the dresser, putting the socks and underwear in the top drawer, the shirts in the second, the pants in the third. But the dresser looked so empty. He liked his clean clothes in plain sight, liked them the way they came out of the dryer, twisted together in a ball from which he could extract what he needed.

He followed the noises next door and found Bob sitting in his truck, trying to start it.

"Sounds like you flooded it, Bob," he offered.

"Jesus Christ, of course I flooded it. You think I don't know that?"

"Let her cool down for fifteen minutes."

"Sharon's having the baby," said Bob. "I don't have fifteen minutes."

"Where's Sharon's car, anyway?"

"She loaned it to her damn sister."

"Call up her sister, have her take Sharon to the hospital."

"I'm taking her," said Bob. "Let me borrow your truck."

"Hell, Bob, I haven't let anybody drive my truck."

"All right, then you drive us to the hospital."

Sharon appeared at the back door with her bangs falling over her eyes. She looked desperate, the way a person who is never helpless looks when she is helpless. Tommy felt that pang again, that unholy desire to throw himself at her feet, and though he meant to speak, his mouth just hung open. He worked his moustache with his thumb and forefinger.

"Are you going to get your truck or am I?" Bob looked about as big as Thor standing there in his driveway.

The keys were in Tommy's pocket, so without even bothering to go in and turn off the TV, he crossed the lawn to his truck. He touched the tailgate as he passed and let his fingers trail along the left rear body panel. Tommy started to like the idea of driving Sharon to the hospital—Bob couldn't get her there, but Tommy could, by God, quickly and safely, and in the comfort of his new faux suede upholstery. He backed into their driveway with his arm over the back of the seat, stopping in front of Sharon, who stood there waiting like a lost stormcloud. Tommy leaned over and opened the door, but Sharon stood until Bob appeared carrying a duffel bag. The truck sat pretty high off the ground and Sharon, who was short to begin with, was in no condition to jump. First Bob boosted her up into the passenger seat, but she couldn't wedge herself over the gear shift in the middle, so she slid back out and insisted that Bob get in first. Then Bob about pulled Sharon's arm off getting her up after him.

"Damn stupid truck," she spat, once she was inside. She was panting hard and rubbing her shoulder. "Don't ever ask me to get in here again."

Bob reached across Sharon's belly to slam the door.

This was the first time Tommy'd had two other people in the front seat, and with one of them as big as Bob it was a tight squeeze. Good thing it was dark so nobody'd see Bob and him pressed up against each other. "I'd rather have sat next to Sharon," Tommy mumbled.

"Well, she doesn't want to sit next to you," said Bob.

Sharon held her stomach and squeezed her eyes closed. "Shut up and drive," she said to the air inside the truck cab.

Bronson Methodist Hospital was in town, ten miles away. When they turned onto M-98, Bob said, "Step on it, Tommy."

"Dealer said I ought not go over 55 for the first 3000 miles."

"Listen, Tommy. All you care about now is getting us to the hospital."

Tommy edged the speedometer up to 60 mph, then to 65, but no faster. Bob's right foot was pressed against the floor as though he was working his own accelerator pedal. The road poured out dark and empty before them, and the railroad tracks sped along beside. Tommy had to admit that driving fast on this dark, smooth road felt good.

As they passed the Ford dealer, Tommy searched the lot for his old blue bomb, but the spot where it had been sitting this morning was empty. Somebody else would be busting his knuckles on that hunk of junk now. Somebody else would be driving with his hand rested on that oversize gearshift knob that he'd taken from a '56 junkyard Ford. Somebody else would jiggle it carefully into reverse.

"Why you slowing down?" asked Bob.

"You know, Bob, you ought to buy yourself a new truck," said Tommy. When Bob didn't respond, he continued. "I always know that my truck's going to start, every time I turn the key. Ford dealer's got good financing, too."

Bob said, "I'd buy a Dodge."

"You'd be crazy to buy a Dodge."

"I always buy Chrysler."

"I know a guy bought a new Dodge Ram truck," said Tommy, "Ten thousand mile warranty runs out, he's got that thing in the shop every week. First it's his front end, then it's his midship bearing. Mopars are nothing but trouble. Like that truck you're driving now, flooding out, backfiring. That's your Mopar."

"That truck's over twelve years old. And it needs a new exhaust. In ten years your Ford's up on blocks. Fix Or Repair Daily. That's your Ford."

"Will you two shut up!" yelled Sharon. "Just shut up and drive!"

"Honey, aren't you supposed to be breathing deep or something?"

As they came into town on M-98, lights hit the truck from all directions—the overhead street lights, lights from the Hot 'n' Now drive-through and the Total gas station. Tommy made a lot of deliveries downtown, so he knew this stretch of road, knew to slow down over the first set of tracks so as not to cause Sharon any discomfort. The hospital was almost within sight. And just as naturally as night follows day, when the lights began to flash red and the gates fell across the road, Tommy pulled to a stop and shifted into neutral.

"What are you doing?" asked Bob.

"There's a train coming," said Tommy.

"You can make it," said Bob. "Go around."

"I can't take a chance like that with Sharon in here."

"Tommy, you idiot!" screamed Sharon. She opened the door and let herself slide out onto the road.

"Honey, wait!" said Bob and jumped down after her.

Sharon supported herself against the side of the truck, but when Bob stretched an arm around her, she pushed him away and headed toward the tracks. But before them all, as big as a movie screen, the locomotive engine appeared, oily black and unforgiving. It riveted them all in their places, approaching in what looked like slow motion. Tons and tons of steel, enough to mangle flesh and pulverize bones, enough to crush Tommy's truck and wrap it around him. A second engine followed the first, then a boxcar from the Chessie System with "Red + Julie" spray-painted on it. Then a hundred more.

With his automatic window button, Tommy lowered the passenger side window and yelled down to them, "Get back in. We're almost there." But Bob and Sharon were arguing.

Luckily, the train kept rolling, and it didn't stop and back up the way they sometimes did. When Tommy saw the last train car, he looked behind him to see about thirty-five vehicles spread out across four lanes. As the gates lifted, cars started honking, but he couldn't pull out because Sharon and Bob were still in the road. Tommy put on his flashers, desperate at the prospect of somebody hitting Sharon or crashing into the back of his truck. Cars swerved around them. This wasn't how it was supposed to be, thought Tommy. He'd wanted to help Sharon, wanted to do the right thing for her.

"She's got to get in, Bob."

"I know that. We're working on it," said Bob. "Honey, you can't walk to the hospital."

The first time Bob tried to help Sharon back up into the cab, she slipped back down on him. "I hate this goddamn truck!" she yelled, punching the side of the seat. She kicked the rocker panel and then walked back and kicked the rear tire. She leaned against the rear fender like a girl on a real bad drunk and moaned as some sort of a spasm took hold of her. "God, I just want to have this baby."

"Sharon, honey, we're almost there," said Bob, "I promise it will be all right." Tommy wished he could say something to comfort Sharon, but the more he tried to think of something, the more blank his mind went. Bob finally got Sharon up inside the cab, sideways onto the seat so that her back pressed against Tommy's shoulder. Bob got in but couldn't shut the door, so they drove the rest of the way with the dome light on and the door buzzer screaming. When Sharon turned to face forward, Tommy saw tears raining down her face. He shifted gently so as not to move the shoulder that supported her. Tommy wondered if he was going to have to sleep alone for the rest of his life.

"Lay on the horn," said Bob as they pulled up to the emergency entrance. By the time Bob got Sharon out, a nurse and an orderly appeared with a wheelchair. Evidently Bob had called ahead. Tommy tried to assist, but they didn't need him, and as Sharon rolled away, he felt himself bobbing in her wake. Her moans trailed behind her until the glass doors swung shut, and she was immediately around a corner and out of sight. Back in Tommy's truck, all that remained of Sharon were her fleece-lined slippers, one on the seat, the other on the floor mat. Like his wife, Sharon had rejected all Tommy had to offer—she even hated his truck. Tommy thought of all the things his wife had taken when she moved away: stacks of neatly folded jeans, the couch, a plastic basket of make-up she kept in the bathroom, a brass floor lamp. It was hard to get used to the empty places where those things had been. The hood of the truck glowed shiny purple in the sodium lights of the hospital lot.

He loved its clean bed liner, the flare of the wheel wells, the toolbox stretching across the back, the tapering of the windows, the heavy smooth feel of opening and closing the tailgate. He hadn't been able to talk to anybody about his wife's leaving, but buying this truck had made him feel better. He hadn't cared how much it cost; the payment and insurance now took most of his paycheck twice a month. And yet ever since he'd passed the Ford lot, he couldn't stop thinking about his old truck, too. After all the hours he'd spent lying underneath it, replacing the starter and the clutch and the U-joints, he should have been happy to be rid of the dang thing.

He ought to just start up the new truck in neutral, skip first, shift from second to third to fourth, head out some dark farm road, drive past dimly lit houses, quiet barns, and acres of pumpkins lying tangled in fields. But what about poor Sharon up there, Sharon with tears pouring down her face, Sharon whose baby was about to shed her like an old skin?

Tommy leaned back against the seat and let out a breath he must have been holding for a long time. He felt raw, as if all his own outside layers had fallen away. He chose one square window on the third floor and pretended it was Sharon's room. Brushing the back of his hand across the upholstery, he thought of the perfect skin of the new baby, as soft as the velvet lining of his wife's wooden inlaid jewelry box. Sharon was probably cursing Bob and the doctor as she performed her miracle, pushing out something the color of a pumpkin, new life which would fill a small place in the world, a place where before there had been nothing.

The Smallest Man in the World

BEAUTY is not a virtue. And beauty is not in the eye of the beholder. Beauty is a fact like height, or symmetry, or hair color. Understand that I am not bragging when I say I am the most beautiful woman in the bar.

Normally I can make this claim without hesitation because this is my regular bar. But tonight the circus is in town, and there are strangers here, including four showgirls at a table between me and the jukebox drinking what look like vodka tonics—tall, clear drinks with maraschino cherries.

Whenever the circus comes to the Palace, I attend, as I did tonight with my sister, who now drums her fingers on the bar beside me.

"What did you like best?" she asks.

I shrug. My sister gets annoyed when I refuse to talk, but I do not like to answer questions that I have not thought about.

"How about that rhinoceros?" she says. "It was sweating gallons out there. I'm surprised that woman didn't slide off."

"Yes."

"Why do you come here?" asks my sister, spinning around once on her barstool. "There's nothing to do." She spins again. "You should tell them to get magnetic darts or something."

My sister always chatters this way. She is warm, communicative, and generous, and I am not—just ask any of my three ex-husbands. If you want to know the other difficulties of being close to me, you will have to ask them or her, because I do not intend to enumerate my faults. My sister and I have similar green eyes, high cheekbones, and thick dark hair, and it is a puzzle why I am more beautiful than she. Perhaps it is because she has developed so many other interests. She is a social worker in a hospital, helping fifty families a day in whatever ways she can, she belongs to a softball league, and she has a husband who is crazy about her. Within a year, she will probably have her first child. I work at a hotel, where part of my job is to look good.

"If you're not going to talk to me, I'm leaving," my sister says. "I've got stuff I can do at home." She downs her cranberry juice and heads for the door.

This is a typical end to an evening we spend together. I cannot explain to her that, though I love her company, I do not want to talk. As she exits, two big men in circus coveralls enter, accompanied by the Smallest Man in the World. The big men have identical builds, but one is white with blond hair and slightly crossed eyes, and the other is black and scruffy-headed. Both give the impression that the coveralls are the only clothes they own. When they reach the bar, these two bend in unison, and the small man straightens his arms and allows himself to be lifted onto a barstool, where he stands and looks down on the bartender. To his credit, Martin the bartender does not ask for identification, but brings the small man his whiskey and soda in a professional way that does not suggest surprise that such a tiny man would want a drink, or indeed that a man would be so tiny.

As usual, I sit at the far end of the bar, on the brass and leather barstool nearest the wall so I can see everyone in the place. The wooden bar curves away from me and stretches thirty feet, halfway to the front door, and is stained a reddish color beneath layers of polyurethane. The wall opposite the bar is raw brick, lined with low wattage fixtures designed to look like gas lanterns. After working all day in bright light, I find the dimness comforting.

The Smallest Man in the World looks at the patrons one by one, then settles his gaze on me and nods. His hair is thinning. With a closed mouth, I smile. He holds up his drink in my direction in appreciation of my beauty, and I lift my drink in appreciation of his smallness.

I have compared beauty to height, but there is more in common between beauty and smallness: conciseness, the correct arrangement of parts in a confined area. Space has not been wasted on the Smallest Man in the World. He is perfectly formed, with limbs, trunk, and ears all in proportion. Only at the most perfunctory glance does he look like a child, for he has a serious forehead and a square jaw. His face is slightly swollen, most likely from drinking, but his size obscures this fact. An art teacher once showed me the trick of making a black ink drawing and then shrinking it on the copying machine—in the reduction, the flaws are less perceptible.

As appears to be the case with the Smallest Man in the World, I sometimes drink too much. When I develop that swollen look, I disguise it by loosening my hair. Drinking is, of course, an ordinary addiction; it is not peculiar to persons who possess extreme qualities. Plenty of plain, normal-sized people drink too much. Take, for instance, the sweaty man who has been coming in for the last few months with his shirt buttons more and more strained—he has the look of a person embroiled in an unpleasant divorce. That woman at the other end of the bar must be seventy, maybe with grandchildren, and she drinks to excess nightly, done up in foundation and blusher. The edge of her glass is smeared halfway around with lipstick.

My sister appears in the doorway behind the made-up old woman and makes her way along the bar to me, jangling her keys.

"I forgot that I drove you here. How are you getting home?"

"I can take a cab. Do not worry about me, little sister."

"Okay, take care of yourself. I'll see you soon." She touches my shoulder to prove her concern. My sister is a caring person, no doubt, but I get the feeling she is worried less about me than about the people around me. "Wherever I came I brought calamity," Tennyson quotes Helen of Troy. My sister knows that when I get drunk I become friendly, and she knows that men who came into the bar with perfectly nice women, or who have left women as pretty and caring as my sister at home, will risk future happiness in order to spend the night with me. You may consider my willingness to go home with such men reprehensible; you also may blame the Trojan War on Helen's misbehavior. Keep in mind, though, that Helen did not herself launch a single warship or burn a single tower. And in the end she paid a great price for her affair with Paris: while you and I are able to toss off married names for fifty dollars and some paperwork, she remains Helen of Troy for all eternity. No matter that she settled peacefully with Menelaus in Athens and had a child.

My sister almost brushes against the circus men on the way out, and the white guy turns to watch her leave. She has a friendly, bouncy walk. She does not look back.

A pale-skinned couple enters and sits on stools halfway down the bar. Perhaps they have been to a play. They move in unison, their once-independent bodies working as complementary parts of a whole. He helps her take off her coat, and she gets him something from her purse. The Smallest Man in the World jumps down and moves across the room toward the jukebox, onto which his friend lifts him. When a song skips, Martin the bartender looks over coolly, but to his credit does not yell, "Get off the jukebox." Though it has never occurred to me before, I consider this bartender a good friend.

Twenty years ago, when I was in high school, my mother and sister encouraged me to enter my first and only beauty contest, hoping that I could make friends. But even then I recognized most of those girls as shallow and hopeless bits of fluff, unaware of what freaks we were making of ourselves. And then, of course, they hated me for winning. It should not surprise anyone that P.T. Barnum himself pioneered the modern beauty contest, recognizing that striking beauty was fundamentally no different from any other aberration. Such absurdly perfect integration of a woman's bones, flesh, and features was not unlike a third arm growing out of the center of another woman's back. Barnum was the first to figure out that strangers would pay to see this sort of female oddity paraded before them.

The sweaty man with the strained buttons walks by on his way to the bathroom. When he glances at me, he trips over a runner on the carpet; he catches himself and regains his balance awkwardly, as though his own body has recently become a stranger to him. I tend my own body with such care that I cannot imagine losing touch with it—I am far more likely to lose my mind, something nobody notices. The man looks away as he straightens himself up, and a few minutes later he returns to his seat by a circuitous route.

In a thick accent, the Smallest Man in the World yells something to the table of showgirls, and at first they ignore him. "Brandy," he then shouts, several times, and I first think he is ordering a drink. "You looking pretty tonight." His voice is nasal and high-pitched, sadly comical.

The red-haired woman turns and shouts. "Why'd you follow us here? Find your own bar, Shrimp."

"You are my loving, Miss Brandy." His strangely-accented voice is far more sad than comic, I decide. The showgirl shakes her head and turns back to face her friends, who laugh. She lights a cigarette.

At the jukebox the two men who accompany the Smallest Man in the World stand near him so they form an equilateral triangle, as if this can protect him. They are heartbroken at what transpires between their small man and the showgirls. After all, they must love him; they have become attached to his smallness the way men become attached to my beauty. When a man is with me, he cannot forget my beauty the way he forgets everything else. Intimate conversations and promises are forgettable, as are meals created with attention to every detail of taste and presentation. Even the loveliness of naked breasts can mean nothing when the skin remains covered for too long. But his size is a constant reminder, as is my face.

I do not like to see my own face, because, despite my make-up, I look sad—sometimes as sad as that rouged old woman slumped over the bar opposite me. When I fix my face in the morning, it sometimes occurs to me to make myself up as a clown by lipsticking a massive smile onto my cheeks. Or exaggerating the sadness by painting a frown and a few shiny tears. I have heard that each circus clown must register a face with the national clown organization, that they cannot co-opt the faces of others. Maybe women should have to do that, for we are famous for reproducing the full lips and long curving eyebrows of teenage runway models; perhaps women could be forced to be themselves, the way my sister is herself. This clown urge of mine becomes so overwhelming some days that I even fantasize about becoming a clown, although anyone, including my sister and ex-husbands, will tell you that I am not funny.

The Smallest Man looks away from the showgirls and over at me. He sways slightly, drunkenly, against the music. He whispers something to the black man, sending him to the bar. The Smallest Man then jumps down, walks over to the showgirls, and disappears from sight.

Martin brings me another drink before I have finished the one in front of me. He gestures with a nod toward the jukebox and says, "The small guy sent this to you, says it's for 'the most beautiful woman'." From him the compliment means something, and it means something to me that Martin conducted the message. "Have you been to the circus?" Martin asks.

"I went tonight with my sister. That was my sister with me." My arms stretch out brightly on the bar, my skin a bronze color which makes unclear precisely what my race is. Some people assume I come from an island where all the women are beautiful.

"She looks like you," Martin says. My hair is swept off my face, twisted softly at the back of my head, so that my neck is bare. Martin's gaze sweeps over me; he never lets his eyes linger, perhaps out of respect or maybe because he doesn't trust me, having seen me leave the bar with dozens of men. Martin is about to lift his foot and place it on a shelf under the bar so he can lean toward me and say something privately. But the look-alike couple interrupts our moment by motioning to him. They want a bag of nuts.

Shrieks erupt from the showgirl table, and I do not see the Smallest Man, but soon the red-haired woman screams, "You little pervert midget." The Smallest Man emerges from under the table on all fours, brushes himself off, and returns to the jukebox. He holds up a black platform pump and sniffs it, until the redhead marches up in bare feet and grabs it from him. Her skirt is short and filmy. The Smallest Man grins, but the two big men look worried.

Though there is no table service on week nights, Martin walks around the bar to the showgirls and brings them another round. The women must have been wearing wigs during the show, because all of them have close-cropped hair. Their eyes are painted large. The redhead has long, muscular legs, the legs of an athlete, legs smooth and strong enough to lure a bartender away from his post. Martin lets his gaze wander all over those legs, even after he returns to the bar. These are probably the kind of women he prefers: energetic, acrobatic, clever.

One showgirl holds her fingers an inch apart toward the jukebox, and when the Smallest Man looks over, all the women burst out laughing. Their mouths seem large enough to swallow his whole head. When the red-haired showgirl notices me staring, she narrows her eyes. I turn back to the bar. I am accustomed to the looks she and the other showgirls give me. They think I have cheated in order to look this way. Have I had surgery? they wonder. They assume that, one way or another, I have sold my soul to the devil.

And I understand why the Smallest Man in the World cannot leave them alone. For the same reason that I cannot resist beautiful new men who come into this bar, because desiring them is uncomplicated. It is not the showgirls' fault that the Smallest Man humiliates himself—their cruelty is ordinary, and they could not possibly know what it means to be tiny.

The showgirls were best at half-time, when all the animals and performers came out in a Wild West spectacular; the showgirls wore fake leather miniskirts with oversized pistols on their hips. I should have told my sister how much I liked the half-time show. My sister was right—the girl riding that sweaty rhinoceros practically had to do the splits as she bounced on its wide, slippery back. During this event, the Smallest Man in the World stood on top of a fancy horse-drawn wagon and waved. He appeared also in the grand finale, standing and waving from an elephant's back.

There is no separate sideshow tent in the circus anymore. You have to go to county fairs for that kind of grotesquerie, or else watch television. This July I traveled thirty miles and paid two dollars each to see the world's smallest horse, the fattest pig, the longest alligator. You must take for granted that they really are the longest, the smallest, and the fattest. Who is to say that the posted weight, height, or length is even honest? Who is in charge of freak show weights and measures?

Surely the man who bought me this drink is the true Smallest Man in the World; the Greatest Show on Earth would not lie so boldly. Before I finish my second drink, the Smallest Man has ordered his third. He seems drunk already, the way a regular-sized man would be drunk had he taken six or eight.

On my way to the bathroom, I look straight ahead, avoiding the eyes of the red-haired showgirl, but on my way back, I walk slowly enough to study their heads and shoulders and to smell their perfume, which is flowery and applied too heavily, perhaps to disguise sweat. Though they portray beautiful women, they are not particularly beautiful. Real beauty would be too quiet on the arena floor, and it could not compete with the menagerie of elephants and horseback riders. Beauty cannot transmit over long distances, could not possibly stretch into the upper tiers of a stadium; costumes do a better job than the real thing. Helen's beauty was transmitted by hearsay; how many of the men who died at Troy ever saw her? These showgirls are not as young and foolish as they seem in costume. They are actors and magicians, good with the sleight of hand, the sleight of face.

Even the Smallest Man in the World used a few tricks. When he appeared in the center ring at half-time, sitting and then standing on the seat of his circus-painted stagecoach, he wore a suit jacket that had been cut long so that his legs, which are actually in perfect proportion to his body, looked short. The horses pulling the wagon were draft horses, beasts that would dwarf any human.

A crack like thunder sounds through the bar, but the showgirls do not look up. They are accustomed to elephants stampeding, vendors hawking, cannons blowing humans across arenas.

"Off the jukebox," says the bartender. He says it quickly, directly, without sharpness, and he is already turning away to avoid a confrontation. Martin is a genius. The Smallest Man in the World has not taken offense. He holds out his arms, signaling to his friends that he wants to be carried.

A man in a dark suit approaches this end of the bar and catches my eye. He has not been in here before. He is perhaps twenty-five and has on his face a look of mild astonishment. If my attention were not elsewhere, I might nod to him and invite him to sit beside me. Instead, he leaves one empty stool between us and motions to the bartender. His jacket hangs from broad, straight shoulders.

Perhaps I will see him tomorrow at the hotel desk, or later tonight in a hotel bed.

At the hotel, I mostly work behind a glass wall, filling out forms, designing staff schedules, and making phone calls, unless there is a problem. In that case, I walk on three inch heels from behind the glass, and I say in the most elegant voice you can imagine, "Is there a problem?" My mouth is perfectly darkened, and I do not open it again until the customer and the clerk have said all they want to say, and still I wait a little longer in silence. Only occasionally do I have to refund money.

Before I have an opportunity to speak to the man in the dark suit, the two men in coveralls carry the Smallest Man in the World to the bar. From here I cannot tell if the jukebox glass is cracked. Hank Williams Senior continues singing a very old heartbreak. The circus people have been playing country-western all night.

I wonder if the Smallest Man in the World thinks about growing the way I think about growing less beautiful. Perhaps he and I could live together, drink less, entertain in our home. I know how difficult it would be to really know the Smallest Man in the World, to see beyond his height, and I would work for us not to be strangers. Along the stairway leading to our bedroom, beside the studio shots of our children, would hang photos of our old deformed selves. Thirty-five is not too late to start a family. My second husband, who already had two daughters, said I was too selfish to be a mother, but I could change. My own late-born children would have an easier time than his girls. When my girls looked at photos of me they would say, "You were so beautiful, Mommy," and that past tense would be much easier on them at thirteen than, "You *are* so beautiful." My husband would say, "I used to be the Smallest Man in the World until I met your mother."

You might suggest that if I genuinely look forward to growing plain, I should skip the facials, the weekly manicures and the constant touch-ups for my auburn highlights; I should let my hair hang in an easy style like my sister's, or cut it short and convenient as the showgirls have done. Well, you may as well suggest to a tall man that he slump; for me to neglect my beauty now would feel like a denial of the facts.

Though I try to ignore the stranger beside me, my body moves toward his the way a flower bends toward the sun. I close my eyes in an attempt to resist, but when I open them, he is looking into my face. He smells musky and a little smoky, and his eyes are cocktails with tiny black olives. I would continue to slide closer, except that the Smallest Man in the World is making a fuss. He has jumped onto the bar and is standing with his hands on his hips, like the most outrageous, arrogant child in the world. Perhaps Martin has refused him a fourth drink.

"You're going to have to get down," says Martin.

The Smallest Man shouts in a language that I have never heard in the hotel—Hungarian, perhaps. He is angry and hurt, but his two big friends continue to man the second and third corners of his triangle. They love him too much to encourage him to get off the bar. He is not a child after all. He wears what looks like a boy's sneakers, but his pants are tailored, and his safari-style jacket is cut to his figure. He stands tall on the bar, enraptured in hostility toward the bartender, and I hope I do not have to choose sides. The showgirls have finally noticed, and they are watching too—everybody loves a spectacle.

The Smallest Man in the World turns and looks across the room, not at them but at me. "Beautiful Lady!" he shouts. "Help me!" He hands his drink to his white man, and he starts down the bar toward me. The old woman with rouge clings to her drink at the other end. The Smallest Man leaps over most of the glasses between himself and me but knocks over both drinks of the pale look-alike couple. They lean back from the bar, Siamese twins, both mouths limp in one expression of confusion. The man beside me jumps up and gets out of the way. The Smallest Man in the World holds out his arms to me, and without hesitation I put down my drink and open my arms. With my beautiful but sad eyes I promise that if he reaches me, I will protect him. I will hold and shelter him like my own first child, embrace him as my blood brother, honor him as my true husband. He crushes a bag of potato chips and kicks loose peanuts into the air. I stand and step slightly back from the bar. If he is brave enough to jump, I will catch him.

Bringing Home the Bones

LIKE hundreds of times before, Charlotte had lifted the eight-quart canner off the stove, only this time she'd lost her grip on one of the handles. Gallons of near boiling water cascaded over her lower leg. For a stupefying moment Charlotte had stood rigid, listening, as if waiting for her name to be called, and then the pain began to boil in her skin. Before she lost her nerve, she had wrapped the blistering, slippery tissue in bandages made from a torn sheet and smeared with salve. Ten days and ten throbbing nights later, she opened the bandages and discovered the flesh had turned gray. Still, she had waited before phoning her daughter Andrea. She didn't even remember arriving at the hospital, but now, when she looked down, it became all too clear. Her left leg ended bluntly just below her knee, a stump wrapped in beige bandages, the butchered aftermath of these people's human body experiments. She shook off the smooth thin hand that touched her hand and threw aside a bed sheet the color of skimmed milk. Each attempt to focus on the limb was like falling off a cliff, like being dragged over a waterfall in a current of thinned pigments. She dropped her head back onto a foam pillow and stared up at ceiling tiles.

"Mrs. DeBoer." A nurse appeared beside her.

"What the hell did they do to my leg?" Charlotte asked, in a weak voice she didn't recognize as her own. The surgical tubes had ruined her throat. An antibiotic drip invaded her through a needle stuck just above her wrist. Charlotte resisted an urge to give it a yank and disengage herself. Andrea pulled the bed sheet over Charlotte's knee with long, smooth fingers, the nails painted translucent ice-cream pink. Charlotte pulled off the bed sheet again to expose the atrocity.

"It was gangrenous, Mrs. DeBoer. The doctors had to amputate." The nurse looked not at her, but at Andrea.

"Don't you remember, Mom?"

"I remember I came in here with two legs. If I'd thought you'd send me home with one, I wouldn't have come." Charlotte's whole body felt waterlogged, but she refused to sink. "Look," she said to Andrea. "Look at what they've done."

"These are for pain," said the nurse, offering her a tiny plastic cup.

"I don't need your damn pills." Charlotte's eyes watered at the strain of speaking.

"Doctor's orders are for you to take these. You don't want to make a fuss, do you?" The nurse had wide cheek bones, shaved and painted eyebrows.

"All right, give me the pills and go to hell." As the nurse left, Charlotte turned to Andrea. "I suppose your sister knows I'm here."

"Liz came while you were in surgery."

"She was here?"

"She was here for thirty-six hours. You saw her in the recovery room. You kept telling her she was named after your mother."

"Is she coming back?"

"She's in court this morning. It's only her second case ever and she can't miss it. She'll come back from Chicago as soon as she can."

Andrea stepped out, saying she wanted to get some coffee. Charlotte didn't acknowledge her leaving, but missed her the instant she was gone. Had Lily been milked? she needed to ask. Had somebody fed the chickens? If nobody fed them, they'd start pecking apart their own eggs. Ragweed, pokeweed, and burdock would eclipse her tomato plants within a week. They held you prisoner in these places with no regard for what you had at home. And she didn't like the way colors of objects faded into one another here. She liked her colors strong and separate: the greens of ryegrass and alfalfa, the blue of sky, the darkness of garden soil, and the colors of cows. Brick and white Herefords. The pure black of a Black Angus. Her fawn-colored Jersey against the grasses of her field, against a clear horizon.

Jersey milk had the highest fat content so it tasted the best and it made good butter. Charlotte used to make ice cream for her daughters, but when the girls got to be teenagers, they wouldn't eat butter or ice cream—they'd even skimmed the cream off the milk they used on their breakfast cereal. Two decades later they were still keeping themselves skinny like little girls, like starved Jews. Their underdeveloped muscles hung slack on thin arms.

"I should have had sons," she mumbled.

"What'd you say, Mom?" Andrea had come back and was sitting beside the bed. Charlotte wanted to say something less mean, but she didn't know what. Feathered sections of the girl's hair yearned toward her bony shoulders. When Andrea was young, she used to wear her hair long in a braid the way Charlotte still did.

"Who's milking Lily?" Charlotte asked.

"You told me to let the calf back in with her. Remember? That was a sweet little calf. What do you call him?"

"Veal. I was going to butcher that calf out for veal this week." Charlotte turned to see Andrea's reaction.

Andrea rolled her eyes. "Mom, do you have to say that sort of thing?"

The girl faded and grew distant. A blood-purple stripe of headband rose from her hair, then plunged beneath it. Charlotte struggled to stay conscious. "Oh?" she said. "I suppose you're a vegetarian now?"

THICK snakes of poison ivy grew up around the biggest oak in her stand of woods by the road. The vines slithered into the branches, unfurling triple green leaves in every splotch of sunshine, sucking the life from her tree. Clouds of ash and rage pressed on Charlotte from all sides, gray and suffocating. She lifted her axe and chopped at the vines, but the axe was dull and it bounced. She swung again, and again the axe flew off. When she glanced down, she discovered that she had cut off her leg below the knee. She dropped her axe and sat up in her bed, eyes wide open.

She was alone, thank God, not that she believed in any God. She clutched the edges of the hospital bed and waited for her heart to stop pounding. For more than fifty years her dreams had done this to her. More than fifty years ago, as a girl, she had left the Netherlands and come to Michigan, but each morning she still had to adjust to what felt like a strange, new country. At home, she got right up and made coffee and eggs. Lying useless in this hospital was worse than enduring the burn. She'd been in agony then, but she'd been home and she'd refused to feel sorry for herself. After all, she had been spared the terrible pain her parents must have suffered at the hands of the Germans who arrested them in their newspaper office in Amsterdam. Before they were taken, she'd been sent to her father's brother in America. Her mother had said Charlotte could come home when the occupation was over, but by that time there was nobody to go home to. From the age of eight, Charlotte was dressed up and taken to the Dutch Reformed church with her cousins on Wednesday evenings and twice every Sunday for the routine care of her soul. But Charlotte's parents had been communist and atheist, and Charlotte honored them by never giving in to the minister's temptations of forgiveness and rescue from hellfires.

Charlotte's Uncle Peter—Andrea and Elizabeth called him "Grandpa Peter"—told her as a child that nobody knew what had happened to her parents, but Charlotte had read the letters written to Peter just after the war. Someone had seen soldiers put her parents on a crowded eastbound train in the middle of the night. Since then Charlotte saw her parents in every one of those concentration camp pictures, a blurred mother with shriveled breasts, a father with dark holes for eyes.

"WHERE'S my leg?" Charlotte asked when the daytime nurse came in, with another plastic pill cup.

"You remember, Mrs. DeBoer. It's been amputated."

"I asked *where's* my leg. I sure as hell noticed you cut it off."

"It's probably in the lab."

"What are you people going to do with it?" Her voice had recovered and was her own again.

"You'll have to ask the doctor, but they usually incinerate necrotic tissue after a biopsy." The eyebrows snapped up and down like little whips.

"Oh, that's just fine, Nurse. You've got a crematorium here, too?"

"Ma'am, I just want you to take your pain medication." She left it on the bedside table.

"Well, I won't have my leg burned, damn it!" Charlotte shouted after her. "Tell the doctor he's not going to burn my leg!"

WHEN Andrea came in that evening with her hair pulled into a small, shiny ponytail, Charlotte was desperate to communicate. She leaned out of bed toward the girl, her face turning hot as she started to speak. "Andrea, these Nazi doctors—they want to burn my leg, toss it in the furnace like a piece of garbage."

"Well," said Andrea, "I guess it's for sanitary reasons."

"I've got a right to that leg. Call your lawyer sister! Ask her what I can do!"

"Mom, her name is Elizabeth. You should say her name."

"Maybe I'd say her name if she'd visited me once in three years."

"She was just here. And she was at Grandpa Peter's at Christmas."

"She hasn't come to the house for three years."

"Have you invited her to the house?"

Charlotte leaned back against the pillows. "Did those bastards even try to save my leg?"

"Of course they tried, Mom. It was full of infection. Why didn't you go to the doctor when you first burned yourself?"

"They're all a bunch of Doctor Mengeles. Just look what they've done." Charlotte nodded toward her leg but stopped herself from looking and held up her chin stoically.

ON her last morning in the hospital, Charlotte came out of the bathroom on crutches to find Andrea sitting beside the bed. The sun had risen while Charlotte was using the toilet.

"So, how are we feeling today?" Andrea asked, her voice cheery. Sometimes the girl talked to Charlotte as she would a stranger, as though her own mother were some good-works charity case. Nonetheless, Charlotte was feeling oddly sentimental this morning.

"I was just remembering, Andrea, that you used to ask me to squirt milk into your mouth right out of the cow." Charlotte had a clear picture in her head of Andrea in a red snowsuit sitting in clean straw in the barn. The steam rose off the warm milk.

Andrea stared. "I don't really remember that."

"You were three. You watched me squirt milk into the cat's mouth, and then I aimed the teat at you. You used to love Jersey-cow milk."

"I don't want to talk about it, Mom." Andrea adjusted herself in the chair.

They waited out a silence. Charlotte finally sat on the edge of the bed. "They can't burn my leg, Andrea. Did you call your sister?"

"You know, I figured Elizabeth would just say you were crazy and forget about it, but she is actually working on it."

"Fine."

"She says we're claiming religious objections. Strict Jewish law requires people to be buried with their limbs. You buy a regular cemetery plot for the leg, and you join it later."

"I'm not Jewish," said Charlotte.

"But she figured you'd be willing to say you were."

"Fine." Charlotte considered telling the girl she was grateful. At times she would have liked to tell Andrea about everything, about her frightening dreams, about her parents being noble and selfless and murdered by Nazis.

"But there's another problem, Mom. I just talked to the social worker. You've got no insurance, and by the time you get the prosthesis, the hospital bill is going to be upwards of twenty thousand dollars. You can't get Medicare, because you and Dad were self-employed and never paid in, and you can't get any public assistance as long as you own the land and the livestock."

The blood stopped in Charlotte's veins. "They can't take my property."

"Mom, somebody's got to pay the doctor. Liz and I don't have much right now, but the social worker said we can make a payment plan and chip away at it."

"I don't want your money." Charlotte's regular farm losses had eaten up what money she used to have in the bank. "Does your sister know about this?"

"Not yet."

"Don't you tell her."

"Why?"

"Just swear you won't tell her."

"Okay, fine, I won't tell her."

Charlotte paused. "Did they cut off my leg just so they could steal my property?"

"Don't be melodramatic, Mom. They're not trying to steal your farm. You could probably sell it for two hundred thousand, maybe more. Then you could buy a smaller place, closer to town, closer to me. Your place is too hard to keep up."

"You think that's what I want to do, 'keep up' a place?"

"You can sell just a part of it, then."

"What am I going to sell, the pasture? The house? The hayfield? Next time I'll just let myself die and you and your sister can sell and be done with it." She felt her eyes watering, but she knew she wouldn't cry. She hadn't cried since she was eleven and Uncle Peter told her she would never go home.

"Maybe the woods," suggested Andrea. "Actually, I talked to a real estate agent today. You could sell the woods near the road."

THAT night, at home, Charlotte dreamed her stand of woods by the road caught fire. The smoke curled through the branches, thick and deadly. The trees had burned so that each one she touched turned to ashes and shivered to the ground. The raspberries, the morel mushrooms, the dogtooth violet, all were burnt to dust. Only the poison ivy remained, immune to the heat, falling in dumb coils from the disintegrating trees, groping along the floor of the woods. Her parents stood perfectly still, staring out at her as if from a photograph in black and white. A wind blew them into powder and they sifted away. Her leg was in place, until it too fell as dust to the woods' floor.

THE Saturday after Thanksgiving, a month after she'd gotten the new leg, both her daughters were coming to supper. In the last few weeks, she'd dreamed repeatedly of the girls as babies, dressed in white wool, squirming from her arms, wiggling toward open doors, heating ducts, laundry chutes. At first she just watched them crawl away, but then she urgently tried to gather them together, as though they were limbs she needed to piece into one body. On Saturday evening, Elizabeth arrived for dinner first, but she sat in the driveway in her low-slung, shiny car the color of broken egg yolks, waiting for Andrea.

Andrea briefly hugged Charlotte, hung her coat on a hook, and headed into the kitchem. Elizabeth mumbled a greeting, then hugged her own skinny body as she walked around the living room, reaching out and touching book spines, the arms of chairs, dusty window ledges. Elizabeth's hair was pulled up and held loosely by a gold barrette. The girl held her head proudly, as though she were continually rising above something.

"Your hair is darker," said Charlotte. "It used to be blond."

"It was this color when you saw me last Christmas at Grandpa Peter's. And the year before that."

"You two need to see each other more than once a year," said Andrea from the kitchen. She emptied saucepans into chipped blue-willow serving dishes and carried them to the table. Elizabeth lifted curtains and peered out through each of the windows. Charlotte kept her west-facing curtains closed now, so as not to see the sign advertising "Wooded Glenn Estates," a subdivision going up on the property she had sold in order to pay the goddamned hospital bill.

"You're getting along so well on that prosthesis, Mom," said Andrea, once they sat. "We knew you would, didn't we, Liz?"

"Like hell you did." Charlotte spooned herself a generous portion of stuffing. She presided at the end of the table, a daughter on either hand. "You said I wouldn't be able to 'keep the place up.' "

"We worry about you," said Andrea. "Daughters worry about their mothers."

"If you were worried about me, you'd have helped put up those four hundred bales of second cutting. There's half a load dumped on the barn floor, and another hundred and twenty bales sitting on the wagon."

"Maybe I can help when I come next Sunday," said Andrea.

"Oh, never mind. You'd just break those pink fingernails. Besides, you've got no muscle. I don't understand how you two got to be such weaklings." She pushed the bowl of stuffing toward the girls. Their father, Mr. DeBoer, with all his faults, hadn't been a weakling.

"Can we do without the criticism?" asked Elizabeth. "Can we just eat and get this charade over with?" Elizabeth had been Mr. DeBoer's favorite, always prettier than Andrea, and though younger, she was more clever and opinionated. At age thirteen, Elizabeth had insisted that Daddy was right, that they should sell the farm. Charlotte had been furious at the girl's nerve and slapped her full in the face. Twenty-one years had passed, but Charlotte knew Elizabeth hadn't forgiven her. Charlotte still felt the chill of the fourteen-year-old face glaring at her during Mr. DeBoer's funeral, as if Charlotte had caused the heart attack which sent Mr. DeBoer's tractor into a tree.

"Liz, come on. You said you'd try to get along," pleaded Andrea.

"And what do you think about your sister driving that new car," said Charlotte, looking at Andrea but pointing at Elizabeth with her fork. "What do you think that cost her?"

"You'd probably prefer I drove a farm tractor to the Cook County Courthouse," Elizabeth said. "You are hopelessly rural, Mother. It's amazing you even have indoor plumbing. I couldn't live like this again."

"Nothing wrong with the way I live," said Charlotte.

Andrea broke in. "Mom grew these vegetables in the garden, Liz. They're organic."

"That just means she grew them in cow shit. And I'll bet a week's salary she chopped off this chicken's head herself."

"Well, they don't chop their own heads off. At least I know where my food comes from. You buy food all wrapped in plastic, you don't know anything about it."

"Just because I buy my food at the grocery store, she thinks I have no soul. Well, I'm actually going to help people in my life," Elizabeth said to Andrea. "Part of my job will be pro bono work."

"It's true, Mom," said Andrea. "You've always made us feel bad for not wanting to farm."

"Hell, do whatever you want," said Charlotte. "You can become Nazi doctors for all I care. Cut off people's legs."

"God, Mother." Elizabeth folded her arms.

"Andrea, don't you want more chicken than that?" asked Charlotte. "And you're not eating your potatoes. They're from the garden."

"These potatoes are gritty," said Andrea. "Did you wash them?"

"They seem fine to me," said Charlotte, but when she took another bite, she felt the dirt grate between her teeth. "Just don't bite down hard. Eat some of those beans," she said. "They're the bush Romanos I planted this year. They canned real well."

"They are good, Mom," said Andrea. "Don't you think, Liz?"

Elizabeth reluctantly picked one up on the end of her fork and ate it.

"They'd better be good," said Charlotte. "That's how I got the burn, you girls know, canning these Romanos. They cost me my leg, these beans."

The girls stared at each other across the table. Charlotte couldn't remember just the three of them ever sitting together like this. She found herself enjoying the agitation, the eye-rolling, this stunned silence.

Elizabeth shook her head slowly side to side.

"Acorn squash is good, too, Mom," said Andrea.

"Elizabeth," said Charlotte, "you try some squash." There. She had said the name. Elizabeth. For the first time that evening, Charlotte looked into Elizabeth's face. The girl took after Mr. DeBoer's family—the high forehead, the long, thin nose. For weeks after Mr. DeBoer died, the girl had mostly sat on the edge of her bed, staring out her second-story window toward the road, long blond hair streaming down her back.

Elizabeth spooned some squash onto her plate. Charlotte watched her, searching for a resemblance to the other Elizabeth—Elisa*bet*, her own mother. Charlotte's mother Elisabet had been dark-haired and dark-eyed, of untraceable mixed stock, born of generations of city dwellers in Amsterdam. Elisabet, herself a journalist, would have thought it odd that Charlotte married a farmer and became a farmer.

"I put lots of butter in the squash," said Charlotte. "That's why it's so good."

Elizabeth stopped eating. Andrea slowed. The sun was setting and the west-facing curtains glowed golden, the color of squash.

"Mother," sighed Elizabeth, returning her cloth napkin from her lap to the table. "You know I try not to eat too much fat."

"You girls follow every fad, don't you? I've been eating beef and cream every day of my life."

"Don't you worry that one day your arteries will just explode?" asked Elizabeth.

Charlotte swallowed a last mouthful of gritty potatoes. "I got better things to worry about than my arteries, child."

"The physical therapist did say you should consider losing weight," said Andrea.

"Everybody wants to look like starved Jews these days. I butchered that veal calf. A hundred thirty-four pounds. Got $1.30 a pound. Neither of you weighs that much, do you?"

Andrea spoke up. "We haven't eaten Thanksgiving dinner here for seventeen years. I was just counting."

"It's not Thanksgiving," said Elizabeth. "I spent Thanksgiving with Nathan and his parents and sister, a normal family."

"But this is like a Thanksgiving dinner," said Andrea.

"This is like a nightmare," said Elizabeth.

"This is like a visit from the Holocaust victims," said Charlotte. "Maybe your stomachs are so shrunken that you couldn't eat even if you wanted to. After they freed the people from the camps, a lot of them couldn't eat, you know, so they starved anyway."

"Oh, this is cheerful dinner conversation," said Elizabeth. "Let's talk about concentration camps."

Charlotte scraped her plate with the side of her fork, and pushed it aside. Even without her leg, she had more meat on her than the girls combined. "It's part of our history, the Holocaust. No sense pretending it didn't happen."

"We should do this every year," said Andrea, forcing a smile. "The three of us. Meet on the Saturday after Thanksgiving. And we'll try to teach you to cook with less fat."

The same way she had eaten every bit of food on her plate,

Charlotte wanted to say everything that came into her head. And she had the right. These girls had screamed in their cribs, and she had picked them up and nursed them with her own breast milk.

"Worrying about fat is for city people," said Charlotte. "Country people can eat anything they want because they work hard."

"You already killed Dad with this stuff."

"God, Liz, don't say that," said Andrea. "Mom, thank you for cooking for us. Everything is delicious, especially the stuffing."

"That's because it's made with lots of pork sausage," said Charlotte.

Elizabeth clanked her fork on her plate and stood. "This is ridiculous, Mother." She walked over to the window and opened the curtains. The girl probably didn't even remember that oak trees with trunks six feet thick had stood on that property, some of them seventy feet high, more than a hundred years old. The developers had cut down nearly every one. Charlotte hadn't been able to escape the noise of the chain saws anywhere on her property.

"It's like you're trying to poison us," said Elizabeth.

"She's not trying to poison us, Liz. This is how she eats."

"I wish I were back in Chicago. Everything makes sense there. You know, people there actually respect me." Elizabeth's features suddenly looked fragile.

"Liz, we respect you," said Andrea.

"Maybe you do, but *she* doesn't."

"Of course she does."

Liz returned to the table and sat decisively. "Mother, do you know what law school is like? You should be so goddamned proud of me for graduating at the top of my class. But you don't know anything about law school. You have no idea about anything but beef prices and alfalfa and fat."

Charlotte had intended to tell the girl she was proud of her, somehow, but she couldn't do it now. "I know you never came home at all, not even during the summer. You never helped me can tomatoes or put up hay."

"I had to work during the summer, Mother, to earn money to go to school. Daddy would have helped me."

"You wanted to sell my house!"

"Stop it, you two!" shouted Andrea. "I can't take this." Her hands went up as if to cover her eyes or her ears but stopped stiff in midair.

"I'm getting the dessert," said Charlotte. She walked slowly, dishes in both hands, to show that she was doing just fine with the artificial leg. In reality, it pinched with each step, and there was another pain, waxing and waning, connected to a leg that lay a mile and a half away in a nondenominational cemetery in River Oaks Township.

Elizabeth spoke quietly to Andrea, but Charlotte could hear. "Let's just mix pure cream with sugar and butter, and eat it by the spoonful until we're fat monsters. Hell, let's just smear it all over our bodies." Charlotte stacked the dishes on the counter as quietly as she could so she could overhear them. These daughters were her flesh, just as surely as that leg had been her flesh, as surely as that land in the subdivision had been her land.

Elizabeth asked Andrea, "Does she have coffee in there?"

"Oh, definitely. She drinks a whole pot every morning." They joined Charlotte in the kitchen as she was slicing a pie into six pieces.

"You made an apple pie!" said Andrea, who in many ways had been an agreeable child.

"Lard crust?" asked Elizabeth. "Or suet?"

"You can't make a pie crust without fat."

"Do you remember when you used to make ice cream?" asked Andrea.

"Look in the chest freezer." Something had come over Charlotte when she was in the township center yesterday, and she had decided to make ice cream, actually bought a twenty-pound bag of ice at the Harding's grocery—paying for frozen water, that was really the limit, all right. She had turned the handle on the ice-cream maker for hours last night.

Andrea carried the silver two-quart tin from the utility room into the kitchen. "Liz, can you believe she made ice cream? Jersey-cow ice cream."

"God, I haven't thought about Mom's ice cream in years," said Elizabeth. "But none for me, please." She was trying to fit together the pieces of the stove-top percolator from the dish drainer.

"Let me make that." Charlotte took the pieces from Elizabeth's hands, which were not pretty like Andrea's, but shaped like her own, large with crooked fingers.

"Look, Liz," said Andrea. "I'm just putting a tiny bit on your plate."

The ice cream melted onto the pieces of pie and when the coffee was done, Andrea brought it out in cups with saucers. Charlotte poured an inch of ivory cream into her cup; Andrea poured a few drops into hers.

"Since when do you take cream?" asked Elizabeth.

"I'm just trying it this way."

Elizabeth shook her head. In near silence she ate the ice cream and pie filling, but left the empty shell on her plate. Andrea finished everything except a ridge of pinched crust.

"I guess I should start dishes," Andrea said.

"I'll do them later." Charlotte looked out through the curtains that Elizabeth had left open and saw a sliver of a moon, thin as a fingernail clipping, the kind of moon that would not rise too high. "Right now I want your help with something else." Charlotte had been waiting all night to start this conversation. "Tonight I want us to bring home my leg."

"What!" shouted Elizabeth. "We are done with this leg thing, Mom. Case closed. It was hard enough to get it where it is."

"Mom, you're not serious," said Andrea.

"I want my leg. I want to bury it on the hill in the pasture."

"This is crazy talk," said Andrea.

"I need a drink," said Elizabeth. A lock of hair fell from the clip which held the rest of it above her neck.

"Bringing it here is out of the question, Mom," said Andrea. "Anyway, it's not really your leg. It's just rotted flesh and bone."

"Andrea, is there any whiskey here?" Elizabeth's eyes searched the edges of the room. The proud look had fallen from her face. She looked like the girl who had lost her daddy.

Andrea shrugged.

"Hell, you think I don't got whiskey, child?" said Charlotte. "I got whiskey." She pushed her chair back and hurried into the kitchen, not bothering to conceal her limp, then returned with a full bottle and one water glass which she set in front of Elizabeth. The label was so worn that the words "Old Crow" were barely visible. It had been in her cupboard since Mr. DeBoer died. Elizabeth poured half a glass, and Charlotte and Andrea watched her gulp most of it down without a breath.

"Hell, I didn't know you drank like that," said Charlotte. "That's how Mr. DeBoer drank. They say a Dutchman doesn't drink, but Mr. DeBoer drank, all right."

"It's no wonder he drank if he lived with you," said Elizabeth, leaning back in her chair. The words stung, but Charlotte savored the attack.

"I've already dug a hole five feet deep," said Charlotte. "I want to put the leg there before one of the cows falls in." She'd been digging for weeks, sloping one side of the hole so she could drag herself in and out.

"I didn't go to law school so I could rob graves," said Elizabeth.

"The leg is all infected," said Andrea.

"It's sealed in a damn box. Pour yourself another drink, Elizabeth," said Charlotte. For the first time in her life, Charlotte wished she were a drinker herself. "Did I ever tell you that I named you after my mother?"

"Yes, but I'm starting to wonder if you really had a mother." Elizabeth drained the rest of her whiskey and banged the glass on the table. "I think maybe you grew out of the ground like a goddamn tree."

"Let's take that yellow car to my grave, child." Her mother had been just as opinionated, just as direct, but would this Elizabeth risk her life to tell the truth the way her mother had? And would this Elizabeth have sent her only child across the ocean to live with strangers in order to save her?

Andrea looked lost, her eyes moving between Charlotte and Elizabeth.

Elizabeth asked, "What happened to your mother, anyway?"

"She died in the war, with my father."

"I know that, but *how* did she die?" Elizabeth shouted. "Tell us!"

"Stop it, Liz!" said Andrea.

"The way a lot of people died." Charlotte looked hard at Elizabeth. "Hungry."

Elizabeth looked back at her just as hard.

Nowadays there was little shame in admitting her mother was a communist. That wasn't the problem. And the girl had a right to know about her grandmother. So why, when Charlotte wanted nothing more than to tell them the truth, was her throat closing?

THE sign at the graveyard read "No visitors after 9 P.M." Elizabeth shut off the headlights and drove in the dark along the paved path. The three got shovels out of the trunk and searched the headstones until they found the single marker, "Charlotte Elizabeth DeBoer, 1932–." Mr. DeBoer had been buried near his own family in the graveyard behind the church. Mats of sod had been laid over the soil here but hadn't thoroughly rooted so Charlotte was able to roll them aside with her shovel. Beneath, the dirt was loosely packed and moved easily. Both girls wore white tennis shoes. Charlotte's work shoes were hard-soled. The night was warm for the end of November—their breath was barely visible—but Charlotte had worn coarse leather work gloves.

Elizabeth carried the whiskey bottle in her bare, crooked fingers. "Some families go to the park and have picnics in the sunshine," she said. "But we go out at night and dig up graves."

"I should have my head examined for even coming out here," said Andrea.

"But don't go to Mom's doctor," said Elizabeth, laughing now. "He'll cut it off."

"Very funny," said Andrea.

Charlotte thought the two might have been digging with spoons, such was the tiny amount of dirt they moved at first. Charlotte's power was not what it used to be since she had to balance on the fake leg as she drove the shovel into the earth with her good one. Andrea, more quickly than Elizabeth, seemed to figure out the angle at which she could best force the blade into the ground. Though her daughters were skinny, they were three and four inches taller than she was, and she had not been considered a short woman in her time.

"How did you get to be such a hard person, Mom?" asked Elizabeth.

"Liz! Leave her alone!" said Andrea.

"Me leave *her* alone? She's got us out here digging up a grave and I should leave her alone?"

Charlotte didn't respond, but absorbed their voices. She liked Elizabeth drunk and loose-tongued. Charlotte hoped that with their careers, the girls would accomplish more than she had. If they married, she hoped they'd marry men they liked and that they'd keep their bodies intact, every limb, every digit. If only she could meld into words the clouds of poison ashes which settled around her each day, then they would understand why she had to bring the leg home. And then she would find a way to tell them everything, about her parents, about Mr. DeBoer, about her terrible dreams. Her eyes watered so she redoubled her efforts, pushing the shovel with more force. As the pile of dirt beside them grew, Charlotte felt her strength infusing her daughters; she felt their small muscles tighten. And as they dug, she felt a shimmer of her own mother's presence.

"My mother died in a camp," said Charlotte, crashing the shovel into the dirt, but not stopping her work. "Along with my father."

The girls worked without speaking for what seemed like a long time. Finally Elizabeth said, "We knew that, Mom. Grandpa Peter told us a few years ago." Elizabeth looked at Andrea, then back to Charlotte. "I just wanted to make you say it back there. I don't know why."

Charlotte kept her head down and did not ask why they had talked to Peter about it instead of her. She didn't ask them if they knew more than she did.

"What was she like?" asked Elizabeth, "Your mother. Grandpa Peter said she was a communist."

"Maybe she doesn't want to talk about it," said Andrea.

"She was a journalist." Charlotte's voice sounded unnaturally loud in the graveyard. She felt as though this simple fact was the first thing she had ever told her daughters. Maybe this was the beginning of telling them everything. But right now they had to keep digging. This was their chance—if they worked hard enough, the three of them would unearth not only her own leg, but her mother's bones as well. By the light of this thin moon, Charlotte's parents would finally awaken from their unholy and emaciated sleep, and they would forgive her for leaving them and for surviving. Charlotte balanced on her artificial foot, and with the real foot pushed her shovel deep into the ground again. She imagined a system of roots growing beneath her, stretching into the dirt, wrapping around lost old bones, reaching toward her daughters' feet.

Elizabeth stopped to rest and leaned on her shovel like the country girl she'd never be. She was gazing up at the sky as though she hadn't seen stars or the moon in a while. After she took a swig from her bottle, she handed it to Andrea who reluctantly sipped and then, instead of giving it back to Liz, held it toward Charlotte. Both daughters watched as she tipped the bottle up and let the whiskey burn her lips.